continued . . .

The Spanish Bride

A NOVEL OF CATHERINE OF ARAGON

LAURIEN GARDNER

BERKLEY BOOKS, NEW YORK

THE BERKLEY PUBLISHING GROUP
Published by the Penguin Group
Penguin Group (USA) Inc.
375 Hudson Street, New York, New York 10014, USA
Penguin Group (Canada), 90 Eglinton Avenue East, Suite 700, Toronto, Ontario M4P 2Y3, Canada
(a division of Pearson Penguin Canada Inc.)
Penguin Books Ltd., 80 Strand, London WC2R 0RL, England
Penguin Group Ireland, 25 St. Stephen's Green, Dublin 2, Ireland (a division of Penguin Books Ltd.)
Penguin Group (Australia), 250 Camberwell Road, Camberwell, Victoria 3124, Australia
(a division of Pearson Australia Group Pty. Ltd.)
Penguin Books India Pvt. Ltd., 11 Community Centre, Panchsheel Park, New Delhi—110 017, India
Penguin Group (NZ), 67 Apollo Drive, Rosedale, North Shore 0632, New Zealand
(a division of Pearson New Zealand Ltd.)
Penguin Books (South Africa) (Pty.) Ltd., 24 Sturdee Avenue, Rosebank, Johannesburg 2196,
South Africa

Penguin Books Ltd., Registered Offices: 80 Strand, London WC2R 0RL, England

This is a work of fiction. Names, characters, places, and incidents either are the product of the author's imagination or are used fictitiously, and any resemblance to actual persons, living or dead, business establishments, events, or locales is entirely coincidental. The publisher does not have any control over and does not assume responsibility for any author or third-party websites or their content.

Copyright © 2005 by The Berkley Publishing Group.
Cover design by Erika Fusari.
Cover illustration: *Henry VIII and Catherine of Aragon Before the Papal Legates at Blackfriars in 1529, Cowper*, Frank Cadogan (1877–1958)/www.bridgeman.co.uk.
Text design by Kristin del Rosario.

PRINTING HISTORY
Jove mass-market edition/November 2005
Berkley trade paperback edition/January 2008

Library of Congress Cataloging-in-Publication Data

Gardner, Laurien.
   The Spanish bride : a novel of Catherine of Aragon / Laurien Gardner—Berkley trade pbk. ed.
      p. cm.
   ISBN 978-0-425-21996-6
   1. Catherine, of Aragon, Queen, consort of Henry VIII, King of England, 1485–1536—Fiction.
2. Queens—Great Britain—Fiction. 3. Great Britain—History—Henry VIII, 1509–1547—Fiction.
I. Title.

PR6107.A73S63 2008
823'.92—dc22
                                                                                    2007027181

PRINTED IN THE UNITED STATES OF AMERICA

10 9 8 7 6 5 4 3 2 1

The Spanish Bride

One

❦

ROUGH sailors' voices brayed and hollered from the deck and from the masts and spars above, and Estrella's ears perked with a surge of excitement to hear them tell of land. All the girls looked up from their work and glanced around at each other, eyes wide and smiles playing at the corners of their lips. Distant thumps of bootfalls on the planks above betrayed the hurry of men to their stations. The girls began to chatter, and only Princess Catherine's head bowed quietly for a moment over the book she'd been reading aloud, before turning toward the cabin window. This view was of the empty sea over which they had come, but there was light from outside the cabin, and it was through these windows the men's voices drifted to the passengers from the decks above.

The tension in the voices of the Spanish sailors was somewhat alarming, for it told Estrella the men to whom their lives were entrusted had been as apprehensive of this trip as they. Not very comforting, for the weather had been dangerous and the crossing filled with the terrors of mighty storms. Most of Catherine's household of sixty advisors, maids, and servants, never having been on the ocean before, were pale with seasickness or fear. Many with both. Their guide across the channel was an Englishman, but who knew what good that could be? Even the English were subject to the whims of weather and fate. Relief now flooded the room, and Francesca de Carceres leapt to her feet, tossing her sewing onto the stool where she'd been sitting.

"Thank God! We've come through safely!" She gathered herself and reached for her cloak to throw it over her shoulders without even asking for permission to withdraw.

"We've not landed yet." Catherine's voice was soft as she stared out the window. "Let us allow God to fully accomplish His task first. Let us have patience."

Estrella leaned forward and murmured to the princess beneath the chattering of the other maids of honor, "May we at least watch Him accomplish it? May we go to the deck for some fresh air?" She was heartily sick of the "fresh" sea air, but the rolling of the ship was far more difficult to take belowdecks, and even the captain's quarters they'd been given were dank and smelly. Water-soaked wood was sharp with blackness growing across it, and there was a heavy whiff of the bilges below, like rotting fish, and the stench of the quarters of the unwashed crew drifted up the ladders and passages. Those who wished to watch the approach to England from above clamored for permission to leave.

Catherine looked back at them all and smiled, and now Estrella could see the bright excitement in her eyes. "Lita, you are more clever than you would have us believe. I know you only wish to eye that ship's commander again." Though she was every bit the daughter of the the Queen of Castile, born to rule with royal grace, she was also the same age as Estrella and had many moments when she seemed even younger than fifteen. The suite of girls giggled and squealed, and Estrella flushed as she denied.

"No! He is a pig."

"Indeed, but he is a very beautiful pig." That brought a wave of high giggling.

"Your Highness, I only wish some fresh air." Estrella couldn't help the smile on her face, for though she did want to see the approaching land, she also would not mind a chance to glimpse again the handsome features of their captain.

With a chuckle, Catherine nodded. "Very well, Estrellita—all of you—let's see what we can see." Her gentle, oval face brightened with her warm smile as she reached up and lowered her veil over it for an excursion outside the cabin.

The nine girls, some as young as twelve and two or three older than Catherine by as much as three years, rose with their mistress in a burble of barely controlled energy. Maria de Salinas settled Catherine's cloak over the princess's shoulders, and Francesca brought her gloves, then they followed Catherine from the cabin and down the passage, up the ladder, and out onto the upper gun deck. With most of the crew climbing the masts above, the black artillery pieces stood alone and aimed out over empty water. The smell of gunmetal and grease was a relief after the stench belowdecks, and added to the ambience was a whiff of earth from off on the horizon. Fresh vegetation now, not rotting wood or badly preserved food.

Along the gangway and upper deck overhead, sailors hurried back and forth, shouting to each other, and all of them looking out across the bow. The girls made their way forward, stepping over piles of rope and around puddles of water on the slick and rolling deck. Rigging creaked everywhere, and the cry of seabirds mingled with the rushing sound of water against the wooden hull far below. Catherine led her suite up another ladder to the forecastle. There the stunned officers of the ship, surprised by their royal passenger, all bowed as she passed, then glanced around for someone to tell them it was all right for the princess to be above decks. Doña Elvira, Catherine's duenna, was nowhere in sight, so nobody raised any objection. Catherine went forward to gaze out through the archery screen toward their destination.

The ship's commander was there, and Estrella was pleased to watch him from behind her veil, for he cut a fine figure among his subordinates. He seemed younger than he could possibly be for a man in his position, broad of shoulder, strong of limb, and with a face with clean, even planes. His gaze moved over the girls, and Estrella imagined it rested just a fraction of a moment longer on her as she passed. Then when his attention returned to his maritime duties, and he ignored the young passengers who had little to do with his running of the ship, she turned her attention to the view ahead of the approaching land.

In spite of the screen above the wales, through the gaps between its panels the cold, wet English wind buffeted them and their clothing about. Estrella missed Spain, where the sun was warm and the air dry most of the year. Already two girls in Catherine's household were sick with a cough. Estrella had never been ill in her life and was terrified her health might fail here in this cold and damp.

But as she watched Catherine, there was an excitement in the air. The princess of Aragon looked out over the water for her first glimpse of her new home, and a light shone in her eyes. A smile played about her mouth, and she held the book in her hands tightly to her breast. Though the headland sheltering the port of Plymouth was still but a dark line on the horizon, Catherine said, "It's terribly beautiful."

"It's a piece of rock," said Francesca in all practicality. She was right, of course. So far the only Englishman any of them had met was the pilot, Stephen Brett, who had guided them across. He, of course, had made the trip in his own ship. That vessel bobbed on the waves ahead of them, slightly to their right, its rigging straining with the wind in its sails. Catherine's Spanish escort knew nothing about England, its land or its people. What they saw on the horizon was only a bit of land, and that poorly visible in the misty distance.

"It's England, my dear friends," Catherine replied, her voice heavy with wonder. With a single finger, she discreetly lifted her veil just enough to see a little better, then let it drop lest Doña Elvira spy it or hear of her doing it. "This is the land where King Arthur lived, and all his knights of the Round Table. England, where my own Arthur awaits me." Estrella had glimpsed bright roses blossoming in the princess's cheeks, and whether they were from the chill wind or her anticipation of marriage to England's new Arthur, Prince of Wales, Estrella couldn't say. She glanced at the beautifully bound volume in Catherine's hands, of rich, embossed red leather. In the cabin she'd been reading aloud to them the stories written by Sir Thomas Malory. Catherine had always adored the Arthurian saga. The old French romances, told and told again, were as familiar to her as scripture, and when she read them to her maids of honor Estrella could hear in her voice the regard for the bold, devout knights of old.

And that made them come alive for her. As the young maid looked through a gap in the archery screen and across the water to the land that was also her own new home, where she would more than likely marry and remain for the rest of her life, the thrill of finally seeing this place she'd heard so much about also rose in her. She, too, imagined stout men in burnished armor astride magnificent warhorses. Men filled to bursting with God's grace, chivalrous and honorable. Excitement fluttered in her belly, and she couldn't help but smile. She pulled her cloak around herself as a shiver ran through her slender frame, and she wished this ship would hurry and land. She wanted to be in England finally.

They landed the next day at Plymouth, but once on terra firma, the journey wasn't nearly finished. Now the princess and her household faced the passage overland to London, and now more people were involved with their progress. The arrival of the princess was huge news to the entire country, and every opportunity was to be made to encourage her acceptance by the populace. The trek from the port city toward London was a bright, sparkling parade of celebration, a grand procession to last over the following weeks. In each town the Spanish arrival was greeted with displays of joy from commons lining the roads to cheer their new princess. Slowly the Spanish train made its way, for they wished to greet Catherine's new people as much as the people wanted to view and welcome her. At a town called Exeter, Catherine was welcomed with banners of bright colors and imaginative design, flying from every rooftop and edifice. There were enormous bonfires, and it seemed every bell in Christendom was ringing for happiness. Estrella was beginning to like these English, and she could see Catherine was appreciative of the welcome. Tired though she was of the travel, the princess maintained a warm and cheerful demeanor to all. When she looked out over the crowds, she saw and responded to the individuals rather than the mass. She looked people in the eye and even sometimes addressed them with greetings in Spanish-accented English. Those so graced seemed to blossom under the attention, and responded by waving or even throwing kisses. Estrella marveled at the joy abounding between Catherine and her new people.

When they rested of an evening, the food was always plentiful, if bland. Accommodations seemed the best their hosts could offer, though the girls found them somewhat drab. Catherine's permanent household wasn't particularly large for her status, but often they stayed in places where there was not enough room to sleep everyone comfortably. Some of the lesser servants—the launderers, bakers, and cooks—had to sleep on bare floors with nothing more than straw and blankets beneath them. There were plentiful straw and blankets to be sure, but still . . . Estrella often shared a bed with Francesca, who always took more than her share of the mattress and rolled around at night in the bargain. It would be good to finally arrive in London and have a bed of her own, even if it were a poor, ugly one.

There was great curiosity about the Englishmen they met along the way. They all seemed terribly pale to Estrella, whose family was fair of skin though dark of hair. Even she seemed dark compared to most of the English. Many were even more pale than Catherine, whose exquisitely royal blood and distant English ancestry showed in her auburn hair and delicate complexion. Here in England, even the men's cheeks glowed with roses, and their lips seemed thin and pink and miserly. Some were like old women, the sort who were disappointed with life and pressed their mouths closed in a lipless gash, though they smiled tightly and constantly. At the distance from which the girls were kept from those men, Estrella gazed across at them and wondered what they were truly like. Were English knights anything like Spanish caballeros, filled with fierce pride and glossy with smooth style? They didn't seem so. They seemed plain: a little dull and not terribly fierce. Estrella thought the best thing to recommend them was that they were all so very cheerful. Cheering. Amused by everything around them and speaking in light voices that seemed to dance in spite of their guttural-sounding language. Her English was spotty at best, and she could only pick out some words here and there, so it all sounded to her like gibberish spoken in the backs of their throats. No grace to the sound at all, but all was certainly lively. In the streets as the carriages bearing Catherine's household passed, even the young nobles, who might have had more dignity, were noisy and boisterous in their welcome. The common people waved their arms and danced as the Spanish procession moved past.

"What a demonstrative people they all are," Francesca commented. The dimples in her cheeks were deep with smiling, and she gawked out the window of their carriage. Theirs was the one directly behind the princess's, so they were able to watch without being noticed by the press of people outside.

"They certainly don't let one wonder what they're thinking." The edge in Maria de Salinas's voice suggested she thought they should.

"Yes, Maria, and how excellent is your English to know just what they are all thinking? They could be shouting vile epithets at us, and you would never know the difference."

Maria flushed. "And do you think they are?"

"I'm only saying that some of them could be."

Estrella laughed. "You two are too silly. They're happy to see us; it's as plain as can be. Princess Catherine, I mean. Of course they're happy to see Catherine. They don't want war, and her marriage to Arthur will assure their succession. It's simple enough for anyone who thinks about it. Besides," she grinned at her fellow maids, "who wouldn't want an excuse for such revels? If someone said to you, 'Here comes our new princess, let's welcome her with entertainment, food, and drink for everyone,' would you say, 'Oh, no! We cannot make merry, for we must work today!' They are not so stupid, I think."

The other girls laughed, and all agreed. It was all fine enjoyment, and they proceeded through the town with smiles for everyone and high anticipation of what they might find.

That evening the travelers were joined by an official welcome contingent led by King Henry's high steward. Aflutter with bright banners, each man decked out in his finest attire, the escort accompanied the Spanish train on toward London. Now there was entertainment at every turn, and their progress became even more slow. Musicians, mummers, and acrobats performed each night and often along the way, during meals and whenever someone new came to join the procession.

Catherine now met the Spanish liaison officer, Don Pedro Ayala, who was the Spanish king's ambassador to Scotland. Don Pedro was an expansive sort and outgoing in the extreme. When he walked into a room he filled it with his presence, and everyone nearby turned to look. It was a magnetism that had served him well in his career, for it allowed him to stay away from Scotland. Reportedly, he'd come from his posting in the north to visit England years ago and simply never returned. Also reportedly, he got along far better with the English king than with the Scots. Estrella gazed at the hale, hearty, and cheerful Spaniard in his rich robes and thought how well this place agreed with him. She thought there might be hope that she, too, would find her place here as comfortable. The future brightened, and she looked forward to what was in store for her with a glad heart.

Nearly two weeks into the journey, by all accounts a week before they expected to arrive in London, they stopped at a castle called Dogmersfield. Catherine and her suite of maids had retired to the apartments given over to them, to freshen themselves before supper. The rooms were awfully small, and though recently hung with rich tapestry and the beds and floors sprinkled with fragrant herbs, there could be discerned a dankness sharp in Estrella's nose. The stone here was ever cold and damp, even this high in the keep. It seemed the entire country was given over to things that grew in the cold and damp. The smell of the fuel on the fire was odd, also. Musty. Nearly as if the fires were burning dirt, and she could taste the smell in her mouth. Though it wasn't entirely unpleasant, it was nevertheless alien, and she wished for more real wood and a higher flame to take the dampness out of the wooden floors and stone walls. An ache began to creep into her bones.

Outside the keep, a commotion arose at the gate in the inner bailey below, and Catherine moved to an arrow loop to look out. A peep of exclamation escaped her. *"Ay,"* she whispered, and the girls crowded around, standing on tiptoe and craning to see through the narrow opening what could have piqued the interest of the princess so.

Before anyone could say anything, Doña Elvira swept into the room like the north wind, a forceful rustle of silk and fragrance and jewels, her majestic bearing nearly eclipsing that of the princess herself. She was tall and vigorous and not to be resisted or doubted by anyone with any sense. As Catherine's guardian she held a position of power even over the princess herself, and that alone made her someone to fear. All the girls did. "Come, Your Highness," she said in a low, clipped tone. "Hurry. The English king has arrived." An excited murmur ran through the suite, and a few squeals as well. The duenna then fell into a murmured monologue to herself regarding the insolence of the English, their disregard for propriety, and their ignorance of civilized manners, as she went to the princess to assess the state of her attire.

Catherine turned from the loop, blinking and taking deep, careful breaths. "*He* is here, also," she said.

Doña Elvira clucked at the disgracefully wilted dress Catherine wore, and muttered, "There is no time."

"Who is here with the king?" asked Maria de Rojas of the princess as she peered out through the loop.

"The prince. Arthur. The king has brought my husband to me." The thrill in Catherine's voice was unmistakable. She was like a little *niña*, on the edge of ticklish laughter at the prospect of finally meeting the young man to whom she'd been married by proxy the year before. The moment she'd talked of and speculated about for months was near.

The girls erupted in fresh excitement, and Estrella clutched her skirts to hurry to the loop to see out herself. But there was no longer anything to see down in the bailey other than a few lackeys milling about. Nobody of importance was in sight anymore. She turned from the loop, disappointed.

The girls hurried to help Catherine pull herself together. After the arduous day of travel and presentation to the local commons and gentry, her attire was somewhat the worse for wear and her demeanor worn. Even her eyes showed the strain of her travels; they were lined with red and surrounded by dark bags. Estrella understood Doña Elvira's irritation at the intrusion of the king. Catherine would not be giving her best first impression, and if King Henry were inclined to balk at the marriage, he could claim her countenance to be unsatisfactory. Diplomatically it would be risky for him, but one never knew with him what might be on his agenda. Henry was known as a tight and shrewd man, if not a particularly skilled monarch, and his reaction to Catherine could take any form.

But there was nothing for it but to brave the meeting. The journey through Spain to the coast, and then across the sea, had taken several months, and now finally the princess was going to meet her prince. The dress she wore might be stained and wilted, but there was no time to wash and change clothes. The King of England was there to see her, and he wanted to see her immediately. There was no putting him off. Muted voices came from the hall below the girls' chamber.

"He wishes to see your face," said the duenna.

The princess looked up at her with wide, surprised eyes. The room was stunned into silence and stillness. "And you told him he could not, of course."

"Of course, Your Highness." Elvira brushed a bit of lint from Catherine's skirt, then took a sleeve of her dress to pick at a dirt spot and see if it would come loose. Then she clucked at the unsatisfactory result. The mud crust was gone, but a dusting of earth remained in the weave.

"I would be mortified to be treated that way. He wishes to examine me so he can reject me if I'm deemed not pretty enough." The surprise was gone, and now her demeanor showed only calm despite her words.

"He insists, I'm afraid. He is a stubborn, stubborn man and apparently has no knowledge of how things are done among true royalty. And he is the law here. He's made it clear there will be enormous trouble if we refuse. He may reject you out of hand for defying him."

The duenna paused a moment, then added, "And there is that if you hide behind the veil he will think there *is* something wrong with you. At the very least he will think you are not confident of your own beauty and intelligence. You wouldn't want this Englishman to think the daughter of King Ferdinand of Aragon and Queen Isabella of Castile is unsure of her own beauty, would you? Prince Arthur is the son of only one monarch, and that one holds his throne by his fingernails. Henry's claim to royal blood is tenuous, at the very least. You are the daughter of two monarchs, both of whom rule in their own right. There is nothing you should fear from the English king, for there is nobody who would dare to call you anything other than the perfect bride."

Catherine gazed at her guardian for a moment, and Estrella knew the situation was far more complex than that. The English king was also testing her compliance. Her willingness to bend to the rule of her husband. He was seeing how far he could press the Spaniards who protected the princess, and by extension her parents who were powerful monarchs and Henry's rivals in European politics. The princess thought hard.

"Very well." Catherine waited while Elvira removed her veil and set it aside. The princess looked nearly naked without it, and she patted the tiny bit of hair that showed from under her headdress as if to assure herself it was still there to cover her head.

Catherine's maids hurried to smooth the overdress. A shawl was brought to cover the small stain where a smudge of grease from dinner earlier in the day had marred the fine silk. Maria de Rojas picked some more at the dirt smudge. Then, arranged and orderly, Catherine went to meet her prince.

In the chamber next to the great hall, the girls pressed close to their mistress, fussing with her hair and the shawl, each eager to be part of this event as well as wanting to protect the princess. Estrella saw, however, the suppressed eagerness in Catherine's eyes. The princess would never admit it, and it would never have been said about her, but she was fairly trembling. All these last months—even her entire life—had come to this moment. What would Arthur be like? Would he live up to the legend of his namesake Malory had wrought? Would he even be the sort of man one would want for a husband? Or a king? Each girl burned with curiosity.

The king and his escort of guards and courtiers entered through the narrow door. Mud had spattered his boots, and his fine tunic was as road-weary as the dresses worn by Catherine and her suite. Estrella thought how much more pleasant this meeting would be if they'd all been given a chance to clean up and rest. But Henry was impatient, and his chin rose in his determination to say how things were done here. It was almost a defensiveness, as if the Spanish contingent were an invasion of some sort, and he was there to make certain they didn't overrun his kingdom. Estrella found him as graceless and uncivilized as Doña Elvira had said, rawboned and high-cheeked. Crude. He removed his riding gloves and handed them off to the man at his right before stepping forward to greet Catherine. The cluster of girls parted and stepped slowly away from their mistress.

He spoke English, which language was a mystery to Estrella. Neither did Catherine speak it, but they all assumed the words were the normal courtesies, and she replied in Spanish, "Good evening, Your Majesty." She made a deep, graceful curtsy, nearly kneeling in it, then stood to face him with a bright face and warm smile.

At that moment a commotion rose from the next room,

and all turned to see. Through the door came a teenage boy followed by a line of sumptuously dressed men, all talking. On sight of the princess, the boy halted, and the men followed suit behind him.

Estrella's heart fell for Catherine, for this boy—plainly the English prince—was small and sickly. Even more pale than the most wan commoner she'd seen in this sunless country, his thin, sallow cheeks had no blossoms, and his eyes were weak. And he was short. A half head shorter than Catherine and even smaller in weight than Estrella herself. His blond locks were to his shoulders, and there was no luster to his hair. Arthur was a year younger than Catherine, but he looked even younger.

But the princess never showed the slightest moment of reservation. Her smile never wavered as she listened to the formal speeches of greeting from Henry and Arthur, translated by the Spanish bishop attached to Catherine's suite. In fact, she seemed overjoyed to finally meet the young man. When she replied, while her Spanish was translated through the Spanish and English bishops, she stepped forward and embraced the thin prince.

His response was to smile, though he didn't seem to have much to say. He seemed embarrassed but struggling to hide it. He spoke a few halting sentences, which the translators gave as "I've longed to see your face, and find it exactly as I'd pictured while reading your letters. Though perhaps even more beautiful."

That made Catherine let go of a slight giggle behind her hand, and her maids hid their smiles behind their hands also.

In a bright, musical voice, the princess called for entertainment, and musicians were summoned. The meeting of prince and princess was transformed into a celebration. Refreshments were brought, and both English and Spanish occupied the great hall to enjoy performances of musicians and jongleurs. There was a recitation by a bard who told his tale in Latin, and who Estrella thought quite good. Her Latin was not perfect, but the storyteller's demeanor and expressive voice made the performance as entertaining and enlightening as if it had been in Spanish. Throughout the evening, tired though they all were, Catherine maintained her cheer and her grace.

Estrella watched the blond prince the entire time, heartsick for Catherine. At supper the slight young man ate little, and in conversation said less. His face wasn't even as animated as the stern and subdued Englishmen around him. Estrella gazed at him over the rim of her cup and thanked God she wasn't the one betrothed to the little fellow. Surely her own husband would be an energetic and handsome man, and rich. It made her smile to think of the future.

But that night as the suite readied their mistress for bed, Catherine still smiled as she had all evening. "What a lovely prince he is!"

Maria whispered, lest someone lurking nearby hear, "But he's so small! He doesn't look well."

"Nonsense. He's but a boy and hasn't got his full growth yet." She sounded like his mother, making excuses for his slight build. "Give him a chance, and he'll soon be a strapping, handsome man like his father. Did you notice his father? The king is a big, healthy man. There's no reason why Arthur shouldn't grow up to be exactly as handsome a king."

"He's not nearly as fine as our king."

Catherine chuckled. "No. Nobody is as fine as our king. So I must settle for second best, because I could hardly marry my father."

The girls laughed.

"Arthur will be wonderful. I know it. I *feel* it. God would not want me to marry a weak man."

Estrella watched the face of her mistress and thought Catherine truly believed what she said. It made her ashamed of her own misgivings.

Two

1527

So many years had passed and so much had happened since she'd first arrived in London as a young girl! It seemed an eternity since the Dowager Countess of Whitby, the former Estrella Juanita de Montoya, had been to court. Estrella's marriage had taken her north, where there was little opportunity or need to lurk among the courtiers in Henry's palaces in the south, and now she looked forward with great eagerness to her return to the center of political power in her adopted country. Age and wisdom had impressed on her the advantages of keeping a distance from the often capricious King Henry, but she longed to see her former mistress again. Her queen had once been her pillar as well, a source of strength in their youth, and on this damp, gray, typically English London day she craned at the carriage window for a first glimpse of the familiar stone, livery, and banners that would tell her she'd returned to a place of happiness. The jouncing was even worse on the paved streets than it had been on the muddy, rutted roads to London, and her two young maids complained, whispering to each other in their northern dialect even as they gawked at the fine London architecture along the way, but Estrella paid no mind. Her heart skipped as she looked toward her new life in her old position, serving the Queen of England.

Since the death of her husband the year before, there had been not a great deal left in her life to recommend it. Geoffrey's passing had not been a surprise, but the void he'd left behind was. Over the previous fifteen years of marriage she never would have suspected how much she could miss him. The match had been loveless, as most were. He had been a good man, though a tightfisted one and none too inclined to generosity in purse or intellect. Nevertheless, he'd always spoken kindly to her, allowed her freedoms she would never have known in Spain, and never condemned her difficulties in childbearing.

The greatest heartbreak of her life was that none of their children had survived. The two that had lived past infancy had been taken during a scourge of the smallpox seven years before. Geoffrey had never been the same after that, and Estrella allowed as she was also no longer the woman she'd once been. Her husband was gone now, his title and lands passed to a nephew. Geoffrey had been a good husband of her assets as well as of her, and with her dowry returned to her she was left with enough for a modest life. Now she longed to return to court, where her old friend waited.

Inside the palace she was escorted by a squire to a chamber in the lodging range, two rooms of adequate size for her and her two maids. There was a private garderobe, which was a very nice thing to have in a residence where every amenity was sought and battled over as a sign of favor. Estrella directed her younger maid, Mary, to bring water for washing, and the girl hurried away on her errand with the pewter pitcher from the ewer stand. Then the other girl, Joyce, helped Estrella undress and slip into a robe. She lay for a few moments on the well-appointed bed while Joyce began the arranging of her trunks and the unpacking of some of her things. The girl bustled about the suite, moving this or that trunk and hanging Estrella's finest dresses in the small armoire in the outer room.

The bed was hung with sumptuous curtains, bringing Estrella to mind of the terrible years when such luxury had seemed impossible. She closed her eyes and wished Mary would hurry with the water. She wanted to clean the dust of her travels away. A tapestry hung on one of the short walls of the chamber, a small one but finely crafted. It showed a religious scene, of Jesus arguing with the devil. Other demons stood about, grinning and grasping toward Satan's target, but Jesus stood calmly, his palms spread wide and his face utterly at peace, a glow of halo about his head and seraphim hovering. Estrella stared sleepily at the golden halo and the watchful angels. For an odd moment she wondered if ordinary people on earth ever had halos that nobody could see. Angels, certainly, but could there be some whose grace was so sure that they would glow with it?

Mary came with the water, and some towels she'd borrowed from a steward, and Estrella rose to wash before she would be presented to the queen. Then her girls helped her dress in blue silk sewn with a galaxy of small pearls. Her coif was in the English style, conservative as she knew Catherine would like to see her. French fashion tended to be too revealing for the queen, and she preferred her maids to have their hair covered entirely. Once ready, she went with an escort from the palace guard to Catherine's apartments, where she was granted admission by the queen's steward.

"Ah, Lita!" Her Majesty was found in her gallery, gazing out the window at the river below, and turned to greet the arrival upon her announcement. Three other maids of honor, all young girls in their teens and twenties, sat nearby, at work on some embroidery. At Estrella's approach they paused to ready themselves to greet the newcomer. With nimble fingers they tied off their threads or tucked their needles away, then folded the fabric and prepared to stand.

Catherine came to Estrella, as warm and approachable as ever, though she had changed so much in other ways. Her hair had grayed, and her many pregnancies had ravaged the figure that had once been pleasing. The oval face was now puffy, and the years had etched many lines into her face. Both forty-two, neither of them were the fresh young girls come from Spain, and Estrella felt a twinge of disappointment she knew was ridiculous. As if she'd expected the years to fall away and restore them all to the glories of the first days of Henry's reign and Catherine's marriage. Estrella knew the heartbreak of lost children, and though she envied Catherine her one surviving child, she also knew her friend had borne a terrible cost for little reward.

"Your Majesty." Estrella paused to curtsy, then stood to receive an embrace from the queen in a rustle of silk and clink of jewelry. "I was overjoyed to receive your summons. I came as quickly as I could." The younger women came to hover and listen in. Catherine introduced her as Lady Whitby, and each greeted Estrella as their mistress had. The queen named them for Estrella: Jane, Margaret, and Anne. Jane was very young and seemed terribly demure for her age. She said nothing beyond a proper greeting. Margaret seemed also of conservative bent but was far larger than Jane and had a head of thick red hair that was barely controlled by her coif. Anne was a dark one and seemed on the verge of laughter though her speech was as strictly proper as Jane's. Each of the girls was English. It was remarkable how English Catherine herself seemed to Estrella now, though she shouldn't have been surprised at all. She had lived in this country as long and knew how far away Spain had become for them both.

"Look how English you've become!" said Catherine, and Estrella had a dumbfounded moment of wondering if the queen had somehow read her mind. "You speak just as if you had been born here, and you don't even address me in Spanish!" There was a teasing light of humor in her eyes.

A bit flustered, Estrella replied, "In the north one finds fewer who are not native here, and so I found them all more willing to accept a foreigner if I spoke like them. After so many years of imitating them, I'm afraid it's become habit. Besides, it would be rude to your other girls here, were I to speak Spanish without need."

"Of course. It's a good thing to have the regard of those around you, and not such a terrible sacrifice to speak their language. All in all I've found my subjects a generous, just, and pious lot. One could do worse than to be like them." A warm, regal smile was bestowed on the cluster of young maids who stood by, and Estrella thought she saw a flicker in the eye of the dark-haired one. The humor was replaced by a look of challenge, which shocked Estrella to her slippers. She'd heard rumors and knew the queen's household was not entirely loyal to her. Not that any household was ever completely free of intrigue and treachery, but bold defiance of Catherine was more than she'd expected to see.

"How was your journey, Estrellita?" Catherine continued. "Tell me all about it."

"Long and tiring, Majesty, but the weather held warm enough. I ache so terribly in winter, it's been lovely to thaw my bones of late."

"Indeed." The queen moved off down the long, narrow room, then turned and gestured to Estrella. "Come." To the other three she said, "Ladies, do take your work into my privy chamber with the others. I desire some privacy."

The maids responded with acquiescence and curtsies, though Estrella sensed a reluctance to leave the queen and the discussion they knew was coming. Curiosity lit the three faces. Women in their position, like the men who maneuvered in the court of the king, hated to be left out of anything, for their futures rested on where they stood with the queen. Marriages could be arranged or lost by her influence, and even the smallest edge on the next courtier for favor could be realized in terms of rewards not just for the maids but for their families. Today, however, Catherine waited until the women had moved entirely from the room, then drew Estrella away from the gallery entrances. At the far end was an alcove accessed by a narrow opening.

Once they were out of earshot of the guards, Catherine sat on a chair that had a plush cushion for a seat and gestured to the one next to it. In Spanish and in a very low voice she said, "Be seated. You must be exhausted from your travels."

Estrella touched a hand to her coif to see if it were awry. But as far as she could tell, she was as pulled together as she'd ever been. She settled into the soft seat and placed a hand over Catherine's. "Are you well? I've heard talk."

"I'm certain you have." Catherine smiled and raised a hand

as if to wave off Estrella's concerns. "Henry, you mean. He's got a new mistress; it's no secret. They never are, and we only pretend we are fooled. Just as in the old days when we used to pretend to be fooled by his masquerades. Remember how he liked to dress as Robin Hood or some such, and his favorites as well, then pull off his mask and reveal himself. As if his own wife couldn't recognize the very shape of his gloved hand, just as she would recognize a look in his eye or know his whereabouts more surely than his steward." She chuckled for a moment, and her gaze drifted off, remembering. "I'm afraid men never grow up; they only come of age."

Estrella had to laugh, for it was so terribly true. "Oh, yes. Dear Geoffrey had mistresses as well, and went through terrific gyrations in pretending I didn't know." Bittersweet memories of Geoffrey crowded in on her. There was a twinge of heartache, for men were as whorish as any woman, yet they pretended to unfailing honor and loyalty. "He was awfully creative about it and had quite a talent. He always told the most outrageous tales of where he'd been, in a style worthy of Malory." Catherine gave an appreciative chuckle, and Estrella continued. "He worked so hard at it. Dear Geoffrey was quite scrupulous about keeping certain people from ever seeing or speaking to each other. It was like a game to him, I think, as if the thing were not a sin so long as he kept it secret."

"He didn't wish to bruise your regard for him."

"I daresay he had no care for my regard, for we both accepted the world for what it is. Even so, sometimes I wondered whether he was disappointed I never confronted him with his infidelities; it was such an exciting challenge to him, and he never knew whether or not he was successful."

"More than likely he assumed he was, and that you were

entirely in the dark. To a man's ego, anything less would be unthinkable unless he *were* confronted and made to face his failure."

Estrella chuckled again. "Indeed. My opinion was that if he ever spent so much energy minding his lands and his favor with the king rather than his mistresses, he might have risen higher in the world."

"I must say Henry certainly has had fewer illicit liaisons than most men, and for that I can be thankful."

"A testament to how he values you as a wife. It is you whose husband cares for your esteem."

"A testament to his loving nature, I think. He cares deeply about everything that reaches his notice and doesn't take other women lightly. Even the most base whore receives his true regard; an irony that cuts to the core, but there you are." There was a long pause as she gazed out the open window on the murky river below. It moved between its banks, carrying boats and barges to and fro, a bustling passage of Catherine's beloved people. "But as a queen, he thinks I have failed him." Her voice trailed off. When she spoke again, it carried an edge. "He believes Mary cannot succeed him, but he is wrong."

Estrella hesitated to say what she thought but also thought her mistress would want her to be honest, so she spoke. "The English won't accept a woman monarch; they are not like Queen Isabella's Castilians. After all this time, surely you know how they are different. There would be war if Mary ascended the throne. Henry's claim to the throne isn't strong enough for her to carry it."

Catherine's lips pressed together, and she frowned. "Nonsense. There's no reason why Mary shouldn't rule, just as my mother did. The lack of a son is not such an important thing. Henry has even made Mary Princess of Wales. Few think it remarkable."

"But what of Fitzroy?"

"He is illegitimate." By the tone of the queen's voice, Estrella knew Catherine thought Estrella was talking silliness to suggest Henry's son by a former mistress could ever rule England. "Were he to attempt the throne even after reaching his majority, he could never hold it." An ugly cloud of anger drifted over Catherine's face at the subject of the ten-year-old boy. Then it passed, and she returned to her calm.

"But he is Duke of Richmond. Some say he was created duke to place him in the succession. Some say Mary will never be queen so long as there is Fitzroy to take the crown."

"A legitimate daughter is always—"

The sound of voices down the gallery caught their attention, and Catherine waited. One of the voices was Henry, loud and strident, reverberating down the room and reaching them in perfect clarity. He was telling of his hunt the day before, of a hart that had evaded him with the wiles of a pixie, then boasting of how he'd outsmarted the animal. Those with him supported the tale with admiration.

One of the courtiers' voices was the Earl of Hartford. Estrella's memory picked it out of the mix of voices with a gut recognition that brought back the past with a clarity of sharp, broken glass. A cold chill skittered up her spine, and her heart beat a bit faster. *Hartford*. She hadn't seen him but once since her marriage, and that briefly on a short visit to London more than a decade ago. They'd passed in a corridor and not spoken, and the incident had retreated quickly to the back of her mind. She wondered if he would try to speak to her ever again, and hoped if he did it wouldn't be today.

When Henry had finished his story he called out in the gallery, "Catherine!"

The women stood. The hall was long, and it took several moments for the group to traverse the remaining distance from the entrance to the alcove. Catherine and Estrella waited in demure silence.

"You are somewhere in here, I trust?" the king shouted out. Then, to his companions he said, "We can't have mislaid the queen, can we?"

A murmur of laughter reached the women, who glanced at each other and still waited.

Finally the cluster of men reached the alcove, and the king entered with several of his ministers. Not eager to place herself forward under the circumstance, as the men crowded in, Estrella allowed their movements within the small area to maneuver her unobtrusively to the rear and to the side, away from Catherine and behind a candle stand. There she stood, unnoticed by the self-absorbed king and his courtiers, and certainly unacknowledged.

Except by Hartford, who spotted her in an instant. His eyes flicked toward her, held her for a moment, then glanced away. She watched him. He'd not changed much, beyond his grayed hair and slight jowls of age. Still handsome, but with a look of strain about his eyes. Weariness, and perhaps wariness. It was a common enough expression for men in his position. His glances in her direction, puzzled at first but then coupled with an emotion she couldn't identify, cut to her core, and she had to look away from him. It had been many years since she'd seen him, and he'd quite slipped from her mind, but now it felt like only yesterday, and the memories crowded in on her like children clamoring for attention. They snatched at her, sending her thoughts into disarray thorough enough to make her forget where she was. She turned her gaze from the earl and focused on the king.

Henry had changed a great deal since she'd last seen him. Though he still seemed healthy enough, he was heavier than he'd been, and jowls had begun on his face as well, though he was a good deal younger than Hartford. His hair was receding, a common enough thing even in a king.

Henry addressed his wife, his demeanor of a sudden serious. The jollity he'd displayed a moment ago was nowhere to be seen, as if it had never existed, and he lowered his chin toward Catherine like a schoolmaster about to lecture an ill-behaved child. There was silence among the men as they hung on what Henry would say next. It seemed each of them knew more than the women did. "Catherine," he began, "there is something I must tell you."

Her head bowed slightly. "I'm eager to hear what you would tell me." She appeared happy to see him and truly interested in what was on his mind.

He straightened, took a deep breath, but didn't seem to have the words for his announcement. Catherine waited patiently, and Estrella remained as still as her mistress. The tension among the men was palpable. Something very important was going on, and by the expressions on their faces the odds were good it would be unpleasant. But Catherine betrayed no apprehension. She was as calm as the placid river below her window. Estrella found herself irritated that the male courtiers seemed to know better than Catherine what the news would be and thought it was a low thing for the king to put her at such a disadvantage among the others in the room. Or himself at the advantage. This was an intimidation tactic familiar to her.

"My dear Catherine, this is unfortunate, but there is the

consolation that we have realized the truth and can rectify the situation. Mitigate our sin."

"What sin, husband?" Now, at the mention of sin, uneasiness grew in her voice, and her head tilted slightly as she peered at him, unsure of what was happening. Catherine was the most pious person Estrella had ever known, and that included many cardinals and bishops. Few clergymen held a candle to her for strength of faith. Estrella's hands gripped each other with white knuckles. She knew Henry well enough to know this reluctance to say what he was thinking was most unlike him. She couldn't imagine what might cause him to hesitate in anything, let alone something that involved his wife, who had never crossed him in eighteen years.

The king continued, "Our marriage. For a time, now, I've had reservations about the circumstances of our marriage, and lately those suspicions have been confirmed by learned men. Pious men, who are the most expert in canon law of any in the world." His voice took on a defensive tone as if Catherine had offered an argument, though she hadn't. "Surely you understand I can hardly ignore the opinions of such authoritative theologians." He paused, as if waiting for her to say something.

Catherine said nothing but only stood with a bland, frozen expression on her face.

Finally, the king continued. "Dear Catherine, it is the opinion of these men that you and I have been living in sin these past eighteen years. They've examined the papal dispensation that allowed me to marry my brother's widow and found it wanting. The passage in Leviticus is most clear, and we cannot argue against the law. By all accounts you and I have never been man and wife, and now we must separate."

Still Catherine didn't speak, though her cheeks turned a bright, burning red. Estrella's heart pounded.

Henry sighed, as if relieved to have gotten that burden off his chest. "You must understand," he said, "in all good conscience—"

Catherine's mouth opened as if to speak, but no words came. Only a sob. Then another. Her hands went over her mouth, and the next sob shook her shoulders. Estrella wanted to go to her, but didn't dare move and attract the attention of the king, who was clearly embarrassed. The other men were looking at the floor, at each other, out the window—anywhere but at Catherine and Henry.

Henry shifted his feet, and his own face flushed. "My dear, you mustn't cry." It was a command. He didn't wish for her to cry, so he ordered her not to. But though his voice was stern, his words were an effort at comfort. "It isn't that there has been no love. Nor that the love is gone. But my conscience will not allow me to continue as we are, living contrary to God's law. I am a pious man, and nobody can say otherwise, as you well know."

Catherine continued to cry, tears streaming from beneath her palms and dripping from her chin.

"Catherine," said the king, even more stern now, "do not cry. Perhaps all will turn out well. This must be the best for us, for we have lived contrary to God's law for so many years, and surely it has not gone well for our souls. Think of all the poor children we were denied because our marriage was hated by God." At that, Estrella blanched, remembering her own dead children. Her face flushed, and she glanced at Hartford. She caught him looking at her, and he looked away. She stared hard at the floor and listened as Henry continued. "If we rectify our situation, end the sin, we will return to grace, and all our lives will be the better for it. You must believe it to be so."

But Catherine only continued to cry.

"*Catherine!*" Henry was growing impatient, his frustration evident in the shifting of his feet and glances over his shoulder at the men behind him. Estrella saw Hartford stifle a smirk, and her eyes narrowed at him. This was not funny to her at all. "Catherine, be reasonable!"

The queen sobbed more, her shoulders crumpling with the weight of her grief.

With a long noise of exasperation, the king turned and made his way through the cluster of men and left the alcove. His courtiers followed without another glance at the queen.

Hartford, however, had a glance for Estrella, and she ignored it.

Estrella went to Catherine and put an arm around her shoulders, but the queen only continued to sob. "Come, sit."

Catherine allowed herself to be guided to the chair, where she sat with her hands over her face and continued weeping. Estrella sat next to her and placed a hand on her knee. "Your Majesty, he can't mean what he says." Though she knew he must. The accusation had been of an abhorred sin, which no woman of even ordinary virtue would countenance, let alone Catherine. Surely he would never have said such a thing casually.

The queen sighed and struggled to regain herself, then sat up and looked out the window. One hand remained across her mouth, and her eyes, damp and swollen, seemed lost. She stared at nothing outside, thinking hard, disturbed only by an occasional hiccup of a sob. Finally she said, her voice gummy with tears, "Mary. What will become of Mary?"

"He loves Mary. Nothing will happen to her."

"But if he would call her illegitimate and me a whore . . ."

A sudden calm came over her, as if she'd decided something. "He means to replace me with another."

"You don't believe he's sincere about his misgivings? You think he only wishes to be rid of you?"

Catherine turned a horrified eye on Estrella. "The pope declared our marriage lawful. All the canonists and theologians in Christendom cannot defy the authority of the pope. Henry has pledged his loyalty to Rome. The pope has named him 'Defender of the Faith.' My husband's misgivings contradict everything he has supported for nearly twenty years of rule, and his desire for a legitimate male heir is far too well-known to be ignored in this circumstance. I may be just a woman, but I am not an idiot. He wants a legitimate male heir and will set me aside to have one. Mary would be called bastard, and all hope for her future would vanish."

"What will you do?"

Catherine gazed at her old friend, and the loss returned to her eyes. "He loves me, I'm sure of it."

"Of course, he does." Estrella knew no such thing, but she said it to calm her friend.

"Then he cannot mean to do this terrible thing. He must see his error and know he cannot destroy me this way. He will not say to the world that I have shared his bed as a whore, for I am his lawful wife. By all law, and before God, I am his wife. For if I am not, then I am nothing." Another sob shook her. "Worse than nothing."

Catherine dabbed at her eyes with wet fingers, and Estrella handed her a handkerchief. The queen dried her tears with it, and gradually the calmness returned to her. Her oval face, now puffy with crying as well as years, began to return to its pale color, and the redness receded. She drew a deep breath and sat up straighter in her chair. When she spoke, her voice was firm. Hard, like iron.

"I must learn what Henry intends to do and how he will go about it. And I must learn it quickly."

Three

❦

Having recovered herself and dried her tears, Queen Catherine went to her presence chamber so Lady Whitby could take her place among her maids. To Estrella's great joy, she learned her old friend Maria de Salinas was also a member of the household, having rejoined it three years before. It was a spirited reunion of hugs, laughter, and rapid Spanish that rolled off Estrella's tongue as if it hadn't been more than a decade since she'd spoken it. She found herself talking like a young woman again, speaking in terms and thinking in ways she'd thought she'd left behind. But all it took was to see Maria again, and the years fell away to reveal the girl she had once been.

Catherine sent all the English maids from the chamber, then withdrew to her bedchamber with Estrella and Maria to sit at a table where there was a writing desk. Her moment of disarray was over now, and the characteristic royal poise had returned. It was with a steady hand she drew a sheet from the desk, and a new quill, and dipped it in the ink. Quickly, but in a flawlessly royal hand, she wrote out her missive. As the quill scratched across the page, she spoke to neither of her maids. Estrella and Maria were silent, waiting to be addressed, and it wasn't until Catherine reached the bottom of the page that she looked up at them and spoke in a voice so hushed she could barely be understood.

"I must learn what my husband intends to do. And I must protect myself and my daughter. You two are among the few I can trust implicitly, and a third is Francisco Felipez."

"Cisco?" He'd once been Catherine's page, and last she'd seen him he was her sewer. "He's still with you?"

"He's a good man. I do well to surround myself with loyal people." The tilt of Catherine's head gave Estrella to know she was considered one of those loyal retainers. The queen folded the letter and sealed it, then held it out to her. "Lita, you were there when my husband spoke to me. You know the situation. Go to Cisco and tell him he must take this to my nephew Charles; the emperor will be at Valladolid, I believe. Tell Francisco everything you saw and heard today. Further, tell him three things to relay to Charles: that he must confront Henry personally on this matter; that he must go to the pope and plead my case; and that he must convince the pope to revoke Cardinal Wolsey's legatine authority. He must do it immediately, before the cardinal can do damage. Wolsey is my greatest enemy at this moment." Estrella thought Henry might be, but she kept that thought to herself. She nodded as Catherine continued, "Do not let Francisco write any of it down, but he is to commit it to memory and relay it to the emperor personally."

Estrella took the letter and slipped it inside her overdress. "Yes, Your Majesty."

Catherine continued, "But he cannot allow the king to know his mission. He must ask for passport to Spain under pretense. He will know what to do."

"Yes, Your Majesty."

"Go now. Hurry. Do not be seen carrying your message nor talking to Felipez."

"Yes, Your Majesty." Estrella hurried from the room, her heart pounding in her ears, and hurried through the palace corridors. So strange to find she remembered the place so well after so long. She found her way unerringly and took little time finding Felipez to deliver the letter. He loitered in the corridor outside the king's presence chamber, and he was easily recognized, for he'd not changed much since his youth. He'd never been a handsome boy, and even now his looks were rugged and craggy. The years had been kind to him only in that he no longer looked older than he was. When she approached him he recognized her, and his eyes lit up. In short order, after a brief exchange, he met her privately, and when she delivered the queen's message, those eyes hardened with a steely resolve for his mission. Estrella watched him go away and knew he was the right man for the job. Perhaps at this moment he was the only man for it.

News of the king's intention to set his wife aside spread through the palace like plague. Estrella learned by this gossip that Henry's new mistress was one of the maids she'd met on her arrival. Anne Boleyn, the one who styled herself a Frenchwoman, whose dresses were too revealing and whose costume boasted jewels above her station. By all accounts the tourmalines and pearls she had been wearing had recently given way to rubies and emeralds, and acid speculation flew as to whether they were gifts of the king. She was a commoner; there was little other possibility, and all the ladies of the court whispered when they saw her. Often they whispered if they didn't see her.

The woman had a reputation for attractiveness, but Estrella couldn't see it. Though Anne was often criticized for her darkness, Estrella's own hair was dark, and she saw nothing wrong with that. It was Boleyn's sallow skin that made her unattractive. Estrella herself had a fair, clear complexion. The king's mistress appeared to Estrella as a fishwife or farmer. But it was said she could talk any man into doing whatever she pleased. As if there were some sort of magic to her. A charm men couldn't resist. Apparently she'd charmed the king, and though Estrella thought long and hard on what wiles Anne must have used, and watched her from beneath lowered eyelashes whenever she could, she was ever at a loss to know. She grew to hate the common maid who thought herself the better of a dowager countess.

Of course, taking a liking to such a whore was out of the question. The woman was a rival to Catherine, who was Estrella's mistress and longtime friend; there could be no possibility of any feeling toward her but revulsion. Not for any virtuous woman who wished to maintain her reputation. But even so, though Estrella tried to understand what a man might see in the cold, selfish slut, what she saw was a woman who put herself forward at every opportunity, as if she were the rightful center of attention instead of her mistress. Anne Boleyn was not exceptionally beautiful, but she carried herself as if she were, and she spoke to everyone she met with the condescension of a queen. The jewels, the haughty voice, the foreign fashion in hair, dress, and conversation made an overwhelming impression. In the face of such a presentation, weaker minds tended to believe her pretense. They responded by treating her as such a queen, and those who knew better hated her with the intensity deserving of a pretender. But Estrella was rarely in the path of Anne's attention, and besides was far too old to be susceptible to a young woman's manipulations. Also, she was not a man. She would never be among the charmed. She watched the maid from afar, appalled that some thought here was the woman Henry wished to make queen. Surely if he were successful in putting Catherine aside, he would choose for his new queen someone far more suitable. Not a commoner and a whore. Surely not. Estrella made frequent prayers that the rumors would prove false, they had been a terrible mistake, and there would be another woman intended for the throne. Any other woman would have done, because the king's choice was a humiliation to his rightful queen.

A month after Henry's revelation to Catherine, two letters came for her. She received them in her presence chamber and noted the seals didn't seem to have been breached. One was from her nephew, Charles V, the other from Francisco Felipez, and the courier swore they had not left his hands since his departure from Valladolid. Though Catherine tried to hide her relief, there was a sense she would have leapt for joy if not for the presence of her husband's mistress in the chamber. Anne's eyes followed the packages in Catherine's hands, and when she noticed Estrella watching her, she looked away. Estrella wondered what would be said to Henry about this delivery, but knew by the time the news of it reached his ears it would be too late for him to do anything about it.

Catherine thanked the courier, ordered a page to escort him to the kitchen for a meal, then gestured to Estrella and Maria to follow her into the bedchamber. They obeyed quickly but without fuss.

Catherine sat in her favorite chair, and the maids gathered

to her. She broke the seal on the first packet of pages, Charles's letter, nodded toward the oratory and said, "Maria, make certain the page posted at the other entry is aware of how much he has to lose if someone were to slip in and listen just now."

"Yes, Your Majesty." Maria went to her errand and returned quickly to hear the letter. It was brief, and Charles assured her she would have his support in this crisis. She nodded, as if she'd been utterly confident of his reply, and Estrella knew she had been. Family ties were everything, and Charles would no sooner abandon his mother's sister than he would abdicate his own throne.

Catherine then opened the letter from Felipez and began to read:

> *Your Majesty;*
>   *As you now know, I have arrived safely and delivered your message to the emperor, your nephew . . .*

Francisco Felipez, loitering near the entrance of the king's presence chamber, was pleasantly surprised at sight of Estrella, Dowager Countess of Whitby. At first he didn't recognize her, for her dark hair had grayed to a fine, lustrous silver, and her figure was no longer so curvaceous and inviting as it had been when they were both young. But once he did, joy rose in his heart for the fond memories she stirred, and he greeted her with a wide smile more sincere than many he'd bestowed in these palace halls over the years. He pushed off from the pillar against which he was leaning and reached for her hand.

But she was not in a mood for reminiscences and quickly explained she'd returned to the service of her queen. Then she grasped his hand in return, stepped very close to him, and with her other hand slipped a letter into his as she whispered, "The queen has a request. Meet me in her gallery immediately." Then she stepped back, said clearly for all to hear that she was glad to encounter an old friend after so many years, then made an apologetic excuse to be on her way.

Felipez discreetly slipped the packet of paper under his wide belt, then struck up a conversation with the king's steward about something inconsequential. There was no telling what might be afoot, so it wouldn't do to hurry away too quickly after Lady Whitby. But a few moments later he bade the steward good day and sauntered from the room as if on his way to one of the gardens for a stroll. Directly he went to the gallery, where he found Estrella sitting in a chair tucked behind a pillar. The deep consternation in her expression alarmed him, and he laid a hand on his sword in reflex. He was quite ready to fight whoever may have caused trouble for his old friend.

"What is the matter?" he asked.

Estrella told him of Henry's "misgivings" regarding his marriage. Blood drained from Francisco's face as he realized the appalling monument of the king's intent. "It would fail. He cannot mean it."

"He means to try. He and his cardinal might even succeed if you do not get this message to the emperor so he can intercede. The queen requires help, and it certainly won't come from Henry's advisors. Nor anyone subject to Henry, to be sure."

Felipez nodded and straightened. "Tell the queen to consider it accomplished."

There was a light in Estrella's eyes that made him think she was confident he could do anything. His chest swelled proudly, and he couldn't help a smile. Then he thought of the dangerous journey ahead, and his pulse beat faster. The office he'd been given was of terrible importance. Perhaps the most important of his life. At that moment he decided either he would succeed, or he would die trying.

Before he could leave the country, particularly since England was an island and passage on shipboard was the only route to the Continent, Felipez needed a passport from the king. Not an easy thing to acquire under the best of circumstances, but at this moment it would be dodgy in the extreme. It took a fortnight to arrange a meeting to even discuss the matter. Felipez waited out those weeks, vigilant that nobody should find the queen's letter. He kept it on his person at all times, for it was the only place he could put it where it would never be found accidentally. He sewed it into a doublet, which he wore every day under different cloaks. His sewing skills did him well, and the seam was perfect. Nobody would guess at the message he carried for foreign eyes. Finally, after a period Henry deemed suitable for his wife's sewer to wait, Felipez was permitted to present himself to the English monarch. He knew he was suspected of having word from Catherine, for he was a member of her household, and the timing of his request to return to the Continent was too coincidental. He hoped he wouldn't be thrown into the tower on some pretense, to keep Catherine incommunicado. His heart skipped around in his chest as he approached the king with his request.

"Your Majesty, it is for the sake of my mother I must request passport to Spain." A lie. Henry knew it, and Felipez knew Henry knew it. The question at this point was whether Henry knew Felipez knew they were dancing, or if the king thought the sewer was stupid as well as common. Felipez allowed some of his trepidation to show and hoped it appeared as respect.

The king lounged on his throne in the presence chamber and peered down at the kneeling Felipez. "Your mother?" His voice was thick with middle age and creeping obesity, and the Spaniard wondered whether he also heard skepticism in it. He'd been a minor player in this court for nearly two decades, wending his way between the pitfalls, but occasionally the English could still baffle him. They always sounded suspicious, he thought. Sometimes he wondered if they always were.

He replied with as much faked sincerity as he could muster, "She is an old woman, Your Majesty, and ailing. She awaits me to give me her dying blessing."

Henry eyed him like a raptor his prey, as did the ministers standing about. Felipez felt as if he were a bit of glass everyone were peering through. Every man in the room knew he was a favorite of Catherine's. His ploy was horribly transparent, and he wished he had a better one, but there was no time for putting Henry off his guard. Catherine needed her message to reach the emperor in all haste, and two weeks had already passed.

But the king didn't mull the question very long. "To be sure," he said and turned to address his ministers. "We wouldn't care to stand between a man and his mother's blessing." A glance flashed between the king's courtiers, and Felipez watched their faces for a clue to what they were thinking, but nothing else was offered. It was as if the fleeting glance had never happened, and Felipez was left to wonder whether it had been his imagination. Henry continued, "By all means, you shall have your passport. And a safe conduct for your passage through France, as well."

Now Felipez knew he was doomed, and his heart sank to his boots. A cold sweat broke out at his neck and palms. With such eagerness, Henry had tipped his hand that not only would there be no safe passage, but the king would make certain Felipez did not survive his journey through France. Heart in his throat, he looked up at the king and thanked him with all the manufactured sincerity at his command. As quickly and gracefully as possible, he made his withdrawal and began preparations for the journey. The following morning he departed London, exiting the palace without undue haste but with murmurings for the sake of form about his hopes his mother would still be alive when he arrived in Castile. He doubted anyone in the stable but the youngest pages were fooled. He exited the palace grounds with quick glances all around in search of those who would follow him. He saw nobody, but that meant nothing.

Once on the road to Plymouth, he set a steady, ground-eating pace. He calculated he would be allowed to leave England, for it would never do for Henry to be blamed for his murder. The English king would surely rather point a finger at France. So the straightest, quickest route to the seaport was the one he chose.

In Plymouth he immediately booked passage in the next available space sailing for Le Havre. It would leave in two days. Perfect. He retired to an inn to rest, a small and plain—but clean—establishment and a bed free of lice and fleas. Pricey for its cleanliness and new straw in the mattress, but he couldn't abide tiny passengers and was happy to pay what it took to avoid them when he could. All the night through he slept with the queen's letter tucked inside his doublet, in more of a light doze than real sleep. Part of him was ever alert for the approach of those who would apprehend him on his mission. It was a quiet night, however, and he went undisturbed except by the raucous drunken revelry in the public room below.

The following morning he arose, washed, checked his garment for the letter as he'd done every morning for several weeks, then made his way to the docks once again. But as he exited the inn with his saddlebag over his shoulder, he noticed a familiar face loitering on the narrow street nearby. The man stood amid a cluster of others before a shop, but Felipez picked him out readily. Only a quick glance, and though Felipez didn't know his name, he did know it was a guard from the palace. There would be others with him for a certainty. The Spaniard made no sign he'd seen the guard but strode on his way at an ordinary pace. He even managed to whistle a small scrap of tune and give a bit of a lilt to his step as he went. He was, after all, a Spaniard going home to Castile. He should be of happy mood. He slogged through the street as if he didn't care it was muddying his boots to a disgrace.

At the next turning, he let go the pretense and hurried to slip down an even more narrow lane that zagged between high stone buildings. Then he broke into a run to attain the next turning quickly. But it was too far. The two men running behind him to catch up spotted him as he ducked into a public house. He muttered an eloquent curse at his bad luck, then hurried through the smoky room, past clusters of drunken men and public women. The men were of the poorer sort, roughly dressed, and the women wore ragged dresses once worn by their betters and since stripped of any costly decoration. Most ignored him, but some gaped at his intrusion, for it was plain he wasn't there for refreshment of any kind. The Spanish courtier to the queen did not belong there any more than these common folk belonged at the king's supper table. They knew it as well as he, and they were right in looking askance at his presence. He fairly ran past the enormous cook fire and out another door.

Now his sense of direction was defeated, for the surrounding structures were high enough and close enough to make unbroken shade. He picked a likely direction and hurried.

But once again his pursuers emerged from the public house before he could dodge away, so he picked up his pace. Around a corner he found a ladder and climbed it to the thatching above. As quickly as he could move on the slippery straw and dried bracken, he hid behind a wide stone chimney. As still as a rabbit, he crouched, listening, and hoped the sign of his passing along the roof would go unnoticed.

Footsteps scraped the stone pavement below. The king's guards ran past, but Felipez waited. The urge to descend the ladder was maddening, but he knew not to move so much as a muscle yet. Not yet. Not until he could be certain his pursuers had given up the chase. Soon the footsteps returned, accompanied by irritated mutterings. The two had lost him and were backtracking carefully. Felipez wished he'd been able to pull the ladder onto the roof to keep them from investigating, but that hadn't been a possibility. He now prayed these guards were as dim as the rest of their countrymen and wouldn't think to climb the ladder in their search.

They didn't. After a few moments of discussion about where the slippery Castilian had gone, they separated and left the alley.

Still Felipez waited until he was certain they'd left the area. The sun was well beyond its zenith before he finally descended the ladder and made his way toward the docks once more.

Another ship. He couldn't return to the one on which he'd booked for Le Havre. This time he paid dearly to book passage under an assumed name on a vessel that would take him not to France but directly to Castile. A far longer and more dangerous voyage, and a far more difficult passage to buy, for he no longer dared present his passport. The amount asked of him nearly broke him. But Felipez knew France would be his death, even if he could escape England alive, so the cash sacrifice and the treacherous waters of the open ocean were the lesser evil. Particularly since this small ship was ready to make sail for Laredo that very day. It was his only hope. He stepped on board immediately and muttered a prayer for the skill and luck of its pilot.

The voyage was rough, and Felipez suffered horribly from seasickness. The tiny ship tossed unmercifully on the seas, through several storms, and even when the weather was clear, the rolling of the waves was accompanied by a rolling of his stomach. Nothing he ate the entire time stayed with him terribly long, and when they landed he was never so glad to see any shore. Pounds lighter than he'd been when he'd embarked in Plymouth, his doublet loose now, he obtained a horse with his credentials and began a hard ride to Valladolid. He traded horses three times before reaching the castle, and pressed onward with barely any stopping for food and rest. He arrived dusty and travel-weary, but whole and bearing the desperate message from his mistress. He tore open his doublet to retrieve the packet and prayed he would find the emperor in residence.

He was in luck, for Charles was at Valladolid as Catherine had predicted. Felipez was allowed through the gates and strode directly to the presence chamber. At the entrance to that chamber he encountered a steward who would have turned him away, but the letter packet bearing the seal of the Queen of England gained him entrance. There inside the presence chamber, Felipez recognized the English ambassador, a dull old man with a soft, plummy voice that somehow even the Spanish language couldn't make pretty. The ministers and ambassadors all turned to blink in surprise and disdain at the messenger's dusty intrusion, but Felipez ignored them all and walked directly to the guardian of the private closet. There he whispered his mission into the ear of the man who could take the knowledge directly to Charles, giving away only enough information to guarantee an audience. A murmuring started up in the room, but still Felipez ignored it. He stood in stillness as his request was relayed to the inner rooms. An itch on his head made him scratch, and he discovered a tick on its way to bloating. Revulsion turned his stomach, and he hurried to pinch it from his scalp. Then he flicked the thing to the floor and mashed it with a muddy boot, leaving a bloody smear on the stone floor. He returned his attention to the closet door, one hand pressed to the letter inside his shirt under his tunic and the other holding his cap.

Almost immediately a line of high-ranking ministers exited the door to Charles' closet, filing past Felipez with astonished looks. The muttering in the room rose to a grumble as Catherine's man was escorted inside. Still he ignored them, thinking only of what he would say to the emperor.

Charles V was a short man, dark, with a heavy lower jaw and full lower lip, all covered by a thick beard. His heavy eyelids gave the impression of sleepiness, but Felipez knew the mind behind those eyes was as alert as any bright-eyed young man. He sat in a large carved wooden chair near a window where the strong sunshine made a halo of light atop his head of sleek, straight hair. He wore his robes of state and a deeply concerned look on his face. Felipez knew the English king thought Charles was stupid, but those who knew the emperor also knew he never let on his true thoughts. The holy Roman emperor had been chosen for the position for a reason, and was as sharp a contender in Europe as any who had gone before him.

"What of my aunt?" he said as Felipez knelt and bowed.

The messenger raised his head and held out the letter from Catherine. Charles took it, broke the seal, and unfolded the page to read it. That took but a moment; then he laid the letter on his knee and looked to Felipez again. The messenger said, "She is in desperate need of your help. Her husband would set her aside to marry another."

Charles blinked, then almost impatiently gestured for Felipez to take a seat in one of the chairs emptied by those who had lately vacated the room. Felipez sat. Charles said, "He cannot do that." His voice carried a tone of surprised amusement, so ridiculous was the idea. Other queens might be set aside, but not Catherine. Not his aunt.

"He is trying nevertheless." Felipez relayed the message detailed to him by Lady Whitby and watched the emperor's face as he spoke. Not a sign of what Charles was thinking passed over it, not a muscle moved. Only his eyes moved, sometimes to look at Felipez, sometimes to look away.

When the tale was finished, he asked, "How has she responded to this outrage?"

"She has declined the offer of retirement and refuses to enter a nunnery."

The tiniest of smiles touched Charles' mouth. "Yes. That is Catherine."

"She has asked for legal counsel," Felipez added.

"She will have it, but not from England." He shouted for a scribe, who arrived momentarily with a desk he placed on a nearby table. "Write this," said the emperor, once the scribe stood ready with a quill poised for work. He began to dictate a letter to Cardinal Quiñones, general of the Franciscans, who was the most able canonist in Christendom.

The next letter was one to Catherine, assuring her of his support.

Four

1501

THE city of London decked itself out in all its finery for the wedding of Arthur, Prince of Wales, to Princess Catherine of Aragon. The day before the ceremony, the procession of the participants moved through the city. Streets and riverbanks were hung with draperies of rich fabric, alive with banners, lined with triumphal arches, and at every turn were the resounding of trumpets and colorful performances of actors and musicians. Ale was made available to the public in great quantity and for free, making the demonstrations lively and loud and somewhat disorganized, but it was all in good fun for everyone. From the tower came the thunder of cannon so profuse the sharp smell of powder permeated the air throughout the city. Catherine and her suite were conducted from the river to the bishop's palace amid throngs of celebrants crowding and jostling to catch a glimpse of the princess. This day was something they would each tell their children and grandchildren for the rest of their lives, at every opportunity around family fires, on travels, and even on deathbeds when the good memories would be most important.

There were frequent stops along the way as each of the tradesman's guilds paid homage to Catherine with pageants and pantomimes. The performers were elevated on enormous scaffolds to raise them above the crowds in the streets, all draped with fine cloth and swaying with the weight and movements of their occupants. Choirs before churches sang to her with sweet voices that beseeched heaven to protect her and praise her. Children and adults alike flushed with pride to participate. The enthusiasm was contagious, and the girls of Catherine's household came alive with giggling and grins.

Once again Estrella, Francesca, and Maria were agog with the high-spirited demonstration of joy in the English, and even more exciting were the performers in the streets. Acrobats tossed themselves this way and that, lithe, quick, and fluid, leaping more like monkeys from the Orient than like men and boys. One fellow in multicolored tights of saffron and scarlet, handsome in a rough sort of way, caught sight of the carriage conveying the maids and left off from his attention to Catherine to fall behind to the next carriage. He began to follow the girls, performing backflips along the street and forcing several onlookers to move out of his way lest he barrel into them. Loud complaining followed him, but he ignored it and made many near misses as those around him dodged his antics. Then when the carriage paused, he leapt upright onto his toes, bells a-jangling at his cap and the curled tips of his shoes waving. Tiny copper bells also jangled at those tips, which were ridiculously high and waved with the weight of their decoration. The grinning acrobat held out his hand to

Francesca in mute supplication. Then held it to his heart as if to indicate his hopeless love for her.

The girl laughed, a joyous appreciation for the fellow's outrageous humor.

"He wants you," said Maria de Rojas. "Go to him, Francesca, he's your match for a certainty."

The jibe only made Francesca the more giddy, and she clapped her hands together as she laughed. "He's quite handsome, for a fool. Perhaps he's a prince under a witch's spell, lost to his kingdom, and only needs the kiss of a beautiful maiden to restore him."

"Then kiss him and find out." Estrella giggled. "Go ahead and do it, if you think he's a prince."

Francesca laughed some more but said nothing further and leaned back in her seat to turn her attention elsewhere in the crowd. The dejected acrobat was left behind to pine after her in broad, comical gestures. The crowd around him laughed at his pretended grief, and when the fellow gave up his performance with a wide grin, he returned back the other way in a series of backflips. The wedding procession moved onward toward the bishop's palace.

Supper there that evening was even more than usual a long and elaborate affair involving many courses. Platter after platter of rich meats, soups, and complex dishes of fruits, meat, and confections entered the hall to be admired then distributed among the wedding celebrants. Tartee, noumbles, and blancmange graced the menu. There was goose stuffed with garlic and fruit, the skin browned to a savory turn, tripe in ginger smelling sharp and sweet, thick sweet pea soup, pears stewed in wine, boiled garlic, baked eggs, the list of dishes was enormous and the amounts fed to the party astonishing. Musicians of great skill strolled the hall, and Catherine's girls delighted in the elaborate and delicate strains the gaily dressed men urged from their lutes, whistles, and tambourines. There were jongleurs and actors, and the festive atmosphere pervaded even the most aged and serious of the king's ministers. The most staid of them laughed uproariously at everything uttered at the king's table, and not all of the hilarity sounded obligatory. Voices filled the enormous great hall, and figures in rich clothing and bright jewels moved about incessantly.

The cost for this display must have been astronomical, particularly for a king known throughout Europe as tightfisted with money. But Estrella watched the high table and wouldn't have known by Henry's demeanor whether he begrudged any of it. His smiles were broad, and his laughter at the conversation near him was hearty, reverberating from the walls more loudly than that of anyone in the room. Tomorrow would surely be a happy day for him. Indeed for all of them, for the futures of many people here today would be established or improved by this wedding.

Catherine sat near the king, beside her bridegroom. Her joy radiated throughout the room, and her eyes sparkled as she listened to Arthur's conversation. The prince seemed awfully still. Slow and almost languid in his movements, his gestures were few, and though he spoke a good deal his voice was not strong enough to be heard in the din about the room. Even Catherine, who sat beside him, leaned close to hear what he would say. His attention was on Catherine and nobody else, as her attention was on him, but it seemed more as if his focus was a thing by default, like water that runs along the floor to find the lowest point, then gathers into a puddle. It seemed he attended to Catherine because it would be too much effort to turn anywhere else.

Nearby sat the prince's younger brother, Henry, Duke of York. The boy was only ten years old but had a large, sturdy build that made him nearly as tall as Arthur. He was blond like his brother, but there the resemblance ended, for Henry was as robust as Arthur was frail. His cheeks were ruddy and his smile ready, and he ate as if he'd been starved for a week. Nevertheless, when the bowl came around for alms he relinquished as much of his portion as anyone, and as readily.

Maria leaned over to Estrella and said, "Have you met the Duke of York yet?"

Estrella glanced over at the boy. "No. He's a child in any case."

"He's an unclaimed child."

Estrella peered at her fellow maid. "Not betrothed?"

"The king apparently likes to keep his options open in these matters. Such a handsome *niño*, and so close to the crown, he would be a delightful match, I think."

"Perhaps, but still terribly young. Eight years younger than you. Six younger than me. By the time he will be of age to marry you'll be nearly an old hag." Estrella was only slightly teasing, for there was no denying her words had an ugly truth to them. Time would march more quickly for them both than for any man they could marry.

"Better a boy younger than I than an old man with crusty fingers and bad breath. Also, the most wonderful thing about extreme youth is that it eventually cures itself. I can see that boy is going to be a big, strapping man. With big . . . hands. See how big his hands are. You know what that means."

"I can't imagine what that means." A lie, but Estrella didn't care to discuss it just then.

Maria gave her a look, then shrugged. "In any case, were

my father to have a correspondence with the English king about the future of his little Duke of York, I would get on my knees and thank merciful God for it."

"Indeed, anyone would. But not because he would be such a wonderful husband. Only because of his influence."

"You wouldn't care to marry Henry?"

"I shouldn't care who I marry, except that he be of a status worthy of my family. My father must approve."

"And you think he would approve of the ship's commander who brought us to England?"

Estrella felt herself blush. "Not in the least."

"But you didn't take your eyes from him for the entire trip."

"Neither have I laid eyes on him since we arrived, you'll notice. I never spoke to him, nor him to me. He's gone on his way, and I've gone mine, and we've never exchanged two words. Nor has he seen my face."

"Nevertheless, you pine for him, and that is why you do not notice the young duke."

"Nonsense." Estrella told the truth. She'd not thought of the captain since landing at Plymouth. He'd quite disappeared from her thoughts, what with the excitement of finally being in England and discovering so many new things and people of interest.

"Then who do you notice here tonight?"

Estrella looked around. Most of the men in this room were very old. Older than her grandfather, she thought. The king himself was not a young man, and his ministers and advisors, and especially his friends, all seemed to be at least as old as he. Even the lesser servants appeared more aged than most, the musicians gray-haired even if on the average they were more fit than the highborn courtiers.

But across the way, in a seat respectably close to the king's high table, she spotted one man with a pleasing face, wearing a tunic the color of a fawn's coat with scalloping at neck and shoulders. He lounged on one elbow, leaning back on the arm of his chair, speaking casually to the diner at his right. "That fellow there," she leaned in to say to Maria. "The one in the scalloped tunic and high collar. He strikes me."

"The Earl of Hartford?"

"You know his name?"

"You do not? My dear Estrella, you must learn these things more quickly if you're to get anywhere in this court. Piers Hilsey is his name. His father died recently, leaving his title and an astonishing array of lands and houses. He has three brothers and no sisters. Old enough to be influential in the old king's court but apparently still young enough to catch the eye of Lady Estrella Juanita de Montoya." Maria's tone was teasing, filled with humor.

Estrella threw Maria a cross look, for she didn't find the comment so amusing, then gazed over at the terribly handsome earl. Young enough, she supposed, though certainly not a boy. He had the look of aristocracy about him. Of old family and with a strong confidence regarding his place in the world. It was a confidence rare in this court of a king who had taken his throne in battle from another king who had himself more than likely stolen that throne by regicide. The nose on his highborn face was long and straight, the jaw firm, and the eyes a crystalline blue that shone like jewels even from across the room. "I expect he's married."

"No. He was once, but his wife died in childbirth after only two years of marriage."

"And the child?"

"Dead also." Maria leaned close, eager to impress Estrella with her new and copious knowledge of the English court. "He was quite grieved over it, I'm told."

"Has he any other children?"

Now Maria peered at her with that insufferable grin on her face. "Well, and aren't you far too curious about him?"

"You're the one who asked me to pick out a man I found interesting. We could talk of something else if you like."

Maria laughed and replied to her question. "No children. None that lived, in any case, and I'm told there was more than one false start. They say his wife was a frail thing. Unhealthy and melancholy, hardly up to the task of bearing any children at all. Her death doesn't appear to have surprised anyone except the earl himself."

Estrella felt a slight pang of sympathy for the dead woman but shook it off. Certainly she herself would be up to that task once she'd made her own match. She was young and healthy, and her mother had borne five sons and three daughters, most of whom had survived. Her mother, in fact, still lived, though it had been many years since the last baby. All her father's recent offspring were illegitimate, so it was plain the pregnancies had stopped for reasons other than her mother's health. Estrella was certain she would take after her mother and produce a large family for her husband. Empathy for the failure of Hartford's wife was as lukewarm as anyone's would be for someone who had not lived up to earthly obligation, and it was the childless, widowed earl who received her most heartfelt sympathy.

Maria continued, "They say he hasn't spoken of marrying again, but now that his father has gone and he's got to think of his legacy, he surely will soon." Maria's tone suggested she hoped to be the one to catch the earl's attention once he resumed thinking about his dynastic obligations to his family.

Estrella grinned. "I thought you wanted the young duke."

The maid of honor shrugged. "Only one will have the boy, and I suppose Hartford would be an excellent consolation if I cannot be the one for Henry."

That made Estrella giggle. "Best of luck, my friend. Perhaps I'll have little Henry, and you'll be the one to marry Hartford, and then we could be each other's husbands' mistresses."

Maria let loose with a high, helpless riffle of laughter that took her breath quite away and made her press her palms to her chest. "Oh, wouldn't that be only too amusing? And the intrigue of it! Watching the two try to hide us from each other!" Both the girls dissolved into giggling until people around them stared to know what they could possibly find so funny, and they were forced to quell themselves.

The wedding the next day was every bit as splendid as the street celebrations and supper had promised. The London throngs cheered with abandon. Banners flew so thickly one could hardly see ten feet in any direction, or even much of the sky. Young Duke Henry escorted Catherine through St. Paul's Cathedral to the altar, his cheeks hot with excitement over his important office, and his eyes bright as he gazed upon his charge the princess. Thereafter throughout the day he treated her as solicitously as if she were a treasure for which he'd been given solemn responsibility. As if it were his duty to be certain she was untouched, unruffled, and as happy as a princess should be on her wedding day. Though his voice was a child's, and his gestures still as inelegant as a child's, he imitated his elders with sincerity and played the perfect guardian to Catherine's sensibilities. She seemed charmed by it and received his attentions as if she were Guinevere escorted to her wedding by Lancelot.

There at the altar, in the enormous and unutterably ornate

cathedral draped with hangings of exquisitely fine fabric, she was married to Arthur in a display of wealth and power designed to be remembered well and told and retold throughout the Christian world. Particularly, the exhibition was meant to reach the ears of her parents, Ferdinand and Isabella, who ruled Aragon and Castile, Louis who ruled France, and Maximilian of Austria, who ruled the Holy Roman Empire. All the monarchs of Europe would know the grand status of Henry VII of England.

The wedding supper was as sumptuous as the wedding itself, even more so than the feast the night before; course after course after course was presented, admired vociferously, then consumed. Afterward the palace hall was cleared for dancing. Wine, mead, and ale in plenty moved the celebrants well, and there was much hilarity in the room. Prince Arthur danced but once, and without discernible skill. He didn't seem very enthusiastic about much of anything after his exhausting day, not even his new wife. She was forced to look elsewhere for conversation, while Arthur sipped at his goblet and stared into the middle distance.

But the prince's little brother made up for him by wild, imaginative steps on the floor. The boy danced with his sister, Margaret, flinging himself about and waxing so playful he then began to throw off his overclothes. He ended up in only his silk shirt, tights, and slippers, waving a scarf as if it were a flag. King Henry and his queen applauded the demonstration of boyish silliness with loud laughter and humorous remarks. Estrella eyed him and began to wonder whether Maria might have been right. The duke was more filled with energy than even the average boy his age. He exuded health and good humor. Perhaps he would grow to become an admirable man and an exciting husband.

During the evening Estrella tried to maneuver herself across the floor to be near him, perhaps even to speak with him, but there were too many others with the same idea, and the press was too tight. Too tightly controlled by the higher ministers. Everyone close to the king was in high demand tonight, and the Duke of York was no exception. Catherine herself had little attention for her maids, who did not rank highly enough to enter the inner circle at this event thronging with important folk, and so Estrella found her entertainment with a succession of older men and her fellow ladies.

She looked toward Catherine's new husband and thought him a weak man indeed, for he danced hardly at all. Instead he observed from his seat at the table, a wan smile on his face suggesting he didn't think it odd that he was sitting. Later, when the couple were escorted to their ceremonial marriage bed, it was plain the groom was not well enough for consummation that night. His face was gray and his eyes dull, though he kept up his smile and pretended every intention of bedding his new wife. As Estrella watched Catherine slip behind the bed curtains with Arthur, she wondered how it must be to have such a frail husband. She also wondered whether Catherine looked forward to the consummation. Did she find Arthur attractive? Estrella couldn't imagine it.

She herself had often wondered what it might be like to have an attractive husband, but never let herself set her heart on it. Disappointment was too likely, and she would hope for the best and expect the worst. Those thoughts were only for daydreams and never for serious consideration.

By all accounts Arthur did not consummate the marriage that night. Neither did he participate in the tournament staged over the next three days, though the jousting was done by men who were strictly carpet knights and really had no business carrying a lance at all. Few genuine soldiers came to compete, and the majority of jousters were nobility playing at war, jockeying for attention from the crown and from the ladies present.

The pageantry, however, was exquisite and imaginative. Champions entered the field with as much pomp as could be mustered, each in a pavilion decorated to the fullest and ponderous in its glory. The wealth and position of each contestant was on display, and each man outdid the other for his elaborate presentation of himself. There were dragons and lions done up in painted wood and rich fabric, a hart and an elk, gold and silver everywhere, ships of plaster and lathe, and even a representation of Catherine herself. At sight of it she applauded like a happy child, thrilled at the attention and homage.

Estrella's eye was caught by a glimpse of a knight below, riding an enormous white destrier and carrying his helm beneath his left arm. A dark blue plume waved from atop the helm, a matching blue velvet cape trimmed in silver cloth fluttered from his shoulders, and there was a bluish cast to his polished armor. She would swear she could see from here his equally blue eyes. The entire ensemble was new and perfect. He shone in the sun so brightly the glare nearly hurt her own eyes. The stallion's neck arched, covered in shining crupper and polished mail, and his tail tossed in the air, his knees high and his gait proud. Hooves thumped hard on the sod. The bard covering the stallion was of rich fabric, a dark blue to match the knight's cloak, emblazoned in silver with his motto. Sir Piers Hilsey, Earl of Hartford, proudly and ceremoniously cantered his glorious mount past the stands, where spectators cheered and the crowd was aflutter with handkerchiefs and ribbons waved to catch his attention. Colors upon colors, some among the royalty even glittering of gold cloth. He nodded to certain of them, and Estrella thought his eye might have lingered an extra moment on her own face. But then it moved on, and she watched him go with a tickle in her belly that made her laugh. How dashing he was! How like a true knight of the Round Table!

Like the others who had come to the field before him, Hartford presented himself to the queen, who sat in the stands at the side of King Henry, and saluted her with his free hand. In a strong, level voice that carried across the field, the knight requested permission to joust in her presence. The language of his speech was as elaborate as he could make it, for each combatant tried to outdo the last for gentlemanly and chivalrous formality. The petition matched his armor for beauty and embellishment. Hartford stated his intention to behave according to the strictest laws of gentlemanly behavior, to fight with honor and courage, and he assured the queen in the most flowery terms that if she declined to grant him permission to enter the lists, he would leave the field with utmost grace. Needless to say, the queen's permission was granted and the earl handed his heavy cloak off to his squires. Then he wheeled his destrier to canter across and take his position among those accepted to the tournament. Estrella watched him go, and her heart thrilled at the beauty of his armor and his horse.

Then she turned her attention to the next knight to enter the field, and let the earl slip from her mind. One by one the jousters presented themselves and were accepted to the contest.

Occasionally Estrella watched Catherine and her new husband. They seemed to be enjoying the spectacle well. The new Princess of Wales laughed readily and applauded the efforts of the jousters. Her husband sat as an observer, with a quiet dignity that struck Estrella as even more reserved than the other Englishmen around him. His cheeks were rosy today, though perhaps a bit too much so. There was always a fine line between the glow of health and the flush of illness, and it was no secret that Arthur's health was not robust.

The jousting that day was nearly dance, highly stylized and carefully staged so as to prevent serious mishap to the nobles in armor or their mounts. The contests were well matched, the men suitably fierce in their confrontation, then boisterous and benign to each other in their victory or defeat. The high-ranking ladies in the stands took great pleasure in awarding their favors to appropriate participants, and all was pleasant and ceremonious and utterly genteel.

How like the tales of Camelot, thought Estrella. Camaraderie and goodwill in a place filled with English knights who never really fought, except verbally in the king's court. On this tilting field they only played at trying to hurt each other. Ceremony in place of war, very orderly. Gentlemanly. It pleased her. Perhaps Catherine was right about the English. This might very well be a place where chivalry lived in its truest form, where grace was more important than strength, and justice had a place of honor.

The blue-and-silver figure of the Earl of Hartford caught her attention when it became his turn to tilt against the Duke of Stafford. The duke was as glittery as the earl, perhaps even more so, in gold as well as silver. They rode to opposite ends of the list, scalloped edges of mail lifted from the animals' necks with their gait, and the ends of metal glinted. Each reached his end and lined up facing the other.

Sun sparkled magnificently from the men's armor and the chain mail draped over the horses. Silver and gold, blue and russet, plumage swaying with the movements of the horses and the horses' bards swinging, heavy with embroidery. Hartford's white stallion pranced in his enthusiasm to be off, and it was only by the knight's riding skill he was able to control the animal. The man rode as if he had been born in the saddle and sat his mount as if he were as integral to it as a centaur.

A squire in blue-and-white livery handed up a blue-painted lance to the earl, as the duke was similarly armed by his own servants. Each held a shield bearing his coat of arms elaborately painted on it. Estrella looked over at the duke, so glorious in his display, then at the earl, whose turnout was equally beautiful if not as rich. But the earl had a much better horse, she saw. The white beast was larger and more powerful than the dark bay steed carrying Stafford, and his movements were more smooth and steady. Hartford's destrier would be the better mount, for a certainty, and Estrella knew Hartford had the advantage for it. She whispered to Maria de Salinas next to her, "The earl will prevail. I know it."

Her friend looked over him with an assessing eye. "He is the more handsome and graceful. Younger. But that can be a disadvantage against a seasoned opponent." She nodded toward the duke, who was such an opponent.

"Hartford looks to be nearly thirty."

"No more than twenty-five, I think," Maria said. "And Stafford has certainly seen better days."

"He's a relic."

"But I'm told his victories in the lists are sung far and wide. He is feared by many."

"The earl has the better horse and rides as if he were a part of it. He will stick to his saddle. I know it."

"I'll wager not."

Estrella looked over at her. "What would you risk?"

Maria thought about that a moment, then a sly smile crept across her face. "I would give my token to Stafford in his next tilt. And you must give yours to Hartford if he loses."

That made Estrella giggle, the hilarity rising and bursting from her so that she had to throw back her head. "Oh, you're wicked!"

"Do it! Take the wager if you think you know the horses so well!"

Estrella eyed the knights making ready to charge. Hartford set his lance against his breastplate and held it steady. He was strong. Younger than Stafford, and with the better horse. He waited with a calm Estrella could sense from where she sat. It was as if he also was certain he would win. "Very well. I'll accept. If Hartford loses, I'll offer him the sash from my waist for him to wear in his next tilt." And hope he would accept it, for she would be mortified to be rejected, particularly by a knight who had lost his previous joust. Now her heart thudded with the fear of losing her wager.

There was a shout and a roar from the stands, and the white and bay stallions lunged toward each other. Estrella rose a little from her seat, willing Hartford her strength that he would not fall. Hooves pounded against the sod. Each stride of Hartford's destrier was a thud of Estrella's heart. Plumes flew from helmets like banners, flapping out behind each rider in blue and russet. Lance tips wavered, each seeking a vulnerability.

Then the riders met with a quick, nearly anticlimactic snap and a crunch of metal as Hartford's lance broke, and Stafford flew from the back of his mount to land on the sod below in a heap of shining armor. Onlookers raised a great noise of mixed cheering and disappointment. Estrella was out of her seat, applauding the earl as he circled to return to the center and discard his broken lance. She was no longer thinking about what she would have had to do if he'd lost. She wasn't even thinking about what Maria was now obligated to do. Her smile was for Hartford that he'd won the joust, and he'd won the wager for her. She bounced on her toes with excitement and clapped her hands with the unmitigated joy of the day.

Maria, for her part, didn't seem terribly sorry to have to give up her sash to the duke in his next attempt later in the proceedings. She tossed it to him over the side of the stand with much gaiety and laughter, accompanied by a smattering of applause, and he snatched it from the air with a gallant flourish. With a broad, theatrical, and gentlemanly bow of his head, he then tied the token loosely around his own waist to let it fly behind him as he rode around the tilting yard to assume his position in his next joust, as champion for Maria de Salinas. The duke was married and had at least one mistress, but this was all in good fun. Maria laughed, and Estrella smiled.

It occurred to Estrella she might have liked it just as well if she'd lost the wager and had been obligated to hand Hartford her token. She imagined him taking it with a smile and a bow for her, a fine figure of English chivalry. But she put the silly thought aside and paid her full attention to the next tilt.

The tournament continued with as much festivity for two more days.

DURING the next several months the girls in Catherine's suite settled into their new lives at the court of the English king. Now part of the household of the Prince of Wales, they were far more important than they'd been in Spain. Estrella's father was a duke in Aragon, and she'd spent her first fifteen years being educated and groomed to assume a position such as the one she now occupied. Her mother had gone to great trouble to arrange this for her and had spent many years maneuvering Estrella into the notice of the royal household of Catherine's father. This was a position from which Estrella could find a husband to suit her rank and who would advance the interests of her father by his influence. Not nearly as important a role as the ones her brothers filled, especially so far from Spain, but her life was really not much different from Catherine's. They all were expected to marry well for the benefit of their families, and they all began to learn English for the sake of facilitating good matches. The joy of it was that she had a good chance of accomplishing that goal. She threw herself into learning about England, its language, and its people.

Until Prince Arthur and his wife were sent to Wales. Suddenly the household was moved away from London and to a spot where the people around them were even more strange than the rest of England. If Henry's courtiers might be dull and unsophisticated compared to those of King Ferdinand, Arthur's local ministers in Wales were downright crude. Nearly uncivilized. Estrella decided she would be glad to return to London at the earliest opportunity.

As it turned out, she didn't have long to wait. Arthur's health worsened even more than anyone had feared, and the prince died early the next year. Suddenly the Spanish household of the Princess of Wales was adrift. Princess Catherine was not just widowed and alone, but with her status in question, for even during those months in Wales Arthur had never had the strength to consummate his marriage. Now his widow's dowry, and therefore her future, was under dispute by her father and the king.

Five

1502–1505

FOR the next year Catherine and her suite lived at Durham House, existing as a pocket of Spaniards and not having much contact with the England outside their walled gardens. They were beautiful gardens, but they were a small world compared to court life and the yearly progression from palace to palace. The girls all expected to be returned to Spain without ado, for Catherine's marriage was ended and there didn't seem much for her here any longer. The dowager princess often wondered aloud to her closest friends what plans her father had for her future, but declined to speculate on possibilities. She only waited for word as to what would happen to her, and her duenna, Doña Elvira, watched over the household with complete efficiency. Catherine worried about nothing, and therefore the girls had nothing to worry about. They passed the time with their embroidery, music, shuttlecock games, reading to each other in English for

the practice denied by their seclusion, and as always much of
the day was spent in worship. Whether at Mass, in confession,
or murmuring the rosary, their fingers tracking the prayers on
fine beads of hard and dark woods, Catherine's household
held tightly to her own devout ways.

Then word came there were other plans afoot in England
for the girls. In the midst of questions about whether the marriage to Arthur had been consummated, King Henry claimed
Catherine's dowry as inheritance from his son. If she returned
to Spain, she would be forced to leave behind all that had been
paid, an amount her father could ill afford to replace. Hard on
that development, news flew through the small household
that King Ferdinand was negotiating with Henry for a betrothal of Catherine to the new Prince of Wales. Though it
seemed an obvious solution to many issues for both monarchs, it was also a surprise because it went against canon law
prohibiting marriage to a brother's widow.

During the negotiation, word whispered in the chambers
of Durham House had it that the flamboyant Spanish ambassador to Scotland, Don Pedro Ayala, had been censured by
Doña Elvira for suggesting Catherine's marriage to Arthur
had been consummated. As it was, any marriage between
Catherine and Henry would require a papal dispensation because the wedding ceremony to Arthur had taken place. Were
Catherine no longer a virgin, there would be no question but
that she would be prevented from marrying Arthur's brother.
When Elvira heard of Ayala's comments, the woman came at
him in high indignation, an irresistible force in protection of
her princess's honor and prospect for marriage to young
Henry. Doña Elvira declared before Henry's court as strenu-
ously as she could—a considerable thing—that she and all the
ladies of Catherine's household would swear that Catherine

was *virgo intacta*, as pure as the day she'd first set foot in England. The English courtiers and their king eyed the Spanish matron and considered her plainly biased words. They were skeptical, but their only real concern was for the advantage or disadvantage of the king's position. The doubt cast on Catherine strengthened their position, but to confirm a consummation would bring the entire negotiation to a halt. Nobody wanted that. The arguments dragged on.

Estrella was taken aback when she heard she might be asked to testify on behalf of her mistress, for it was a serious business to swear an oath. Hell awaited those who swore lightly and falsely. As much as Estrella loved and regarded Catherine, she was not close enough to her mistress to be completely certain of the truth in this matter. Only the duenna was in a position to know what had gone on in the marriage bed of Catherine and Arthur every night of the several they had been together. Estrella's best guess that nothing could have happened between the two was based entirely on the obvious ill health of the prince. Arthur had never in those months appeared strong enough to have taken Catherine's virginity. Had Estrella been approached, she would have sworn only because she trusted the duenna. Doña Elvira would never have said such a thing if it weren't true, for the virgin status of a girl was easily proved or disproved. To say it and then have it proved false would have been a disgraceful failing of honor on the part of the princess's guardian. It would have destroyed her reputation. They would all have been ruined. Estrella knew Catherine must have never consummated her marriage to Arthur, because Doña Elvira had said so.

Besides, there was the assertion of Catherine herself. Estrella believed Catherine was incapable of telling a lie.

The wrangling over the issue continued as long as Henry's

advisors could make it, but in the end, Doña Elvira not only drew an apology from the ambassador but ultimately Ayala was recalled to Spain. The testimony and examination were never required. Hope rose for the successful conclusion of the marriage negotiation, for the acceptance of Elvira's word suggested King Henry truly wanted his son to marry Catherine and did not want bad news to spoil the deal.

Finally, in the summer not quite two years after the Spanish suite's arrival in England, it was set that Catherine would marry Henry as soon as he came of age. The boy would be fifteen, and marriageable, in three more years.

So now Catherine's status was settled and she was once again permitted to participate in court life. But on the other hand, she was no longer the dowager princess, and King Henry was no longer obligated to care for her. Suddenly she was without English status of any kind and dependent on her father for support. But Ferdinand was not forthcoming. Catherine and her household remained at Durham House, but now on the charity of the king. Over the next years the Spanish household was forced to live in tighter and tighter circumstances. Though there was an allowance from the king, it was carefully controlled by him, and every bit of it was spent on daily maintenance and food for the suite. No salaries had been paid for quite a long time, and food was growing scarce. No new clothing was to be had, and the girls spent more of their time sewing, turning their old dresses to look less shabby. Catherine made no complaint and only waited for her wedding to take place.

Then the news came of the death of Catherine's mother and the succession of her sister, Joanna, to the throne of Castile. A double blow, for the political situation between the monarchs of England and Aragon worsened as King Henry pressed to gain political advantage over Ferdinand in Europe. Trade disagreements arose. In retaliation for slights to English merchants in Spain, Henry cut off Catherine's allowance entirely, leaving the Spanish household without any support at all. The princess and her maids were no longer invited to the king's court. They no longer enjoyed socializing with the courtiers, rarely even seeing the outside of the palace grounds, as if they were prisoners. Prince Henry was sequestered, kept away from Catherine. And she missed seeing him at court.

It was disheartening to watch Catherine in her loneliness. Left with the company of her elderly suite and unhappy maids of honor, she heard little encouragement from those around her. Francesca, ever the one to point out whatever might be wrong, complained bitterly of their poverty. Sometimes she let Catherine overhear, then pretended it had been accidental. But everyone knew she wanted their mistress to know how displeased she was. Estrella thought she was disgraceful. Over the years they'd been together, Catherine had always been kind to them and had done her best for them. As much as she disliked the situation herself, Estrella thought Francesca to be ungrateful. Tension rose. All the girls were on edge, wondering what would become of them, and arguments became commonplace. Only Maria kept her silence. And, of course, Catherine.

One morning Estrella was helping dress Catherine when Doña Elvira entered the chamber.

"Your Highness," she said, "A letter from His Majesty, your father." She handed the sealed packet of paper to the princess, who tugged herself away from her maids and went to sit on her bed, half dressed in a shift that had been patched and darned, the rents hidden with embroidery more than once.

She broke the seal and read with great excitement what her father would say to her. But as her eyes scanned the page they dulled, and her face fell. A frown creased her brow, and when she finished she looked up at Doña Elvira with saddened eyes. "He says nothing about money."

"Nothing?" Doña Elvira leaned in to look at the letter. "Surely you've written to him of our predicament."

The maids busied themselves with the clothing Catherine had not yet donned, pretending they weren't listening. They brushed off nonexistent lint, straightened already smooth silk, checked the sewing on each pearl and sapphire. But every ear was pricked to the conversation. Estrella found a pearl dangling by a thread nearly worn through, and she reached for a needle to fix it, glad to have something to keep her in the room and occupied so she could listen.

"Indeed I have," said Catherine. "But here in this letter he writes blithely as if all were well and there is money enough for every need. As if I hadn't written to him at all." Her voice faded as she spoke, puzzled and lost.

"Perhaps he hasn't received your letters?"

Catherine gazed at the paper and made a small noise of concern. It would be terrible indeed if the English were intercepting her letters to Ferdinand and not sending them on. "No, see, here he makes reference to the comment I made about wishing to see Henry. He tells me I'll see him soon enough, and that once we're married I'll wish to not see so much of him. So lightly he treats the whole question." She looked up at the duenna. "So, you see, he's gotten the last letter."

"Perhaps he doesn't believe the seriousness of our predicament?"

The princess sat with the letter in her lap, thinking hard, a deep crease in her forehead. "He doesn't think I know what I'm talking about. He thinks I'm still only a child."

"Your father has utmost respect for you, I'm sure of it. However, he does hear from his ambassador. Perhaps Dr. De Puebla has been untruthful in his reports? You can hardly blame your father if the man he depends on for information is lying to him."

"Why would De Puebla tell lies? Why would he want me to live this way?" She gestured to the room, to the shabby bed curtains, bare walls, and nearly ragged maids. Her words defended the Spanish ambassador to England, but her tone had an edge that suggested she thought Doña Elvira had hit on the truth. Catherine had never liked the somewhat furtive De Puebla.

Doña Elvira folded her hands before her. "Perhaps King Henry is bribing him. You know how Henry wants to see you suffer for your father's protection of Spanish trade interests. He would have Aragon a fiefdom of England, so demanding he is to have precedence in over-water trade. King Ferdinand refuses to treat English merchants as if they were his own Spaniards, to welcome the English to plunder his kingdom, and for that Henry would punish you. He wishes to hurt Ferdinand."

"Then he doesn't know my father at all," said Catherine. Estrella smiled at that, somewhat dryly, for it was well-known that Ferdinand's only love was for his kingdom. His daughters were of value to him so far as they could advance the interests of Aragon, and they all knew it. Catherine had been raised to understand that principle as much as she'd been raised to love God. Ferdinand could not be manipulated by threats to any of his daughters, and that made him a stronger monarch, less vulnerable to pressure such as this.

Doña Elvira chuckled. "No, Henry does not know your father. But De Puebla knows Henry, and the wily old ambassador knows what will gain him money and influence. He's been in England quite long enough to have established interests here. Surely he has told lies to your father, then taken gold for his treachery."

A hardness came over Catherine's face. Her lips pressed together, and her eyes narrowed. Her dislike of both Dr. De Puebla and the ostentatious and superficial Ayala was well-known. Also, she knew her duenna didn't like either ambassador and tended to follow her lead in these matters. "Do you think so?"

"It's possible. Likely. That cunning old Jew knows his way around a king's court. He may even be encouraging Henry's coldness toward you."

"But why would he do that?"

"To endear himself to the king. To make Henry trust him. Who knows what a man will say to be on the good side of the fellow wielding the power? This is a golden opportunity for him to place himself in a position of influence, where he controls the lines of communication and lets people think what he wants them to think. With Your Highness betrothed to the Prince of Wales, it is not only Ayala's importance that has increased. De Puebla certainly must be making the most of it. More than likely he thinks you're a simple girl who won't realize what he's up to."

Catherine stared at the floor for several more moments, hard in a frown, but it gradually fell into a wan look of despair. "What am I to do? I cannot continue living like this." She looked over at her maids. "They cannot continue like this."

"Perhaps you need a respite, Your Highness."

"Of what sort?" Catherine's voice was distant. Confused.

"A journey to see your sister." Catherine looked up, and Doña Elvira continued, "Joanna. Surely once Queen Joanna sees the straits in which you are living, she will set things to rights."

"And with what money would I pay for this journey?"

The duenna's voice turned bright and lively, as if there were nothing to worry about and they were planning a picnic in the country. "Write to her and suggest a meeting between Henry and her husband. Surely your sister will embrace the opportunity to see you again and will welcome the king. Henry will think it an excellent opportunity to meet with Philip. There could be great benefits to the entire undertaking, for the two of them would have a unique opportunity for a meeting of the minds in many things. It would be a marvelous diplomatic coup for you and would go far to make your reputation as being a woman of substance, and not just a simple girl."

As Doña Elvira spoke, a light of relief came to Catherine's eyes. "Do you think so? Do you think King Henry would think well of me for suggesting this?"

Francesca whispered something to Maria, but Estrella couldn't hear. Maria shook her head and glanced over at Catherine, then returned her attention to her work.

"Of course he would. It's a marvelous idea. It would demonstrate in plain terms your position among European royalty and that you are not to be taken lightly. You are a princess, daughter of a king and sister of a queen, and as such should be treated with far more respect than you are."

Catherine appeared to be thinking hard on that, and Doña Elvira pressed her case from another tack. "Also, it would show him you have his best interests at heart. And those of England. A sovereign lives as his land does, you know. Your parents taught you that. I'm sure that when you show him you love England as much as he does, he will accept you as a true daughter."

The frown on Catherine's face cleared, and Doña Elvira pressed even further. "By this," she said, "you would not only please Henry, you would also get to see your sister you haven't seen in so very long."

Catherine flushed at the prospect. "Oh, yes! I like the idea very much. It's been so long since I've seen anyone. Doña, bring me my writing things. I'll send a letter to Joanna immediately. A journey to the Continent is exactly what we need!"

A murmur of excitement rose among the maids standing by. They were going on a trip! Though it meant sailing again on a boat across the treacherous channel, it also meant gaiety once they arrived. Music, dancing, and good company. And probably better food than what they were becoming used to these days. Estrella's heart lightened as they finished dressing Catherine, then the princess sat down to pick up a quill and write the letter to her sister. The mood among the maids was joyous.

The reply from Queen Joanna returned quickly. Catherine received a letter from her sister in Flanders that she and her husband Philip would meet King Henry in Saint-Omer, and naturally Catherine would travel with him. Letter in hand, the princess danced around her chamber, laughing with joy at the thought of seeing her sister and her husband, of royal festivities, of having a visit with someone who would not treat her coldly as the English king had. She sat down to write another letter suggesting the meeting, this one to King Henry. At long last the oppression under which they'd been living would be over. Joanna and Philip would see to it she was treated as a princess.

That evening after supper, the maids were sitting with Catherine at their sewing while Estrella played her lute for them. Poorly, she thought, for she loved music and knew her talent was less than she wished it to be. As she played, she thought of the deft and creative minstrels of her father's household, and one in particular who had arrived the year before her departure for England. He'd been young and beautiful, his gray eyes terribly deep and his music so haunting as to give her chills. She'd followed him everywhere, begging him to teach her his skills, and he'd obliged with a gentle smile and kind voice. The way he'd spoken to her, with his smooth, trained voice, made her heart skip in ways she'd never imagined possible. And it quite confused her at the time. His countenance and bearing drew her to him, promising lovely, mysterious things she could suspect but never quite understand in her youth. He'd called her Estrellita, always softly, as if the name were a secret between them. It made her dream of what it might be like to be alone with him, to talk privately and without the watchful eyes of her guardian and others about all the time. But the thought was a silly one, for her reputation was far too valuable to her father to let it come under question for the sake of a musician. The palpitations of her heart meant nothing to anyone but herself, and so she kept them to herself even as she pressed the fellow for music lessons. Manuel, his name was. Beautiful Manuel, whose patience with a very young girl placed him in her memories as a hero. She now thought of him every time she played her lute.

Anymore, the playing was more practice than performance, but even so she was acknowledged to be the best musician of the women in the suite. She allowed as any real skill she might have on the instrument was bestowed on her by her father's minstrel.

Voices rose in the next chamber, and they all looked up when Dr. De Puebla barged into the room. The lute fell silent. His face was dark with alarm, and his eyes glanced about, looking desperately for someone or something. Then they settled on the princess. It was plain he was restraining himself as best he could, but the business he was about was apparently so urgent he must violate every protocol. The strain in his voice as he spoke choked him so he could hardly spit the words out. Lines of sweat ran down the sides of his face from his hairline to his jawline. None of the girls had ever seen him so distraught.

"Your Royal Highness," he said, "I have a matter of utmost urgency to discuss."

Catherine laid her sewing in her lap and frowned at him. Her voice was stern. Offended. "Dr. De Puebla, you forget yourself."

He fluttered but gathered his courage and held his ground. "Indeed, Your Highness. I regret that I must. Something has gone terribly awry, and only you can help me now."

"How?" The princess was not accustomed to being sought for her opinion on anything, and her curiosity seemed to have the advantage over her intense dislike of this man.

"A letter has gone to King Henry, written by Your Highness, inviting him to a summit with Philip."

Catherine shook her head. "A visit."

"A *summit*, Your Highness. I must tell you—and it grieves me terribly to have to say this—that such a meeting would be devastating to your father."

The blood fled Catherine's countenance. Not a muscle moved in her body. Softly she said, "Go on."

De Puebla did. Though Estrella didn't understand the convoluted politics of the situation, she did glean from De Puebla's plea that any alliance between Henry and Philip would cripple Ferdinand of Aragon strategically in Europe. Catherine's sister was the ruler of Castile in her own right, her kingdom more powerful than her father's, and her husband Philip already disliked Ferdinand. With Henry backing him militarily, Philip could rid Castile of Ferdinand's influence. Aragon would then be completely alone on the European stage, with no allies and no money. Estrella felt herself pale at that prospect. Not just Ferdinand, but her own family would suffer. Her father. Panic rose in her, and she listened to De Puebla with increasing interest.

When De Puebla finished, Catherine said, "Why would Doña Elvira suggest the meeting if it were truly so disadvantageous for my father?" Doña Elvira was Castilian, but her loyalty to Catherine's father had never been questioned in all her years of service to the crown of Aragon.

"It is for the sake of her brother. Don Juan Manuel is a Castilian separatist. He wishes for your father to lose his footing there and for Philip to have complete influence over his wife and her domain. Your duenna has led you to betray your father in order to aid her brother."

Now the paleness in Catherine was filled with a flush of anger, and she looked away from the ambassador.

"Do you understand what I say to you?" he asked.

She looked at him again, a hard light in her eyes Estrella had never seen before. Catherine said, "I understand a great deal more than you might think, Ambassador."

For a moment, he hesitated to say the thing that danced at the tip of his tongue, but then he spoke. "Do you believe me, Your Highness?"

She nodded. "Yes. I can see your sincerity. And I can see where I've been remiss in learning the facts. I understand the truth in what you say."

Estrella's mind raced, wondering what would happen next. But she didn't wait long, for Catherine immediately set her work aside and went to the writing desk near a window. "Dr. De Puebla, tell me what I must write." She sat with all the dignity of a queen, picked up a quill, and looked to the ambassador for direction.

The journey would never take place, and for that the maids were all sorry. Francesca, especially, took hard the news they would be staying in London indefinitely. She even had the temerity to suggest that an alliance between Henry and Philip would have been a good thing for them all, for if ever Henry decided he no longer needed a relationship with Aragon, he might send Catherine back to her father. Then they could all go home. Estrella made a clucking noise of disapproval at that. Francesca was Castilian, and so therefore was her family. She had nothing to lose by what she suggested. The fortunes of Estrella's family, on the other hand, went very much hand-in-hand with those of King Ferdinand. What Francesca suggested was selfish and shortsighted, and Estrella did not even deign to discuss it. She kept her head down as her fingers worked her needle and Francesca kept talking on and on.

Doña Elvira, it turned out, lost a great deal by what she had done. As soon as Dr. De Puebla was on his way with the letter Catherine had written for him, the princess summoned her duenna. Then she dismissed her maids for the meeting to be held in private, but Estrella, Francesca, and Maria all picked up their skirts and hurried to a room off the presence chamber that connected by a short, narrow hallway to the princess's oratory. With a rustling of skirts and shushing each other as they approached, they then settled into the small room where a stained glass window let sound in from the bedchamber. There they listened, kneeling in the dimness before a crucifix and a tapestry depicting the pieta. Through the window they heard clearly the conversation between Catherine and her duenna.

"Explain this to me," the princess was saying.

There was a dark silence, then Doña Elvira's voice came. "I only wished for you to be happy. To see your sister after all these years would have been a wonderful thing for you both."

"And convenient for your brother."

"What could Juan have to do with you? Or Queen Joanna?"

"Nothing. But he has a great deal to do with my father. And Philip. But King Henry will not be in the midst of this if I can help it. I will not let your machinations hurt my father." Clear anger crept into the voice of the princess.

Doña Elvira laughed, a light, easy chuckle as if Catherine were simply being silly and overreacting. "Dear, dear Catherine. You know I love you like a daughter. I would never do or say anything that would hurt you or your father in any way. I've sworn loyalty to the king."

Catherine's voice rose. "And you've broken that oath. What you have done could be construed as treason, and it is only your previous years of good service that keeps me from doing so. How dare you claim loyalty, when you know the meeting you suggested would have put my father at a terrible disadvantage?"

"Who told you that?"

"The ambassador."

"And you believed him?"

"Once he pointed out the truth to me, it became plain. I do not like him, but neither will I let that blind me to truth. I do not doubt him in this. You thwarted the marriage offer Maria de Rojas received, and now you've attempted to destroy my father's influence in my mother's realm. Obviously it is you I cannot trust—"

Doña Elvira's voice was conciliatory, and the girls could hear the tinge of fear in it. There was a perverse thrill in hearing the mighty duenna caught so at a disadvantage. "Of course you can trust me! In my service to you I've never had anything but your best interests at heart! I've loved you like a daughter and know you better than your own mother did! I've been your duenna for more than a decade!"

"And no longer. You are dismissed."

"Your Highness—"

"I said, dismissed! Leave! You will make your own way back to Spain. I'm certain Dr. De Puebla will be able to secure your passport from the king."

"Who will watch over you, then?" Doña Elvira's voice became strained and panicky. Clearly, she was at a loss she'd never experienced before with Catherine.

"I am perfectly capable of taking care of myself, Doña Elvira. Apparently I must do so whether you are here or not, so I wish you to be gone."

"You cannot go without a chaperone. Not until you are married."

"My chamberlain will act in that capacity. And I will abide by my own counsel from now on. I am old enough. And I certainly cannot trust you."

The duenna's voice turned wheedling, and the maids' eyes widened. Doña Elvira begging? They'd never imagined it. "Your Highness—"

"Go!"

"Catherine—"

"Leave now!"

There was a long silence. It strung out so long, everyone so still, that Estrella thought she could hear her own heartbeat. Finally Doña Elvira said, "Yes, Your Highness. I only wish to say—"

"Say nothing."

"*Please*. Your Royal Highness, just one thing."

Again there was silence, then Catherine said, "Very well."

"I truly would never have hurt you. I wish you to understand that. What I suggested would have been best for you. I told the truth when I said the meeting between Henry and Philip would have put you in good odor with the English king."

Catherine's voice was low and dark. "Elvira, when you hurt my family, you hurt me. I could no sooner allow you to plot against my father than I could countenance you assaulting my very person with a dagger. And I'm appalled . . . *appalled* you do not understand that when you claim to know me and love me so well."

Doña Elvira didn't seem to have a reply to that and only cleared her throat. Then she said, "Yes, Your Highness." Then, with a rustle of skirts, the duenna withdrew from the chamber.

With that, Doña Elvira was gone from their lives. The maids looked at each other, stunned. For Estrella, the thought was heady. No more scoldings. No longer would the old woman's overbearing presence control their lives. A sly smile spread across Francesca's face, and Estrella was hard put to disagree.

And what of Catherine? When the ladies returned to the chamber, they found her sitting on the bed, her hands folded in her lap, staring at a point on the floor several feet in front of her. At first they thought she was praying, but there were tears in her eyes. None of them spilled, and she straightened to address the maids. It was time to ready for bed, she told them. And so they went on with their day and their lives, but with a mistress who was no longer a simple girl.

Six

1506

B Y the time Prince Henry was old enough to marry, his betrothed was twenty-one, and the king still dragged his heels to allow the wedding. Estrella was also twenty-one, and there had been no offers of marriage for her from anyone in the English court. There had been precious few offers for the maids, and the older they became, the less likely there would be any at all. Passing the lonely, quiet days in the palace, Estrella listened to Francesca bemoan their fate.

"The prince will never marry her. The king has a hundred thousand crowns of the dowry; I'm sure he'd rather keep that and promise his son to someone else than to give up little Henry for nothing."

"Not for nothing. It is for the daughter of Ferdinand and Isabella," said Estrella. "Besides, the prince isn't so little anymore. I caught a glimpse of him not long ago, and he's grown to quite a size."

"Big hands," murmured Maria. Estrella chuckled.

Francesca laid her hands and sewing in her lap and gave her a harsh stare. "We're all going to return to Spain as old maids." The girl who had once been the prettiest of Catherine's maids then ruined her beauty with a frown, bent her head to her work, and yanked her thread through the fabric in her hands.

"Maria de Rojas had an offer. Two offers."

"But she didn't marry Derby's grandson, you will note. That match died a horrible death, and for lack of dowry. The only one who would have her was Doña Elvira's son."

"Doña Elvira made sure of it. Blame her. Maria de Rojas would have had Stanley if not for Doña Elvira taking advantage of her position and our plight."

"Exactly. If not for Catherine's uncertain status, Doña Elvira would never have succeeded in thwarting the match with young Stanley, and she would have made an excellent marriage. She would have been a countess one day. Our situation is hopeless."

"Francesca, don't be so gloomy." Estrella had heard it before. Many times over the past three years, in fact. The refrain had become a daily thing for Francesca, whose bright, lively beauty was fading more quickly and more obviously than the rest. Already her dimples were beginning to turn to deep lines in her cheeks, and the corners of her mouth were turning down. Her habitual frowning encouraged it, and Estrella often thought how Francesca might still be the prettiest of them if not for the set of her face. Today she sewed with highly skilled fingers that had done little else in what seemed a long time, and it crossed Estrella's mind that Francesca's doom-filled thoughts might be more true for herself than anyone.

"Our life here is awfully gloomy; you cannot deny that.

How can I pretend there is hope of any of us making a good marriage anymore?"

"Aren't you happy here?" Maria was the closest to Catherine, and now there was an edge to her voice that Francesca was speaking badly of their mistress. She took sharp glances at her, and her own frown was creasing her face.

"Not to spend my entire life imprisoned by the English. Forgotten and ill-used. They hate us here, you know. They hate foreigners."

"And I suppose all Castilians love foreigners?"

Francesca's voice turned sulky now. "Hostages; that's what we are now. We are hostages of the English, held so the English king might have power over ours. Even Catherine has forgotten us, for she has turned English also, and has become one of them. She's turned against us."

"She can't have. She sees us every day, and she gives us every bit of gold she gets." Maria leaned close and whispered, "And you might wish to keep your voice down, lest she hear you in the oratory. Even in prayer she might still hear what you say."

"Especially in prayer," whispered Estrella. "I think sometimes when she speaks to God, God talks back. And tells her things."

"I don't care what she hears." In defiance, Francesca even raised her voice a little and turned her face toward the small room with the connecting window, where Catherine knelt in private meditation. Mass would be soon, and they would all go then to pray. "In fact, she should know that she has reneged in her duty to us."

"She can't help it." Maria picked with her fingernail at a stubborn knot in her thread, then used her needle to loosen it.

"There has been little money from her father, and that has gone to feed us all. She's done everything she could."

"Except take us back to Spain. She hasn't done that."

"We shouldn't want to return to Spain. Even as things are, our prospects are better here than they ever were there. Not to mention that English men are more willing to marry girls our age than any of the Spanish men we might have married. In addition, it's not within her power to return. She's to marry Prince Henry."

"Well, then, good for her. She can't care what happens to us now that her own future is assured. Which, I don't think it truly is. Henry doesn't wish to marry her. He said so a year ago."

"Surely he was told by his father to say that. It can't be true; why wouldn't he want to marry Catherine? I'm certain the king only wanted to force more dowry from Ferdinand, and so he made the prince say what he did. He made it seem as if the marriage would be thwarted by the prince's childishness if Ferdinand let the negotiation go on too long. I expect he thought the King of Aragon would then collapse in apology at his folly. King Henry knows our princess has nowhere else to go and no purpose anywhere but here, and only wished to let us know his son was the more powerful. Posturing and rattling of sabers, that is what he is all about."

"At least, in this instance he is," Estrella said. "Wait until the marriage takes place, then you'll see who is the more powerful. And the more intelligent. Catherine is her father's ambassador. Ferdinand doesn't want her to leave England and will go to a great deal of trouble to keep her here."

"She's his spy, you mean."

"She was always his spy. Now she's got a place and a task,

and she is privy to information she never had before. She can't take us back to Spain. Our king won't allow it."

"He might reconsider when all the plate is gone," said Estrella. "He'll have to." She relished the looks of surprise on the faces of Maria and Francesca. "Oh, you didn't know that? Catherine has been forced to pawn some pieces of the gold plate she brought with her from Spain. Her dowry is going to support her. And us."

"Then why isn't the food we're given better than it is? Why are we forced to eat fish even on days that are not fast days? And strong fish in the bargain." Francesca held up the sewing in her hands. "And why must we turn our dresses and patch our linen? Where is the money if she's pawning the plate?"

"Should she lose all of it? Should she have all of it gone before she marries Henry? He's been old enough to marry for months, and still the king is delaying. Who knows how long it's going to be; would you have her spend all there is, then not be able to buy food at all?"

Francesca glanced toward the oratory. "Indeed. Who knows how long it's going to be? We should entreat King Ferdinand to return us all to Spain. It's our only chance at any sort of decent future. I think—"

The door to the oratory opened, and Catherine emerged with her Bible and rosary in hand and a warm smile for each of them. The girls stopped talking and rose to greet their mistress. Catherine chatted amiably among them as she picked up a bit of embroidery she'd been working on and settled into a seat by the window. The girls sat again and attended to their work, attempting to restore their worn clothing to a measure of respectability.

Not long after, an invitation came to attend a hunt led by

the king. Excitement swept through the Spanish household, for they were rarely invited anywhere, and it had been years since any of them had been on a hunt. Catherine's ladies set to work on their least worn dresses to make them presentable to Henry and the rest of the court. *Especially* to the rest of the court. Here was a chance to catch the eye of someone eligible to rescue them from obscurity. Estrella took her best dove-gray dress—the one that brought out her eyes—and sewed onto it some pearls filched from another dress that was more frayed at the hems than this one. Perhaps the decoration would take attention away from the age of the fabric. Fortunately, pearls and gems were ageless and caught the attention more brightly than frayed silk.

It was quite an exciting day in the forest near London where the hunt took place. Most of the girls had ridden in hunts back in Spain, but in recent years there had been little opportunity. Estrella would have loved to take a horse through the woods in pursuit of a hart, or even a red deer, but today she was disappointed to learn the hunt would be a bow and stable. Only the hunters themselves would be on horseback, and the game would be taken by archers hidden behind trees and blinds. The animal would be driven into range of the archers, then killed and butchered on the spot for the entertainment of the guests.

As onlookers, the women would spend the day nearby the blinds, enjoying the company and the king's hospitality in the forest setting. A tent pavilion of colorful silk was erected, and though it was well worn and plain, it was also large and comfortable, furnished with plenty of chairs and tables, the forest floor inside strewn thickly with dried straw and bracken. A small, black iron brazier burned in the center to keep the fall chill from biting the guests. Quite a few women were there, wives and daughters of the king's friends in the hunting party and their ladies, all seeing and being seen by those who were closest to the king and his son. In fact, there seemed to be little real conversation at first, for everyone was looking around to see who was there and who was seeing them. Few seemed as interested in the hunt as they were in eyeing each other's clothing and jewels, and gossip was dispensed in low whispers. Some of it also in voices louder than a whisper, where some with an abundance of irritation or overconfidence made certain they were overheard by everyone.

There was good food and drink, plenty for everyone, and Estrella was glad for an opportunity to eat her fill on the bounty of the king rather than of her mistress. The girls happily helped themselves to cold meat and wine while the king and his company lurked in the forest in pursuit of the wily red deer. It was good to be away from the palace. This place had a wildness to it that gave a fluttering to Estrella's heart, and her skin tingled among untamed, gnarled trees, explosions of bracken, and racks of black fungus nestled in deep shade. It seemed a place of magic she'd read about, where one might encounter a wizard lurking among moss-covered deadfall. Where woodland creatures knew more than the men who rode their horses along ancient tracks in the dark stillness of even more ancient and knowing trees. Men on horseback moved in the distance, and for a moment Estrella could almost see a glint of shining armor. But then it was gone.

Catherine seemed to be enjoying the day. She drew deep breaths of the fragrant forest air, and kept a sharp eye out for the hunters among the trees. But neither king nor prince was within earshot, let alone sight. They were busy placing themselves so they surrounded the deer, and would force the animal back in this direction. The onlookers awaited their approach. The princess sat near the opening of the pavilion, on a folding chair draped with red velvet and equipped with a pillow for a cushion, and chatted with her ladies until there would be something to see.

"Do you know the meaning of this hunt?" she asked the group at large in a cheery voice. Her cheeks were bright apples in her oval face.

The young women looked at each other, then Maria said, "This particular hunt?" Estrella wondered whether there might be a political significance she'd missed, and listened closely to what her mistress might say.

"No. The taking of deer. What it means to hunt one."

Estrella was relieved to realize Catherine was speaking only in general, symbolic terms. Today was supposed to be fun, and she didn't wish for a lesson in politics to spoil it. "I know little about deer, beyond that they're delicious to eat and dreadfully hard to catch."

Catherine laughed happily. "All true, but that's not what I meant. You've not read the *Livre du Roy Modus*?" Estrella shook her head. "Did you know that the deer, particularly the hart, is a symbol of eternal life and hope?"

Francesca moved away from the group, and Catherine's eyes followed her for a moment. Then she turned her attention to Estrella, who replied to her question.

"They're beautiful beasts." The first time she'd seen a hart, with ten-point antlers and a long, graceful neck, its flanks strong and powerful, her breath had been quite taken away.

"Indeed. As beautiful as the hope they represent. You see, its enemies are just as the enemies of man. The wolves who seek to devour it are as the devils from which we all must flee. The men who hunt it are the world and all worldliness—"

"How? Why are the men not like the wolf?"

"Because there is no possibility of the wolf ever taming the deer. He would never care to; he only eats the deer. But man would tame the deer if he could. He cannot. The deer must live near men but cannot let himself be tamed by them, just as men must resist worldliness and its temptations. He, like the deer, must live apart, always aware of the dangers surrounding him, yet never changed. He must be who he was born to be, and can never be what worldly influences would make of him." The girls nodded with understanding, and Catherine continued. "The third enemy is his irresistible urge to seek female deer in the rutting season, which is the temptations of the flesh men are prone to. It weakens the hart and makes him easy prey to wolves, and so it is also with men who are slaves to their earthly bodies. When one succumbs to temptation, one is taken down by the wolves and devoured. All hope is then lost, for that is death. True death, of the soul."

"What of eternal life, as you said? How does the deer represent that?"

Catherine was warming to her subject, and her eyes brightened as she said, "It's said that the hart can live forever. But first the old hart must go through a transformation. It must scatter the anthill of lifetime accumulation, tread underfoot and swallow the white snake of avarice, then it must retreat to a deserted place where it becomes as if dead. That is purgatory, where the immortal soul suffers, but only for a finite time. Then comes the marvelous transformation. It throws off its aged flesh, hide, and bone and becomes young again. It emerges triumphant, wholly restored. And we can do that as well."

Francesca, listening off to the side, murmured, "I would like to be young again."

Estrella and Maria threw her cross looks, and Catherine

made no sign she'd heard. The princess continued, "We all have hope. Each of us has the ability to make that transformation if we do what's required of us and bend to the will of God."

Maria said, "That's a good thought. I'd like to believe it."

"I tell you it's true. You may believe it without reservation." Nobody dared to contradict her. Estrella hoped it was true.

At that moment a cry went up in the forest some distance away. Dogs set to baying, and horns bleated signals to the hunters and archers. Crashing of underbrush and a noise of hoofbeats heralded the approach of their prey and the mounted hunters behind it. Catherine rose with an excited smile, quite forgetting the conversation. "Does anyone see Henry?"

"King, or prince?"

"Prince, of course. Does he approach?" They hadn't seen him that morning at the assembly, but it was said he rode with his father to drive the deer.

The girls craned to see, but there were only sounds yet. No sight of men, dogs, or horses. Then, in the distance, there was a movement among the trees, rustling and cracking of branches, and an animal bounded into sight. Then another. Two deer were fleeing, leaping with wild grace and heart-stopping terror, headed straight toward the spot where archers with crossbows stood. The shooters let fly, the thunk of bowstrings sounding like a short drum roll. Each immediately bent to reload another bolt. They hurried feverishly, fingers flying and arms cranking, for the crossbow was slow to cock. Many hunters preferred the sword in spite of the danger of coming too close to a quarry, for it rarely missed and was always ready.

One deer collapsed, but the other stopped in its tracks and stood, confused. Its nostrils flared and eyes looked wildly about, rimmed with white. Its flanks twitched with the urge to flee, but no knowledge of which way to go. Its sides heaved and struggled for breath, but only for a moment, before it bounded off in another direction. The fresh bolts flew, and one found the animal with a dull thud. The creature fell head-long and disappeared from sight among the bracken.

The dogs bounded into view, and not far behind them was the crashing of horses through the forest. Two more deer appeared and met their fates as the others, and the hunters rode in to claim their prizes. With cheery voices they congratulated themselves and each other. The men took care in giving credit to the king and shouted great, loud cheers to him. An excited murmur arose among the onlookers.

King Henry galloped up, and the guests gathered around to see the unmaking of the deer and the ceremonial rewarding of the dogs. Prince Henry was there, on a fine stallion he controlled as masterfully as any of the older men. His face was flushed with the excitement of the hunt, his cheeks a deep, rosy red that covered his jaw and parts of his neck as well. He laughed with a robust joy as he dismounted and let a courtier take his mount for him. The newly arrived men trampled the bracken all around, making it much easier for the women to see what was going on. "Here, Your Majesty," he said to his father. "Here is the finest one." He indicated the largest of the deer, the first one felled.

"Aye," the king agreed and called to the hunt master for the carcass to be taken to the nearby clearing where the pavilion stood. He and some huntsmen obeyed and lifted it by head and hindquarters to carry it.

The king's master huntsman was Sir John Cranach. Estrella recognized him from a time he'd stayed at Durham House for some days the year before, while taking deer for the king's table. Today she noted that when he saw her his gaze lingered far longer than it should have for discretion, and a secret smile touched her lips. He seemed an old man, approaching forty and never married, but he couldn't be considered ugly, by any means. Beauty was a sign of God's grace, so she knew he must be a good man, and that pleased her. His hair was a virile thatch in spite of his age, and his office as huntsman kept him fit as well as moderately wealthy. Though his face was lined, his person seemed more youthful than many his age. The way he'd looked at her, she thought perhaps she'd caught his eye, and that might be an excellent thing even though his rank wasn't worthy of her own station. These days she could no longer afford to be overly fussy about who she would marry. None of Catherine's women could anymore. Without staring, she kept her attention in Sir John's general direction to see if he would look her way again.

The king and his retinue of sportsmen followed the large deer carcass to the clearing, and a leather packet was brought to him, unrolled, then placed on the ground before him. His knives. They were very nice ones, though not as ornate as even those belonging to Estrella's father. The handles were of ebony tipped with pewter, all matching, and the blades were of shining steel. Those blades varied, but most were of a leaf shape, some wide and some narrow, a couple of them no longer than dirks but others nearly as long as swords. Among the set was a long fork, also of ebony, pewter, and steel.

The king rolled up the sleeves of his fine hunting tunic for this task and approached the carcass with something akin to reverence. With the aid of Sir John he hauled it onto its back and embedded the antlers in the earth beneath so that the throat was a long, high arc. Then he selected a short, thin knife and plunged it into the base of that throat. He cut the length of the neck, then adjusted his stance to make another cut downward at each end of the first. The two flaps of hide were ripped back by the king and his huntsman. Blood ran copiously, and Sir John caught as much as possible in a large wooden bowl. The flesh of the neck was sliced to the bone.

Then Henry and Sir John stood back while the death was blown on trumpets and horns. One loud blast, two soft and short, followed by four more, then another loud, and two soft close together. Each hunter repeated on his own horn, then all blew the reply. The sound ended in a long, triumphant blast before all lowered their horns.

The laughter of Prince Henry was louder than the rest of the men, as if he seemed to be enjoying the outing the more. Estrella glanced over at Catherine, who also was laughing, her gaze hard on the prince. The princess wasn't watching the *curée*; she had eyes only for her betrothed. Estrella observed his antics as he helped his father prepare the carcass to be butchered. He was in a festive mood and danced attendance like a jongleur, with flourishes that were quite comical and seemed to annoy the king. But they amused Catherine, and though he never glanced in the direction of his intended, Estrella wondered if the show was for her. It made her smile and lifted her heart to think it might be. If Prince Henry were amenable to the match, its likelihood seemed greater.

By now the dogs were in a happy frenzy for their taste of the kill. They danced and slavered at the ends of their leashes, and all knew what was to come. The baying was loud and frantic, encouraged by the hunters who egged the animals on in great humor. The men laughed and grinned and joked with each other, having as much fun as the dogs. Then the hounds were allowed to run to the carcass and harry the neck flesh. Each dog snatched at the meat running red, but only for a moment. Animals fed daily on bread were encouraged in the hunt this way to crave the meat of the deer and only get it after they'd performed the task for which they had been trained. These dogs would only be used for deer and never any other quarry.

A heavy, forked stick was brought, the *fourchée*, and stuck in the ground nearby. King Henry cut the testicles from the dead animal and handed them to his son. The prince took them, dangling by the skin, between his fingers and swung them back and forth like a little pendulum, causing laughter among the onlookers.

Finally he hung them on the fork, then returned his attention to his father as the king split the hide from the groin to throat. Then down the inside of each leg, and around the neck at the head. He and Sir John yanked at the edges of the skin until it was all peeled away from the meat and flopped back toward the ground. More, smaller, sticks were brought to hold up the edges of the hide so blood would pool inside it, the forks stuck through tiny slits cut in the edges. Then began the cutting of the joints of meat and the entrails. First the tongue was cut from the head with a long knife and hung on the *fourchée*, then the flesh was stripped from the neck. Working the length of the carcass, each piece was cut and set aside and would be given to the person or dog for whom it was intended. Along with the testicles and tongue, the *fourchée* received the large intestines and some other small organs and tender meats that would be for the king himself.

Gradually the deer was reduced to a skeleton, the bones bright pink and gleaming white in their freshness. Then came the *curée*, in which the hounds received their reward.

During the butchering, the small intestines had been washed, then chopped up with the heart, lungs, and liver of the beast, then mixed with bread and the blood saved in the wooden bowl. Once the offering was ready, the hounds were encouraged to bay again, worked into a frenzy, then let go to eat their reward of entrails, blood, and bread from the carcass. The men shouted hunting cries as the animals ate. The on-lookers applauded.

Estrella watched Prince Henry during this and was taken by his lusty enthusiasm. He seemed as excited by the event as the dogs themselves, and shook his fist in the air as he shouted in a voice that cracked with adolescence but showed promise of manly strength. He was tall and would surely grow even more. Maria had been right; he had big hands.

Then she looked over at Catherine, whose gaze was only for the prince. Eyes bright and wide, she followed him with them wherever he walked or stood. Shameless. Catherine didn't seem to care who saw her stare at Henry. Every so often he would glance at her, then away. Estrella wondered what he truly thought. Had the boy meant it when he'd said he didn't want to marry Catherine? She hadn't been deported, and that was good. But it was well past time for the wedding according to the contract, and still it hadn't been set. None of that seemed to matter to Catherine. To her, it was only a matter of time before the event took place, and she acted as if they all had an eternity to wait.

But young Henry did keep glancing at her, and with each flash of his eyes it seemed he gazed longer. Now Estrella really began to wonder.

She also wondered about Sir John, who went about his business, performing a similar but less noisy and theatrical un-making on the other dead deer now that the main excitement was over. Estrella watched him order his men this way and that. They leapt at his command. Below the notice of the

king—who was occupied as the center of the attention of his
guests—Sir John made certain the meat of the other quarry
was taken and distributed according to established practice.
Each huntsman would go home with his portion tonight, the
amount of meat owed to him for his part in the hunt, depend-
ing on his station. Carefully, she eyed the master huntsman
from a distance and noted his strength. The way he manhan-
dled the carcasses himself, rather than standing back and let-
ting his underlings do all of the work. Not very gentlemanly,
to be sure, and it indicated poor breeding, but there was something to be said for a man who was so hale and active at his age.

After a moment of observation, she then retired with the
others for refreshment near the tent.

For the rest of the day, the thick, metallic smell of blood
mingled with the fresh forest smells. It reminded Estrella of
home and her father's hunts. As a child she had loved the festive camaraderie of following the dogs through the woods, the
men's voices hallooing in and out among the trees. The scents
of trampled brush and disturbed earth, the sharp sweat of the
horses, and the blood. It stirred something in her she'd long
missed. She was sorry when the excursion was over, and they
all had to return to Durham House where their furnishings,
meals, and pastimes were terribly dreary. Boredom awaited
her there.

It wasn't long after the hunt that Estrella received a visit
from Sir John Cranach.

Seven

 O N a cloudy afternoon not long after the hunt, the young women of Catherine's suite were at their sewing in an inner room of the apartments. Only one small window gave onto the outside of the stone palace, and the room was not large, so it was quite cozy, though the fire was a small one to save fuel. The wall hangings were shabby enough to be an embarrassment, but for the sake of warmth Catherine was in the habit of asking for the use of whatever tapestries and drapes weren't occupied, no matter what their condition. If any overlapped on a narrow wall nobody minded, for they made for a warmer room which required less wood to heat. Old rushes were left under the new ones more often than in the rest of the house, even though the old were trampled and damp, for the thicker layer was better than a thin one. Some floors were stone, and even on the wooden ones in the upper rooms keeping feet warm in the winter was often a difficult task.

On this afternoon Catherine's chamberlain came with a message that Sir John would like to have conversation with Lady Estrella Juanita de Montoya. A murmur of excitement rose, but Maria said to her, "You can't possibly encourage him."

"I can't possibly let this opportunity pass," Estrella replied, nonplussed by the comment. It was ridiculous to consider rejecting a valid offer of marriage in her circumstances. Maria should know that, but never seemed to face the fact.

"He's only a knight and barely has any lands to his name. He makes his living from his work." Her tone was thick with the disdain such a thing deserved. There was no security in marriage to a man who made his living by fees.

Estrella knew Cranach was beneath her, but also knew it might be the only offer she would ever have. Even assuming this was an offer. There was no dowry, for her father expected Catherine to provide it, and of course the princess had no resources for it. Any man who would make Estrella his wife would have to want her only for the sake of her youth and her connection to Catherine. That youth was waning day by day, and her connection to Catherine became less promising as the king balked further at the marriage to young Henry. There was still a chance they would one day all be sent back to Spain with no husbands, no youth nor beauty, and no prestige in the English court. Here was a bird in the hand, and she wanted it. "If he makes an offer, I will accept it." She set aside her work and readied to stand.

"A huntsman?"

"Master huntsman to the king. And far better than spinsterhood."

Catherine said softly as she slowly pulled thread through the fabric in her hands, "Do you not believe I will marry Prince Henry?"

Estrella's heart fell as she gazed across at her mistress. She was caught, and her mind scrambled for a reply that would not give away her fears. She said, "Sir John is handsome." But her voice betrayed that she knew he wasn't handsome enough to overcome his lack of lands or to win a noblewoman's heart by his looks alone.

"So you would marry him because you have fallen in love with him from afar. Because he is so very comely." A couple of the girls giggled at that.

Estrella said, "Comely enough in spirit."

"You've spoken to him? You know his heart?"

Estrella wanted away, quickly, but she had to reply. "No. But I've seen him at his work."

"I see." Everyone in the room could see that Catherine realized Estrella was afraid her mistress would never marry Henry. "And if the angel Gabriel came to you and said, 'Fear not, young Lita, for your mistress is fated to marry the prince and will one day be Queen of England. You will marry well and soon.' What would you say if that happened?"

"Why, I certainly would know it was true, and wait for it to happen, were God's messenger to tell me to wait."

"Why? Why would you then know it was true?"

"Because the angel said it."

"So, why must there be an angel? Where is your faith? Do you have no faith?"

That stung. "I have as much faith as anyone, Your Highness." Estrella's heart skipped, for she knew how important it was to Catherine that her maids be devout.

"If your faith is so strong, then I ask again, why do you

need the angel to tell you what you should already know?" The princess leaned forward, her interest intense, but her voice remained even and gentle. This mattered a great deal to her, surely, but she avoided condemning her maid's feelings.

Embarrassment reddened Estrella's skin in blotchy patches over her chest, neck, and cheeks. Her head lowered, and she looked only at the work in her hands. "I don't, Your Highness. I shouldn't."

Catherine put her work aside. "Then do what your heart tells you, and not your head. If you know that all will be well, and that God will not allow you to live your life alone, then receive an offer from Cranach in that light and make your decision according to that. If you can accept him, knowing that our situation here is more dire than permanent, then do so, and you will have all our blessings. But do not think for a moment that you have no recourse but to marry beneath you. You must have faith God wouldn't do that to us."

Francesca said, "You're so certain?"

"You are not?"

"He took Arthur from you, didn't he?"

Catherine sat erect, her chin up. "Yes, and for a purpose. It is plain I was meant to marry Henry and not Arthur." Her voice was filled with utter certainty Estrella wished she could feel. "Henry is strong enough to hold the throne after his father, and strong enough to sire many sons who will assure the Tudor succession. There will be no war. Had Arthur lived long enough to ascend the throne, his ill health would have made for a weak king. A weak king is vulnerable to insurrection and civil war, and there are many who feel they are more deserving of the throne than King Henry. God obviously does not want a civil war in England and will make certain the succession holds. I will marry Henry, and the beautiful thing of it is that all I need to do to accomplish God's will is to wait. It will happen, and all I need is to have faith in it."

The girls fell silent in the face of her serene belief.

"Now, go," said Catherine without the slightest hint of rancor, and she patted Estrella's knee. "Go talk with your suitor. If he pleases you, then accept him. If he does not, send him away disappointed. You are not a slave to any man who asks you to lower yourself."

Estrella felt her heart lighten at the thought and nodded. "Thank you, Your Highness." She rose and set her work on her chair, then accompanied by the chamberlain went to greet her suitor in an outer chamber.

"Here is a veil. Wear it." The chamberlain strode beside her and handed Estrella a single layer of dark lace. Since the dismissal of Doña Elvira he'd taken many of the responsibilities regarding the safety and reputations of Catherine's female servants, but now that Catherine had come into her own as a Spanish ambassador, that control was less strict. Unlike the heavy veils Catherine once wore, this one was of a loose weave and only chin length. The bottom hem was of a denser lace weave and dotted with tiny seed pearls. However, beautiful as it was, Estrella declined to take it.

"I don't wish to wear a veil."

"You will wear it." He commanded her in a hard voice accustomed to obedience. Though he'd been in this country a very long time, he was still as Spanish as the day he'd stepped off the ship in Plymouth. His English was not nearly as fluent as her own, and he often tried to use Spanish even when speaking to Englishmen. Estrella thought it would be folly to trust him on what would be best for her in this negotiation.

"I cannot, and I don't even see any point in it. Nobody wears them here. I've been in public without one several times. In fact, I haven't seen one in years."

He stopped in his tracks, and Estrella paused without turning to look. Her heart would surely falter if she did, and she would lose her argument if she attempted to look the chamberlain in the eye. "He will think you're a whore if you don't wear it." His voice was filled with disgust.

"He will think I'm a foreigner if I do."

"You are a lady of Spain. That is why he will want to marry you. You are better than Englishwomen. More demure, more obedient. Surely more devout. Wear the veil."

"If he marries me, I will be neither a lady nor of Spain. He is English, and he will think like an Englishman, even if he is intrigued for the moment by an exotic Spaniard. My hair is dark, my complexion not nearly as pale as the northern Englishwomen. If he cannot see my face, he will think I'm hiding something. Pockmarks, perhaps. Lesions. I won't wear the veil, and furthermore won't hear of it."

"I demand you wear this."

"No."

The chamberlain glared at her in silence. Estrella gazed back at him as bravely as she could. She waited for the world to crash in, or lightning to strike, but neither happened. Instead the chamberlain said in a low, fell voice, "Your father will be ashamed of you."

That struck Estrella's heart like a dagger. But she looked off to the entrance of Catherine's presence chamber where her visitor awaited and drew a deep breath. She could sense the chamberlain's rage, coming from him in hot waves and evident in his hard, stiff breaths, though he was silent. It was like standing too close to a hearth, though Estrella was unable to back away to a more comfortable distance. Slowly, she said as challenge rose in her, "My father more than likely will never know." She now looked him in the eye. "Unless you tell him yourself you failed to make me wear it. And if he heard it on the heels of news I was betrothed, he would more than likely survive the shock. Far better, do you not think, than to hear I lost a valid and respectable offer for appearing too foreign."

There was a long silence while the man chewed on that perspective. Then he said, "The respectability of the offer could well be debatable."

"The respectability of a lady with no dowry might also be in question, were we to press the matter."

The chamberlain made a frustrated clucking noise, then folded the veil and stuffed it into a pocket in his robe. "Very well. But do not be terribly surprised if there is talk of you bandied about in the future."

Estrella had been close enough to the English court long enough to know there would be talk of some sort about everyone, no matter what anyone did. Just then all she cared about was to appear the perfect English bride to one man. "Indeed."

The chamberlain proceeded toward the meeting, and Estrella followed.

They entered the room used for Catherine's presence chamber and found Sir John standing by a small fire in the large hearth. He wore what was obviously his best suit of clothes. It was new, she could tell, and she wished her own dress weren't so well-worn. Sir John was as splendid as could be expected, in green velvet and a brocade of autumnal brown that had an almost golden sheen. As often seen as he was by the king, he obeyed the sumptuary laws to the letter. So the pikes at the toes of his shoes were short, and there was no embroidery anywhere. Nor was there any trimming in fur. Not even miniver. Estrella took a deep breath and told herself this was unimportant, but it struck her as ironic that a huntsman would not be allowed fur in his costume.

Sir John greeted her with a smile and a bow. "Good afternoon, my lady."

She nodded to him. "Good afternoon, Sir John. Would you like to have a seat?" He waited while she took her own seat in a rather rickety chair that boasted a deep rose-colored cushion stuffed with down. Though there was little decoration in this room, the pieces that were here were the best available to Catherine. Only one tapestry graced one wall, but it was large and new, and showed a well-executed scene of Jesus at the wedding in Cana, turning water into wine. The seat taken by Sir John was a finely carved wooden bench before the fire. He seemed reluctant to move very far from the wan source of heat in this rather large and underfurnished room. But his voice was cheery as he said, "I've come to test waters, so to speak, for a suit of marriage, and I hope you'll find yourself agreeable." A plainspoken man. Blunt, even. One could tell he did not make his way through the world by virtue of his way with words. Estrella found it at once alarming and intriguing.

"We shall see." She made a conscious effort to minimize her Spanish accent, for she knew it was not pleasing to some Englishmen. Over the years she'd learned that, while the English sounded guttural and crude to her, to their ears she sounded weak and untrustworthy. Today she spoke clearly and formally, rounding her vowels as he did, opening them so they sounded as English as she could make them, and keeping herself from the rolling R's that were often confused with Scottish speech.

His eyes flickered at her reply, but his smile never faltered.

"I've noted my lady's attention has sometimes been drawn in my direction. I hope I'm not mistaken."

"You're not mistaken. Not at all. I confess I am intrigued. Do go on." Care would be necessary to not be so coy as to discourage this straightforward fellow.

He drew a deep breath and settled his hands on his knees to proceed with his offer. He was terribly transparent, so much so it was nearly painful to watch. One wondered how he ever survived in his post so close to the king, amongst the cutthroat politicking and backstabbing of far more subtle courtiers. But then, it was true he never spent much time at court. His office took him into the countryside more often than it allowed him to be part of palace affairs. His strength as Henry's master huntsman was to keep a low profile and let the king appear to have accomplished every aspect of any hunt. The huntsman wasn't important enough to enter the privy chamber, and so never was allowed deeper into the apartments than the presence chamber. He was ever on the move on his own professional hunts to provide game for the king's enormous and often crowded table. More than likely Sir John survived well because he was beneath too much notice.

Again Estrella's heart sank at the thought of marriage to a man who would ultimately remove her permanently from the court. Even with Catherine's connection to it as ambassador so tenuous, Estrella was now closer to the seat of power than she would ever be as the master huntsman's wife. Living away from the palaces of London might be unbearably dull.

He brightened and said, "Intrigued? You would consider a suit from me, then?"

Estrella nearly snorted with exasperation. Too fast. She was already having to swallow her pride just to speak to him.

He was asking for a capitulation she could hardly afford to give at this time.

The chamberlain leaned down and whispered in her ear, "Do not reply to that. Not until he has submitted a formal proposal to Catherine."

But Estrella knew this man would see silence from her as a rebuff. She ignored the suggestion and replied to Sir John, "That should depend on what you would offer."

Now he sat up straight, and realized he was going to have to talk her into this. He cleared his throat and said, "I'm a good, honest, and devout man. I have lands—"

"Some."

"Enough." His head tilted just slightly as he realized she'd been looking into his background. His voice heavy with emphasis, he continued, "And the promise of more."

"The king is an old man. And not a generous one."

Sir John nodded. "I have a good rapport with the prince. I expect to keep my office into the next reign."

Estrella's heart lightened, and a tiny smile she couldn't help touched her lips. She'd not anticipated this. "That is good." It would also be good if a man could be certain of living into the next reign, but she kept that comment to herself. Death was always a possibility no matter who she married, and not much of a consideration in this instance, for the knight's good health was obvious. It shone from his cheeks like a light. Instead, she said something that was perhaps just as cynical. "Tell me, sir, what gave you the impetus to approach me?"

He smiled, and Estrella didn't care much for that, for it seemed too forward, but then he said, "I've heard you are also honest and devout. A good woman, who would be a credit to me as a man and as a Christian."

That made her blink, though it was certainly true. It was

also a given in her mind, and she had never thought of it as a point in her favor she held above other women who were not known whores. In short, it seemed he was telling her he wanted to marry her because she was not a slut or a heretic. His expectations of women certainly did not seem very high.

Then the knight went on to say, "You believe I wish to take advantage of your awkward position in the court."

"You must know I come without dowry to speak of."

The chamberlain said quickly, "Lady Estrella, it's plain Sir John is aware of your superior ancestry and your position in the royal court."

This time it was Sir John who ignored the comment. He leaned forward and replied to Estrella, "As I said, my position in the realm is not precarious."

"Neither are you ambitious." Now Estrella was forging ahead in plain talk. They were getting to the heart of this matter, and she wanted to know the answer. More than likely this was a man who would tell her honestly.

"I know the limitations I bear in life, and don't wish to stick out my neck for it to attract unwarranted attention from a king who is known to look with disfavor on men who are too ambitious. I offer you a respectable life though not as sumptuous as that enjoyed by your mother. I wish to marry you for the sake of your virtue and beauty, and the grace you would bestow on our children."

A flush of hope rose at the mention of children, and she realized she'd been avoiding the thought for fear of disappointment. It was a struggle to keep to the negotiation. After a moment she said, "Beauty fades. What then? Will your eye wander?"

Now it was his turn to blink, and he sat up straight, his palms on his knees. "And if it does? You would extract a promise from me you would not have expected from another husband?" She opened her mouth to reply, but he continued, "I will promise as much that I will respect your sensibilities as my wife."

"That is to say, if there are mistresses you will keep your indiscretions to yourself?"

"Aye. I will never humiliate you in public."

Estrella took this with mixed feelings. Good that he promised to respect her, but not good that he could already countenance the possibility of one day taking a mistress. Obviously love wasn't a factor here; she hadn't captured his heart, only his need for comfort, respectability, and children.

But then she looked straight at him and considered how it might be to share his bed. He was nearly twenty years older than she, and rugged. Hard. There was a small scar on his upper lip that may have been from an encounter with an armed man or a wounded beast, and brought to mind the warrior knights of old, who spent months and years in the open on campaign. She thought of what it might be like for him to touch her in places no man had ever dared approach. Places she'd long thought she might like to have touched. A flush began at her neck and rose to her cheeks. It was impossible to look him in the eye.

"I apologize, my lady," he said, "I've spoken too plainly."

Estrella threw him a sharp glance, took a deep breath, and let him think she was pulling herself together after all this talk of mistresses. It wouldn't do to let him know the true source of her blush. "Well. Yes. One should assume respect for the wife if not the marriage."

"And that is why I've approached you. I desire a virtuous wife."

But not enough to be a virtuous husband. Estrella knew

the way of the world, but also knew few women who liked it, and she was no exception. Nevertheless, she said, "The man who marries me will certainly have that. And more. My answer to you, Sir John, is to wish you all luck in your negotiation with my mistress. I give your suit my blessing."

A wide smile lit up the man's face, and Estrella found it charming. It disarmed her. Perhaps there was something to be said for a man plain enough to show pleasure at the prospect of having her company for a lifetime. "Excellent!" he said. "I shall present my case without delay."

Estrella rose from her seat, and Sir John hurried to stand with her. "Very good. I'll await happy news of your success." She held out her hand, and the man who would probably become her husband bent to kiss it. He was still grinning like a boy when he straightened and released her hand.

"Thank you, my lady. And bless you. You've made me a happy man."

The overt eagerness was fairly pathetic, but Estrella made a conscious effort to soften her heart toward him in his unseemly display. His was a nice smile, and in spite of his lack of discretion, her heart skipped just a little faster to think of him as her husband. Hope for the future filled her, and she felt lighter than she had in years.

The chamberlain escorted her back to her mistress and her sewing. Though she tried not to show it, inside Estrella was aflutter with a touch of fear for what Catherine would say. Her mind raced with how she would support what would be perceived as a betrayal of her mistress in accepting a marriage that was plainly unsuitable. She told herself Sir John was handsome, virile, and strong. He had a kind face that reflected a grace many nobler men couldn't boast. When she returned to the suite she worked her voice into an excitement she didn't truly feel as she related the details of her exchange with Sir John, emphasizing his virtues of strength and health, and perhaps overstating the value of his lands.

Catherine didn't speak much as she poked her short embroidery needle carefully through the delicate fabric she held and drew it gently out the other side. Estrella felt a bit like a traitor, but there was nothing for it. She wanted to be married and knew that even if one day Catherine married Henry it might be too late for her to make a good match. Especially a match better than this one. Sir John wasn't so bad. In a short time she might be looking at worse. She hoped Catherine would allow the marriage, for an elopement was out of the question.

As if reading her mind, the princess smiled and said, "I'm happy for you, Lita, to have received a suitor who pleases you so well. And I'm certain the arrangements for it will be made to your satisfaction. You've been a good and loyal maid, and I wish you all happiness."

"Thank you, Your Highness." Soon she would learn whether Catherine meant what she said.

Eight

THE arrangements were made. Catherine and her chamberlain managed to pull together a tiny dowry with the aid of Estrella's father, involving a small payment on the wedding day and further money and silver plate to be provided in subsequent payments. Nothing more than a token, but it was enough to stave off complete humiliation for all concerned, and by all accounts Sir John was extremely well pleased by it.

It had come at the price of a stormy argument between Catherine and Dr. De Puebla, who insisted there was nothing he could do to move her father to send money for her. These confrontations were becoming more frequent and uglier each time. The princess was convinced the ambassador was siding against her with the English king, and certain all would be well if he would only tell the truth of her situation to her father. Though he whined he was doing the best he was able,

Catherine would not be moved in her conviction. After one terrible argument, a tiny sum for Estrella's dowry was squeezed from a loan against her dowry plate.

Estrella was awash with gratitude, and though she hated to feel so grateful, she took the successful negotiation as an omen the marriage would be a respectable and fruitful one. The wedding was set for the following month.

During that time Estrella saw very little of her betrothed. Before the wedding there was but one visit from him. He came to the palace, and after Mass she met him in the garden near the river.

It was a bright day, uncharacteristic for London, and the warmth reminded Estrella of her southern home. On days like this, Estrella enjoyed the brightness, reveling in the sight of colors she sometimes forgot existed in England, where gray weather so often prevailed. A tinge of nostalgia touched her soul, and she greeted her eager knight with a wistful smile. Happiness glowed on his face, and Estrella thought it a good sign. That he was visiting was good, for most matches were without affection at all. Sir John might have left it to the wedding day to see her again, and it wouldn't have been remarkable. It was good he was here today, though, and she found herself enjoying his cheerful company. He bent over her hand to kiss it, and they began a stroll through the garden, away from the palace proper, at a leisurely pace.

Catherine's chamberlain hovered behind, close enough to assure Estrella's chastity but not so close as to overhear conversation. She and Sir John moved along a stone walkway beneath spreading oak trees where shade dappled the ground and leaves whispered softly in the most gentle of breezes. The only drawback of the sunshine was that it revealed the shabbiness of her dress. Each time John glanced over at her, she dwelled on the threadbare spots in the fabric and the frayed hems. To have a new dress just for today would have been sweetness beyond compare.

"My lady appears a bit sad this morning."

Estrella shook her head. "It's nothing. Only the beauty of the day has overwhelmed me."

He chuckled. "What a thing to be sad about! Too much beauty. I pray always for weather such as this, to make the hunt easier and more pleasant. Indeed there's more safety in it, for mist and rain can often cause men in the forest to loose bolts at each other rather than the deer. And the bright sun makes for less illness among them as well. Aye, this weather brings more joy than sorrow for me." He took a deep breath of the pleasant air and grinned at her. She couldn't help but smile in return, for his enthusiasm was catching.

"I hope you've an appetite," he continued. "I've brought something for you. I find many women don't eat as heartily as they should, to my mind. Particularly those attached to the court." He pointed with his chin off down the path, and she looked to find a table beneath a tree. It was in an expanse of grass edged by rose hedges punctuated with poplar, under a gnarled and sprawling old oak that threw dancing, dappled shade. The table was small and flanked by two weighty chairs. An excellent, thick red cloth was draped over it, its edges heavily embroidered in roses, and the equally heavy plate was silver and not the pewter one would expect of a man whose only title was knight. This had cost quite a bit of cash to arrange. Estrella wondered where he'd borrowed or rented the plate but was nevertheless pleased he'd gone to the trouble of trying to impress her now that the betrothal was settled. The only gain he could expect from this would be her high regard, and it pleased her that it mattered to him.

A large covered dish sat in the center of the cloth, and two smaller ones at the sides. A squire dressed in green velvet livery stood at attention to wait on the couple. Estrella didn't recognize the young man, but his look was of the higher nobility, with even features, graceful nose, and strong, square jaw. Such an impressive fellow to have as squire! He pulled out a chair for Estrella to sit, then for Sir John. The knight sat back in the chair and allowed his squire to remove the covers from the dishes.

The large one held a roast pheasant, golden and steaming hot. It had surely been roasted on the premises, in the palace kitchen and not the outbuildings where Catherine and her suite resided these days. Some influence had been required for this, or else a significant amount of money. Again she was impressed. Another dish boasted fritters, some of apple and some of parsnip. The third dish was boiled garlic, cinnamon-spicy. The squire reappeared after spiriting the covers away, surprising Estrella with a plate of bread and a jug of wine he poured into the silver goblets. She looked around but couldn't see what table or cart there was for these things. It was as if they'd appeared out of nowhere. She smiled and returned her attention to her intended.

While they ate, Sir John chatted about his work. He tore tender meat from the bird bones and relished the fritters with good appetite and much pleasure. He seemed far more relaxed today than he'd been last time they'd met, and now Estrella eyed him to see the sort of man he really was. Pleasant. More cheerful than most, but that could mean anything so soon before marrying. To be sure, she wouldn't know much about him at all until after she was his wife. Perhaps even well after. She listened to him talk, nudging him with questions that sent him off along storytelling paths that seemed to please him. It was plain he loved his work, and she thought that might explain his lack of ambition at court. He was the king's master huntsman after all, and there was no higher position to fit his talents and inclination.

His face was as sunny today as the weather. Estrella now noticed he was blond of hair. Odd, how she'd never before had a thought for his coloring. His tan face was darker than most Englishmen, but his hair was extremely light and utterly straight, dangling from his cap in feathery locks. It touched the back of his neck just above his shoulders, and the wispy ends wafted lightly in the gentle breeze here in the garden. She found its silvery golden color fascinating. Nearly exotic. The smile she offered him became easy, natural, and she relaxed against one arm of her chair as she nibbled on meat she stripped with her fingers from the chunk of pheasant breast on her plate.

The food was delicious. The bird was freshly killed, she could tell, probably from Sir John's own lands. The other dishes were also well and expensively prepared and far beyond the current provisions of Catherine's household. This was luxury they'd all pretended to for the past several years but had never even come near in reality. She thought it would be nice to be the mistress of a household which, though less ostentatious, would at least be substantive. Even debt free, perhaps. Sir John had a reputation for paying his debts diligently, and so avoided the dunning of creditors. Estrella knew she was lucky her mistress was allowing this marriage.

When Sir John began to run out of tales of his work, Estrella tried to encourage him in conversation about some books she'd read. But that avenue was fruitless, for apparently this knight had done little reading in his lifetime. Not much more, really, than had been required to learn the art, and since then only letters and messages. He faltered, and his discomfort with the subject of literature was evident. Estrella cast about for another subject.

But Sir John saved her. He nodded to the stack of bones before her and said with a twinkle in his eye, "I see you do have an appetite."

She had been more hungry than she'd ever care to admit, and had quite enjoyed the tasty, well-seasoned pheasant. One finger at her lips, she sucked a bit of grease from it, then smiled. "This excellent bird is irresistible, even should I grow fat from it. Did you kill it yourself?"

That made him laugh, a hearty chuckle. "Naturally. And when I loosed the bolt I said a prayer that it would please you. My prayer has been answered."

"All prayers are answered. But not always with a 'yes.'"

"God has been kind to me of late. I prayed you would accept me, and now I fear I've quite exhausted my grace with the Lord in asking for favors."

She had to smile at that. "You seem devoted."

"To you?"

"To God."

He lit up with enthusiasm. "Oh, aye. He's been good to me, and I do my best to return the regard."

Religion. The subject seemed to interest him, so she encouraged him. He rose to it, leaning forward to the table on his elbows, and shared his thoughts with her. She listened with true interest now, and not just politeness. He was, indeed, a devout man, and with little of the cynicism she'd seen during her service here in England. They talked of their views on matters of faith well into the afternoon, until the pheasant was a bare skeleton and the fritters reduced to a plate of crumbs. The shade of the oak quite left them as the sun dipped below the branches. The meal was over, and neither of them wanted it to be. A warmth glowed in her, and the future lay before her in brightness.

It was time for her to return to Catherine and for him to go back to his own work. He stood and reached over to help her rise from her chair. "Thank you for your lovely company today, my lady."

"Thank you for the lovely meal." She'd never been more sincere to any man.

"There's one thing more." He reached into a pocket of his surcoat and drew out a jewel. "A gift for my future wife." He held it out to her. It was a ruby. Small, but nevertheless a ruby, set in a gold brooch. "When we're married, you'll wear this at your throat, sewn to a new dress."

Estrella flushed that he'd noticed her ragged dress. "Sir John . . ." But she allowed him to lay the gift in the palm of her hand and marveled at his willingness to extend himself for her. Though the jewel was paltry in size relative to the norm for the royal court, she realized for him it represented a fortune.

"I wish I could promise such things every day, but you understand I cannot. This is a token of my high regard for you and acknowledgment of your sacrifice for me." Now she realized why the expensive meal. He was afraid of losing her once she realized the relative poverty of her future circumstances.

"I understand," she said, and looked straight into his eyes. They were dark, and darker still with his concern. "And thank you. I'll be a good wife to you."

He smiled. "I know."

That made her smile as well. Then he leaned down to kiss her lightly on the lips. Catherine's chamberlain, who had been sitting by the tree the entire time, rose and stepped forward to make a noise of disapproval, but Sir John quickly stepped back and clasped his hands behind his back. The twinkle returned to his eyes, and it touched her in places deep inside her. Estrella placed her fingertips over her lips and smiled. The kiss had been nice. Gentle. Far more so than she'd imagined it could be from a rough huntsman.

The chamberlain said in Spanish, "Perhaps it is time to return to your duties, Lady Estrella."

With a nod to Catherine's man, she said to Sir John, "I must go."

He nodded, glanced at the chamberlain, then bowed to her. She curtsied, then turned and accompanied her chaperone to the palace.

The next day Sir John was sent by the king to take a number of deer, rabbits, and various birds to provision a coming holiday celebration in the palace. She would not see him again until the wedding.

At night Estrella lay in her bed, listening to the deep breathing sounds of the others in the room, and tried to picture what her new home would be like. It would be small, but how small would it be? More so than her father's main residence? How rough and simple? She could guess there would be few servants—fewer certainly than hurried about in the king's palaces—but she wondered if they were good workers or if she would have to struggle with them. How would she dress? Her fingertips touched the brooch she'd pinned to the neck of her nightgown. Was this ruby the last jewel she would ever receive? She consoled herself on that question with the knowledge she would probably have new dresses and not the threadbare ones from which pearls were falling. Plain, perhaps, but at least new. Once she was married.

Married. The thought sent shivers all through her. She

wondered what it would be like. There was a pang of near regret at having to leave the household to which she'd become
so accustomed, but the prospect of having her own domain,
her own house where she controlled the servants, was heady.
Though it would be small and not rich, it would at least be
hers. It might even seem rich compared to the tight circumstances of the past few years in Catherine's suite.

The wedding day approached, and the day Sir John was to
return from his hunt Estrella found herself anticipating him
with a skip in her heart and a quiet smile on her lips. She found
it pleasant to think of seeing him again, and once more she
thought it a good omen for the marriage. She sat at a window
high in the apartments, overlooking the bailey below, awaiting
the arrival of her intended.

Her heart leapt when a rider approached at speed and dismounted in a hurry. The mount was handed off to one of the
guard, and a discussion ensued between the rider and another
man who approached across the open area near the gate. Estrella leaned as close as she could to the window opening,
stretched across the deep stone of the wall to look out, but she
knew it couldn't be Sir John. He would have returned accompanied, and probably not at a gallop. Surely he wasn't that eager to return to her. So she watched the rider enter the palace,
then continued to wait for her betrothed.

Another hour passed, and there was no sign of him. The
sun was sinking to the west, and the dim light made it hard to
see anymore, so she turned away and went to Catherine's
chamber where the princess sat with her Bible. She was reading aloud to her maids while they embroidered, and Estrella
murmured an apology for disturbing them as she entered.

"No news of Sir John today?"

Estrella shook her head. "Perhaps he was delayed. The last message from him said he would return today, but who knows what need the king might have that would keep him away. Or what weather may have waylaid him on the road."

Catherine nodded. "To be sure, he's certainly at the beck and call of His Majesty." She smiled. "And the weather."

"As are we all."

"Indeed." But Catherine's expression held the same worry that was in Estrella's heart. John should have come today.

Just then the chamberlain entered the room, bearing a letter folded into a small packet and a bloodless face so pale he almost appeared English. His mouth was a thin, lipless line, and he came directly to Estrella. At first she thought it must be news from Sir John, but the look on the Spaniard's face told her something was terribly wrong. It couldn't be John, then. News from elsewhere, certainly. Her father in Spain? Surely nothing had happened to her family. But apprehension crept in on her for the look on the chamberlain's face.

"My lady," he began, "I'm afraid there has been an incident."

She blinked up at him, wondering what could possibly be so dire that had upset him so terribly. Nothing bad could have happened. Not to her. Not to anyone she knew.

He continued, "Sir John Cranach has been killed."

What he said made no sense. They were nonsense words coming from his mouth. She was forced to ask him to repeat himself. When he did, the truth was like a cold splash of water in the face. She bent her head and stared at her hands. The room was silent, awaiting her reaction. But she had none. Not one she could countenance expressing here. In her mind, all the dreams she'd woven over the past month unraveled. The images of Sir John she'd carefully taught herself to cherish fell limp and useless. Her future suddenly yawned before her, empty and black. Not just empty of John but devoid of everything but darkness.

Finally she found her voice and whispered, "How did it happen?"

The chamberlain held out the packet in his hand. "Here is a letter for you from his second huntsman."

Estrella looked up and stared at it. She didn't want to touch the thing, for all it could bring her would be pain. But it was there, and the next hours were a narrow gantlet she must pass through, so she took it. The seal had been broken, the letter read, but that was to be expected. Under the circumstances the king would want to know every detail of the incident and had probably been the first to see all the messages sent by the huntsman. With trembling fingers she opened the pages and struggled to comprehend what was on them.

The script was untidy. Written hurriedly, and by a man whose claim to literacy was tenuous, the words sprawled across the pages in a near zigzag.

My Lady Estrella de Montoya;
  It grieves me to inform you that your beloved intended husband is no more. This morning, while we stalked the wily and dangerous boar . . .

As Estrella read on, she pictured the hunt as the man described it, and Sir John's final moments on earth.

PETER, Sir John Cranach's second huntsman, rode with his master and the others through the forest, listening to the baying of the dogs in the distance. They had the scent and were hard on the trail of an enormous boar. His heart pounded in his ears, both from exertion and from trepidation. The animal was dangerous; he never liked taking them, whether with the king or with only Sir John. These ill-tempered brutes were more trouble than they were worth and always cost the master in dogs when the king requested boar meat for his table. Peter had seen a black monster kill a horse once, and today his own horse wore quilted armor against an attack from below. He himself wore greaves and cuisses on his legs for the same purpose and never mind those who thought it unsporting. Today they were huntsmen, not sportsmen. He was a procurer of meat and nothing more. The party carried spears rather than crossbows, for that was the only weapon that would still protect a man once deployed. Each bore a sharp crosspiece to prevent a pierced animal from rushing him along the shaft of the spear to use its long, deadly tusks.

They were fell weapons, those tusks. The lower ones curved long over the head, sharp and heavy, capable of ripping a man from knee to throat in a heartbeat. The beast was quick and powerful. Fearless. Immune to pain, and that meant going near it without killing it as quickly as humanly possible was foolhardy.

On this day the quarry had turned to confront them once already, grunting and eyes rolling in rage, displaying its tusks in a very real threat, then it fled when harried. The men were beginning to tire. Peter could feel his own strength sagging, for it had been a long flight over irregular terrain. Once the men thought the dogs had lost the scent, but they picked it up again and returned to baying. Now the day was waning and Sir John called out to his huntsmen he thought they might be nearing the end of their pursuit.

He was right. The hunting party burst onto a small

meadow where the dogs had the boar surrounded, barking hysterically and in full-throated cacophony that forced the men to shout to each other over the dogs to be heard. The quarry was huge, black, and extremely angry. It grunted and squealed and charged one of the dogs, which fled while its comrades closed in to harry from the sides. The boar twisted in an attempt to skewer one of them, but the hound dodged, and the boar backed off to fend against the other dogs in a scurry of grunting and growling animals. In this way the standoff was secure. Sir John dismounted with his spear and let one of the lower huntsmen take his horse. He approached the dogs as Peter dismounted and readied his own spear. To Peter's shame, his palms were slippery on the smooth wood of the shaft. His heart pounded hard and fast.

"Call them off," said the master. Sir John's spear was cocked and ready. Somewhere in the woods he'd lost his cap, and his nearly white hair fell into his face. He threw it from his eyes with a toss of his head, then lowered his chin to face the boar. His chest heaved with exertion and anticipation of a fight.

The dogs were called off, and as they retreated, Sir John immediately charged. The boar came at him in a rage, short legs pumping. Peter and the others ran to their flanking positions. It was too fast. They weren't ready. But the master knew what he was doing. He'd taken many boar in his career and had done this more times than most men, with only one bad scar to show for it.

John stopped at that instant and took his stance, one foot forward and the other carrying his weight. One hand steadying his spear, the other at the rear to aim. Peter wheeled into position to the master's left. As the animal neared, John leaned forward against an impact he knew would be devastating. The thing weighed as much as he did and was far angrier. Were he bowled over, he would be lost. His men stood behind him with other spears and bows, but they couldn't protect him. They could only make certain the boar didn't live afterward.

The impact of boar on spear made John reel, but he emitted a loud snarl and kept standing. The impaled animal squealed horribly and tossed itself this way and that, but the crosspiece of the spear held, and John stood his ground against it. Other hunters rushed to stab.

But before they could reach the boar, John's spear broke. Peter uttered a curse and threw his spear in hopes of saving his master, but missed. Without the slightest hesitation, the raging beast rushed onward and thrust a tusk into the hunter's thigh. Sir John screamed. Then his voice jarred in rhythm with the thrusts of the animal. In four lightning-fast jerks of its head it ripped open thigh, groin, and gut, finally catching the tusk beneath the master's rib cage. A cry went up among the huntsmen as each ran to pierce the boar from all sides. Peter could only stand, weaponless, gaping in horror at the scene before him and the realization his master's life was ended.

The boar writhed madly at the spears stuck through him, then weakened and lay still, dying in a bloodied, mangled heap. The men gathered around where Peter knelt beside their master.

Blood soaked the ground, and more was pouring from the violated belly. The tusk had ripped John's quilted armor and laid waste to his hose and tunic. Blood ran everywhere, it seemed, and the hunt master's hands were shiny and red with it. He writhed on the ground and grasped his lower belly to hold in his guts. The stench of blood and bile rose from him, and black goo mixed with the blood and white intestines. Sir

John was silent now, gasping. Unmoving. Tears began to run from his eyes and backward to his ears as he blinked upward at the sky. Then his lips began to move in fluent, unvoiced prayer.

It would be a quick death, the blood running so freely, and that was a relief to Peter. He leaned close to lay a hand on Sir John's shoulder, a small effort to impart as much comfort as he could, then bent farther when his master voiced a whisper.

"Peter," he said, "tell Lady Estrella . . ." He gasped, struggling to breathe, then continued, "Tell her I regret . . ."

Then he fell silent, no longer able to talk, and only gazed at Peter with fading eyes. Soon his eyelids drooped, and then he stopped breathing.

ESTRELLA folded the letter, slipped the packet into her belt, then picked up her sewing and bent her head to it. The other women were silent. She said nothing. She only sewed with trembling fingers and concentrated on not pricking herself.

Nine

❦

1527

WHILE waiting for Henry's other shoe to drop in his effort to set her aside, Catherine studied the law. Days were spent in long discussion with friends who knew the ins and outs of secular and canon law, gathering information and asking what would be Henry's most likely angle of attack. Her friends Thomas More and Bishop Fisher were especially helpful in arming her with understanding of where she stood.

Particularly More, a religious conservative and extremely devout, was highly sympathetic to Catherine's cause, though he was attached to Henry's court. Catherine spoke highly of his defense of the church in the face of Henry's attempt at denigrating the authority of the pope. The two spent a great deal of time in conversation on the subject. They spent long afternoons in the palace gardens, often in the company of others with like minds, discussing the need to protect the Church from this assault on its authority. Estrella found More's coun-tenance severe and his opinions unnecessarily rigid, but they seemed to please Catherine. She'd heard a rumor Sir Thomas wore a hair shirt, and knew Catherine did as well, though she couldn't imagine for what sin the queen felt she needed to do such severe penance. There was nobody she knew more de-vout than Catherine, unless it was More. Were it not for More's distaste for marriage, though he did marry eventually, Estrella thought he might have been a better match as a hus-band for Catherine than Henry. Their friendship now turned to a mutual support regarding what was to be done about the denigration of papal authority that was becoming rampant in England now that the king had an interest in it.

Estrella was old enough and experienced enough in poli-tics to know that Catherine's principles of faith would hold little water with the men who would rend asunder the king's marriage. Some were motivated by simple desire to please the king, some by a Lutheran disposition for discrediting the pope, and some by a genuine and reasonable fear of civil war if Mary should ascend the throne on Henry's death. Even with God on her side, Catherine was going to need all the le-gal help available to her and could have done with some that was not.

The women of Catherine's suite listened and watched, and within their ranks drew away from Anne Boleyn, the one of their number who was the cause of their mistress's distress. For her part, the maid of honor showed no outward sign of concern over the matter. As gay and chipper as ever, she per-formed her duties as casually as any of them, and it never seemed to bother her that the other maids fell silent when she entered a room. Seeming too friendly to Anne would be at the very least a bad idea politically, and most thought it betrayal of their mistress. They whispered if they thought she was near, for she was known to hide for the purpose of eavesdropping. Spying on others in the court was a common enough practice, and everyone had done it at one time or another, but with Anne it was a regular occurrence. It was plain this woman was as dangerous to everyone else in the suite as she was to Catherine. They closed ranks and did their best to keep her out of any conversations of import.

Anne ignored the treatment, or at least behaved as if she cared nothing of what anyone thought. There always seemed to be a smile ready to curl her lips, and her conversation was ever bright and witty. The younger girls seemed impressed by her, but the women who had been with Catherine the longest barely tolerated her presence. Estrella and Maria scrupulously avoided the king's mistress whenever they could. Catherine herself bore her rival with utter grace and nary a cross word. The queen and her rival played card games together, as if there were nothing more between them but casual acquaintance and goodwill.

In Anne Estrella recognized the sort of moral and spiritual cripple she'd long ago avoided becoming herself, and though she understood the pressures on Anne from her ambitious family—both the Howards and the Boleyns—she also knew Anne was the sort of slave to those pressures none of the rest of them had become. That made her a thing to be disdained as well as pitied, for there was no excuse for such weakness. A good woman didn't need to abandon her principles for the sake of her duties to the men around her.

Even worse, Anne seemed to take pleasure in the discomfort of her fellow maids. One afternoon she caught up with Estrella and Maria in the shuttlecock court, and there was no getting away, though Estrella had a mad urge to simply walk from the court without a word. They were playing a light game, batting the bird easily to each other and not seriously trying to beat one another, when Anne entered the court accompanied by her own maids. The three women were chattering in French, a language Estrella had never learned well, but she could tell they were gossiping about someone, and made their way to the net where Maria and Estrella played. They stopped by a pillar, in a little cluster of brightly colored silk and jewels. Anne's decoration glittered in brighter hues than any of the rest of Catherine's ladies, testament to questionable behavior and status with the man who could provide her with the most sumptuous jewels, and who would allow her to wear them. It was as if she wore a sign declaring that she was fornicating with the king.

Anne and her women were laughing with great hilarity; then she turned to the players and said with uncalled-for brightness, "How now, Spanish ladies? Do you not know how to play this game in your country?"

"England, you mean?" said Maria, and she missed her shot. The cock fell to the ground, and she picked it up. "I confess, I've quite forgotten how it's played in Castile. Or even whether it's played at all." Of course it was, and Maria was only trying to annoy.

Anne ignored the tart reply and said in a voice dripping with disdain, "Neither of you will win that way, tipping it to each other as if playing a child's game." She turned to her girls. "Or perhaps they're having a party together? Not competition, but a friendly exchange of pleasantries and cakes?"

Maria glanced over at her maid, who sat on a bench with both of Estrella's, playing a game of cards. The young women stared with rapt attention and listened closely to what their mistresses would say to the woman who was the talk of all England. "If playing to win were the only thing, life would be empty indeed."

"Why play at all if not to win?"

Estrella murmured, "Empty life, empty heart . . . empty head . . ."

Anne cut her a sharp glance, then continued in her cheery hail-fellow tone, "Come, allow me to show you how it's done."

"Perhaps your brother would make a more entertaining opponent for you," said Maria, a sly reference to the inordinate amount of time Anne spent with George Boleyn. Then she served to Estrella, who lobbed the bird back easily.

"Surely he would," replied Anne. "But I've nothing to teach him, do I?"

"Indeed not." Maria batted the cock with a flick of her wrist, and the two continued to send it back and forth as she spoke. Her voice took on an edge similar to the one in Anne's. "He and your father seem to have taught you more than one would care to know. How fortunate for us you've taken pity and wish to deliver us from our deficiency. Alas, I fear we're hopeless and unable to grasp the terribly sophisticated ideas you urge on us." There was a giggle from the small cluster of younger women on the bench. Anne's maids murmured between themselves. Maria added, "We prefer to play in friendliness, for the good of all involved, and never to injure." Estrella missed, and the play was halted for the moment while she retrieved the feathered ball from the ground.

Said Anne, "Those who cannot defend themselves—"

"Have a champion." Estrella turned toward Anne and hefted her racket. She thought of the Arthurian tales Catherine had so loved as a girl. They'd all loved those stories when she'd read them aloud. "A woman of virtue and grace always has a champion to defend her. It is the one who has no grace, or whose virtue has been squandered, who must fight her own battles. No hero of worth would have to do with such a one."

"Do you depend on a man to fight for you?"

"I have no battle."

"You think you don't. But you are a dowager countess, in service to a dowager princess. Your position is not secure." Her voice was weighted with meaning, a tone of near threat.

A coldness came over Estrella, and she glanced over at Maria, whose expression was equally weakened. It was the first time Estrella had heard the queen referred to as "dowager princess" since the terrible days before Catherine's betrothal to Henry. "The queen, you mean."

"Dowager princess. Her marriage to Henry was false. The pope will declare it null. He must."

Anger rose in Estrella, and she said to Maria, "*Mi amiga!* Let her have your racket. Allow her to play a point with me."

Maria hesitated, but Estrella nodded with a tiny frown. So her friend handed over the racket to Anne, who stepped onto the court and faced Estrella.

"You wish to learn how to play games?" That irritating smile was there, taunting. For one terrible moment, Estrella wanted to smack it from her face.

But instead she served the bird gently without reply. Anne's return was not so gentle, but Estrella backpedaled quickly to the rear of the court and lobbed it easily to the rear of Anne's court. Again, Anne slammed the bird over the net into a far corner. Estrella dove for it and caught it to return it nicely, then centered her position. Anne once again whacked the bird as hard as she could, and this time Estrella simply held out her

racket for the bird to bounce off. The force of Anne's own
stroke made the bird zip back across the net, but Estrella's lack
of force on the return made it lose speed quickly. Though it at
first appeared to be a strong hit, the thing barely cleared the
net before it faltered and dropped straight down. Anne rushed
to the net in a flurry of skirts and arms but wasn't quick
enough to recover the shot.

"You lose," said Estrella lightly, as she plucked the strings of
her racket like a lyre so they made a *twang*.

Anne straightened, her eyes narrowed at Estrella, and without a word she returned Maria's racket to her. She left the
court with her maids and as much dignity as she could pull
around herself like a cloak. Precious little it was, with the gig-
gles of the younger maids following her.

Maria whispered to Estrella, "You should hope she never
becomes queen."

Estrella replied, "We should all hope she never becomes
queen."

To the astonishment of everyone except Catherine, Henry
maintained his habit of dining with his wife in her apartments of an occasional evening. Estrella was among those
who served the king and queen as Henry lounged in his chair
at table, behaving as if he weren't trying to divorce his wife.
During these visits Catherine seemed to deny the situation as
much as he did and was as gracious to him as when they'd
been first married eighteen years before. They talked of
Princess Mary as parents would about a child. The girl was
showing intellectual promise and making great progress in
her music studies. Catherine glowed with pleasure as she
spoke, for her daughter was the center of her life, and she
loved talking about the girl and her accomplishments. She focused on Mary with an intensity that suggested to Estrella the

queen was barricading herself against the ugliness of Henry's recent behavior. As if by mere force of will she could make her marriage what it had once been. It occurred to the maid that if anyone could succeed at such a thing, it would be Catherine.

Then a bit of tension slipped into Henry's voice as he finished sucking on the end of a small goose bone, set it aside, then told his wife, "You know I haven't stopped loving you."

Catherine glanced at him and slipped a bit of meat into her mouth. She said nothing but only chewed and gazed blandly at him as if she were taking care in considering her reply.

Henry persisted. "Truly, I do love you. As dearly as the day we married." He stared at the pointed tip of his right shoe, turning it this way and that as if it were the most interesting thing in the room. Estrella noted the shoe was a bit muddy and guessed half his mind was on changing his shoes at the next opportunity rather than on the love he held for the wife he would discard. "You remember that day, my love, don't you?" Now he looked at her as if expecting her to declare her own love for him, for it was, after all, only fair she respond in kind to his admission of love.

Catherine now smiled and obliged. "I do, indeed. You were the epitome of a manhood other men would fain pretend to." Estrella was hard put to know whether she was sincere or merely saying what he wished to hear. But it surely didn't matter to Henry which was true, so long as she said it.

He was the one to glow with pleasure now. "And over the years that love has grown." Oddly, Estrella could hear no hint of insincerity in his voice. She knew him well enough to understand this meant he fully believed what he said, though she couldn't comprehend how.

"Has it?" The edge of skepticism that crept into Catherine's voice went unnoticed by the king. He waved an insouciant hand as if to assure her.

"Certainly it has. You have been my companion these eighteen years, and an invaluable helpmate and queen. I cannot deny it."

"Though you might if you could."

Finally Henry seemed to hear pique in her words, and peered at her. "If I could deny it, it certainly wouldn't be true, then, would it?"

A slight flush came to Catherine's face. "True, to be sure, my husband." Her stress on the word *husband* brought a flush to Henry's face. His head tilted for a moment, a sign he was thinking hard, and he seemed to make a decision about what he would say next.

"You must understand, Catherine, my hands are tied in this distressing matter."

"What matter would that be?" The queen focused her attention on the meat before her.

"It is my dearest wish to obey the law of God."

The only visible reaction from Catherine was a momentary closing of eyes, then she gazed at her husband with nothing more than a show of interest in what he would say. Nevertheless, her voice was pointed when she said, "Mine as well, my husband. You know I hold that obligation above all else in life."

"Then we are in complete agreement. It would be a sin to live as we have been, in defiance of the law. Our marriage surely is invalid, and we must bring ourselves to face our error and rectify it." The king was calling her an unwedded whore, and he did it with the same ease as if he were telling of a successful day in the lists. Estrella bit her lips together to keep from making any sound that might be interpreted as comment.

"It would be a sin to live in defiance of any of God's laws. That is why we have His Holiness in Rome to help us determine what those laws are. We can hardly wander the earth only guessing at what God would have us do. Or not do. That would be anarchy. If we do not trust in the infallibility of the pope, we are lost."

Henry gazed at her for a moment, his eyes narrowed. This apparently wasn't going the way he'd expected. A tiny smile touched Estrella's mouth, and she wiped it away immediately with her fingers. Henry's intellect was not anywhere near as nimble as his wife's. In eighteen years of marriage, Estrella had never seen him win a disagreement except when Catherine allowed it. At this juncture he said, "Do you and your friends not believe in the new learning? I've heard you and More talk long on the need for every man to read scripture and have knowledge directly from it rather than through priests and such."

"His Holiness is not just an ordinary priest."

"The pope is but a man."

"A man chosen from among the best and holiest of God's servants. Chosen by men who are guided by prayer. Who else would there be to shepherd us all?"

"A king. Indeed, a king would serve more surely as the conduit through which could pass knowledge of God, for he is placed where he is by God Himself. Born to his position and not made by men."

"As was your father?"

Now Henry flushed fully and shifted in his seat, for his father had won his crown on the battlefield, and his descent from royalty came from an illegitimate ancestor. "Had God not wanted my father to be king, he would have lost the struggle at Boswell."

"Had God not wanted us to be married, Arthur would have lived."

Henry's reply was snappish. "Had Arthur lived, he would be king now. Obviously I was meant to wear the crown."

"And just as obviously so was I. It was, after all, a joint coronation. And quite elaborate, you'll recall. A spectacle worthy of such an important event. And the banquet afterward. Remember it, Henry? It was ever so costly, but worth the expense, for it established us as not only king and queen, but husband and wife."

There was a dark silence of frustration in Henry. Then he said, "Our childless marriage is proof of its invalidity."

"We have a daughter. We are hardly childless." Her voice was hardening with each response in this repartee.

"I have no heir."

"Nonsense. My mother ruled Castile, and more handily than my father did Aragon, I must say. My sister ruled after her."

"England is not Spain. There has never been an English queen to rule in her own right. My subjects would never tolerate a woman on the throne."

"I think you give little credit to your own people."

"I know my people, perhaps, better than you ever could." A very sharp edge had crept into his voice, an implication that her foreignness was barrier to her ability to know her subjects.

"I'm certain you do not." Catherine gazed blandly at him. She was, of course, right. The queen, by her pious nature and gentle guidance of the king, had long ago won the hearts of the English public. Over the years of her marriage to the king she'd become more beloved than many English queens of native birth. And now she took that same gentle and pious tack of guidance, and allowed her husband a graceful way out of the discussion. "What I do not doubt is that you love me. As you said. After eighteen years there is no denying the regard we have for each other, and that no man can put asunder." Catherine took it all with aplomb that also astonished Estrella. The queen's gentle smile rarely left her mouth, and she gazed on her husband with the same sort of adoration Estrella had always seen in her where Henry was concerned. What she'd said was the absolute truth. She did love Henry, with an abiding regard Estrella couldn't fathom.

Estrella herself had never loved Whitby. Not in that way. Only one man had ever commanded that sort of affection from her, and that was not her husband. Though she'd learned to respect the man with whom she'd shared fifteen years of her life, and to think of her life as joined with his, there had never been any question of real love. The spiritual kind, where the other's thoughts and feelings became one's own heart's desire. Estrella had been thankful she'd merely not hated her husband, for far too many women were fated to a daily wrangle with men who respected nothing about their wives. Though benign neglect was the norm, many women, even among the nobility, were beaten. They hid their bruises and broken noses, and nobody wanted to see them, for everyone knew it was a man's right to control his household as he saw fit. Some men were brutal in maintaining marriages only for the sake of status and money, and kept their control by physical means. Whitby had not been like that, and for that Estrella had always been glad. She could just as easily have found herself married to a cruel man.

By all accounts, Henry had never been like that, either, and Catherine's respect for him was well founded. In spite of what he thought of the marriage, he talked to her as a trusted advisor, asking her mind and listening carefully to what she would tell him. Except, of course, for what she would tell him about the validity of their marriage. Estrella thought he deserved her respect, but not her love. For he plainly no longer loved her in the way he claimed. Word was he hadn't slept in her bed in years. There was no longer that light in his eyes Estrella knew signaled true caring. One she'd seen herself a very long time ago. The light Henry had once had for Catherine, he now had for that Boleyn woman.

She'd seen the king and his mistress exchange glances many times, when Henry and Anne thought nobody was paying attention. Or else they never cared about the thoughts of anyone who would see that which they might have kept to themselves. There was an arrogance about it that annoyed Estrella and made her think all the more that the king was unworthy of the queen's regard, let alone her love. But Catherine persisted in her adoration. Estrella wondered why such an intelligent woman would give herself so completely to anyone so undeserving.

One evening as Catherine was readying for bed and Estrella was the only maid in attendance at the moment, Estrella murmured a question to her queen.

"May I ask, Your Majesty, why you aren't angry with your husband?" She lifted the overdress and laid it off over a rack for the purpose.

Catherine turned toward her, eyes wide with surprise. "Why, I'm often angry with Henry. What do you mean?"

"You act as if he's done nothing to you."

"He hasn't. I'm his wife, and there's nothing he can do to change that."

"But he wants to."

"Nevertheless, he can't. And once he sees he can't, he'll stop this nonsense and give up the pursuit."

"I don't need to tell you the king is accustomed to getting what he wants and will persist."

Catherine chuckled. "Even Henry cannot bend the will of God. Nor dictate to the representative of the almighty. God's law is immutable. Henry will see that one day. He's a good man, and ultimately will know the will of God."

"It doesn't matter to you that he wants to set you aside?"

"Surely it's not his wish; it's the wish of his advisors. Wolsey, especially, may God strike him down for a heretic Lutheran. He wished to be pope himself and puts on airs as if he were, and is embittered at his failure. He and the others are the ones who whisper in the king's ear that he must have a legitimate male heir. Evil men tell Henry that Mary can't succeed him because she's a princess, and he has always listened too well to men like Wolsey. Once the cardinal has been discredited and taken down, Henry will see his true error and all will be well."

Estrella frowned as she continued undressing the queen. "But the king has betrayed you."

"I'm his wife. As I said, there's nothing he can do about that. I must behave as his wife, and if I can continue to love him I will be the happier as such a wife. I believe he is still the knight I married nearly twenty years ago, and therefore I must love him. As I believe he still loves me."

The words to utter the truth stuck behind Estrella's teeth. She wanted to say them, but knew she wasn't cruel enough to tell Catherine her husband couldn't possibly love her anymore. But she said, "You think he's your champion?"

"He always was. I'm the same woman I always was. He knows the truth of our wedding night, and he knows the truth of our marriage. I know my Henry, and I know he doesn't have it in his nature to lie before God or deny his duty."

"When he calls you a . . . when he tells people you're something you're not, he's not cruel but he's merely mistaken?"

Catherine nodded, though Estrella had been trying to point out the unlikelihood of the idea. The queen said, "He cannot mean it."

But Estrella wondered what the difference was, whether he meant it or not, if the result was that Catherine would be set aside. Even Whitby had had more regard for his wife than that.

Maria appeared at the door, and curtsied. "Your Majesty."

Catherine gestured for her to enter, and Maria approached with a letter. "This arrived a moment ago." She curtsied again and offered the packet of pages.

"Thank you, Maria." Catherine sat on the edge of her bed, rustling with her silk nightclothes. An excited note came into her voice as she said, "It's from Charles."

Estrella craned to see, curious what the letter might say, but knew Catherine would read it aloud. She could be patient while Catherine broke the seal and opened the stiff, travel-battered pages.

She scanned it for a moment, and her eyebrows went up. "Oh, dear," she murmured.

Still Estrella could be patient. She and Maria only stood and waited.

Finally, after reading the letter through once, Catherine said, "It would seem the pope is the prisoner of my nephew."

No longer able to pretend disinterest, the two maids came to sit on either side of their mistress. "How?" said Maria.

"Charles' unruly Lombard army has sacked Rome."

THE Holy Roman Emperor Charles V was in his privy chamber when a messenger arrived in Valladolid with news that was at once good and terrible. He sat at his favorite desk, writing a letter to his aunt, dressed in his nightclothes. He liked this time of the day, for the world was quiet and his thoughts went uninterrupted by the exigencies of life. It was a brief pause, a suspension that sometimes even allowed him to indulge in the fantasy of peace. He liked to take the opportunity for correspondence of a personal nature and so was irritated when his chamberlain entered to announce the arrival of pressing news.

"What is it?" Charles leaned back in his chair and gazed at the intruder, who knelt before him. The distress plainly evident in the chamberlain's demeanor gave Charles great pause. Something was terribly wrong.

"News from Rome, Your Majesty. A courier has brought a message from one of your generals in the Lombard contingent."

Charles grunted. Trouble. It had been brewing for a while, and now he saw it must have broken out. He gestured for the messenger to be allowed in, then set aside the letter he'd just begun.

A bedraggled soldier entered, knelt, and bowed. He gasped with exertion, having hurried on his mission, but with distress as well. The man was walleyed, not happy to be the one bringing this message. "There is terrible news from Rome, Your Majesty. The city has been sacked, and the pope is exiled to the Castel Sant'Angelo, where he is in custody of men under your authority."

Charles stifled a groan, but took a moment, gazing at the quill in his hand, to consider the broad fact of this thing and his next question. Then he said in a low, even voice, "Is he being treated well?"

The messenger looked up. "Indeed, he is. He's escaped the carnage and won't be harmed."

Carnage. Worse and worse. But at least the pope was likely still alive and possibly even well. "Do you have a letter?"

"My deepest apologies, Your Majesty, but no. I was told only to say that both German and Spanish troops have mutinied for lack of food, they've taken the city and are demonstrating their anger against the clergy, but that the pope himself is safe."

Charles nodded. "Tell me what you saw."

The messenger's mouth gaped for a moment, hesitating to reply even as he struggled to obey, and Charles knew the truth must be even worse than what he'd imagined. So the emperor repeated in a calm, soothing voice, "Tell me."

Still on one knee, the messenger said, "The soldiers are very angry." The pleading in his voice suggested he hoped not to be counted as one of the angry soldiers, that he himself had not been part of the massacre. Charles knew that, for this man would never have been chosen for the mission if he had been.

He ignored the issue and prodded the man to continue. "But not so angry anymore as when they entered the city, I suppose."

"They hate the fat, wealthy priests and have murdered many of them." Tears began to well in the messenger's eyes, and they choked his voice. "They've beheaded monks and raped nuns. The city is bloodied, and littered with bodies and pieces of bodies. They've destroyed relics and altars—smashed them to bits. The pope wept, and begged for terms, but he went ignored. He barely escaped with his life, and most of the clergy in the Eternal City weren't so fortunate. The drunken soldiers have murdered a great many, and others they have auctioned as prisoners. Slaves." Terrible grief was in the messenger's voice and demeanor. His mouth bubbled with his weeping as he spoke, and he had to wipe his runny nose on his sleeve. "I think many would rather have died."

Charles was repulsed by this news. Lutheran sentiment against the clergy flew in the face of everything he believed as a Catholic. He was the grandson of their Catholic Majesties, Ferdinand of Aragon and Isabella of Castile. His faith in God and the authority of the pope was unshakable. He said, "Is there anyone to bring the army under control?"

The kneeling soldier shook his head. "No, Your Majesty."

The emperor gazed at him for a moment, thinking hard. He would need to call for his advisors, and immediately. The pope was in danger, and Charles couldn't let his army be the instrument of the destruction of His Holiness. As it was, the authority of the church hierarchy was at risk. Already damaged, it might conceivably be destroyed. He needed to assure the safety of the pontiff, if nothing else. A brief prayer for the pope's safety touched his lips.

Then he said, "You may go."

The messenger allowed himself to appear relieved, stood and bowed, then made his exit.

Charles called for his chamberlain and ordered certain ministers to be awakened and summoned to the chamber. The chamberlain hurried away on his mission. Then, alone once again, the emperor returned his attention to the desk and the blank sheet of paper before him. A sigh escaped him as he realized there would be at least one person glad to hear the pope was under the power of her nephew. He dipped his quill and set it to the page once again.

CATHERINE sat with her ladies, staring at the missive on her lap. Estrella could see in the queen's face how horrified she was at this news of blood and destruction against the Church.

They were all horrified. Tears filled the eyes of the queen, and
she shook her head slowly back and forth.

"Not for me," she murmured as a prayer. "Please, God, not
for me."

Ten

1528

"WOLSEY would have me painted as a whore," said Catherine to Maria and Estrella. The three of them sat at a large trestle table set in the privy chamber surrounded with chairs. It was crowded with stacks of books and scatterings of aging paper and vellum heavy with the seals of great men. Catherine had gathered as many learned writings as she could that addressed the questions raised by Henry's challenge of their marriage. "That man's existence nearly makes a case for the Lutherans' hatred of clergy." Her voice was thick with disgust, as it had ever been when talking about Wolsey.

Eustache Chapuys, the imperial ambassador to England, sitting at the table, allowed himself a slight curl of the corner of his mouth at her dry wit. He didn't like Wolsey any better than she did. The queen's confessor, Bishop of Llandaff Jorge de Athequa, stood nearby and did smile at the barb for the

English cardinal. His eyes crinkled at the corners, and for a moment he appeared ready to burst out in unseemly laughter.

Estrella certainly agreed, though she stayed in her place and was silent. The cardinal put on terrible airs, as if he were a monarch. When he went a-progress anywhere in the realm or on the Continent he carried with him trappings far above his station, hangings, plate, servants, entertaining in richness comparable to that owned by Henry himself. And Henry was a king known for unwarranted expenditure in his festivities. Even her own sensibilities were offended by the opulent displays put on by that supposed spiritual leader, and she had spent many years as part of a court given to indulgence in wealth and frivolous display. As a Catholic, she was accustomed to clergy who emphasized their authority in the eyes of their parishioners by appearing as powerful monarchs. But Cardinal Wolsey took the practice to such extremes and was of such ignoble descent in the bargain, that it was too much for even her to tolerate.

Maria said, "I'm told the cardinal is trying to arrange for the pope's authority to be transferred to a commission of cardinals he can dominate. If that happens, they would surely make haste, then, to grant Henry whatever the king wished."

"He will fail." The queen held a copy of the papal bull granting dispensation for her marriage to Henry she had been discussing with Chapuys. It was a large parchment, heavy with seals, notarized and authorized. But after nearly twenty years the color was dark and the ink faded. It was barely legible, and she held it up to the light from the windows to her right. "There is nobody in Rome so stupid as to even entertain such a notion," she continued. "France cannot free the pope, either. I daresay Clement isn't entirely unhappy in the custody of my nephew. I think—"

The chamberlain entered. Catherine paused and laid the parchment down to ask him what was the matter.

"Cardinals Campeggio and Wolsey, Your Majesty."

"Ah," she said, a weariness in her voice Estrella had heard more and more lately. "They may come." They were expected. Chapuys rose, and Catherine remained seated.

The queen's maids rose and moved to the wall behind their mistress, emptying the seats at the table for Catherine's conference with the messengers of the king. "Shall I move these, Your Majesty?" Estrella asked, indicating the stack of papers and books lying out on the table. The resources would show the visitors Catherine's recent researches.

"No. Let them see that I am neither ignorant nor without help."

The maids curtsied and went to stand at attention as servants, but with their ears open for whatever information might be revealed to them.

The clergymen entered, both resplendent in shiny, silken red robes and heavy gold collars that lay about their shoulders like fallen haloes. Thomas Wolsey was the king's closest advisor and had been for nearly two decades. Hated and envied by nearly everyone in the kingdom except Henry himself, he had achieved his position and kept it so long by virtue of his keen legal mind and nimble grasp of court politics. Cardinal Lorenzo Campeggio of Santa Anastasia likewise was an expert in canon law. His corpulent body held a fine, persuasive mind. In sending these men to coerce Catherine, Henry was bringing to bear his most deadly guns.

Estrella watched a stillness come over Catherine as the men made their obeisance and were invited to sit. She gestured to her chamberlain to remain in the room, and he took up a position near the door. Wolsey moved the best chair in the room to a position close to the end of the table where Catherine sat, between the queen and her advisor, Chapuys. With a grunt and a long, gurgling groan, Campeggio settled his aging, gouty bulk into a chair on the other side of the table, so the two flanked her like fat, shiny red bookends and she couldn't look at both at the same time. Estrella saw this, and knew this meeting was not going to go well.

But Catherine solved the problem herself. Rather than spend this session swiveling her head back and forth between these men, she rose and went to gaze out the window as if she didn't care where they sat and would do as she pleased. She was the queen, after all, and wasn't required to look at either of them if she didn't wish it. Both men struggled to their feet as she rose, clearly distressed she wasn't going to allow them to sit. For that matter, she wasn't required to allow them here at all. She looked over at Estrella and murmured her name, and the maid went to open the window for her. The vista below was a garden, and a fresh breeze came to cool the queen's face. She smiled and breathed deeply with satisfaction, as if she'd summoned it especially. Estrella returned to her position near Maria.

Catherine addressed the clergymen without looking over at them. "You've come to advise me to enter a nunnery, then?"

There was a slight hesitation in the cardinals.

Catherine said, "London is not so very large a place, and news travels quickly in Henry's court." Her gaze remained on the out of doors, and she raised her chin as she drew a cleansing breath. The suggestion to take the veil was also expected because it was what was usually asked of a queen whose husband wanted her gone. Convents were so crowded with unwanted women of all ranks that it was sometimes difficult to find a nun with a true vocation.

Campeggio said, "It would be best for all concerned."

Now the queen turned to him, taking in both men with a single impassive gaze. "How so?"

"It would allow you to retain your honor and possessions. And those of Princess Mary, as well. You could maintain your own apartments, live as you live now, and lose nothing."

A flash brightened Catherine's eyes, and Estrella wondered if the men even saw it. If either of them did, neither gave any indication. Campeggio continued without pause, and his tone suggested he thought he was explaining the big, wide world to a small child.

"You could hold court in the same opulence to which you are accustomed, just as the queen of Louis XII. Nobody wishes to force you to change your life. What is desired is that there be a viable successor to the throne."

Catherine cut in sharply, "And for Henry to put himself right with God."

There was a short pause as the two clergymen realized their tactical error, then Campeggio cleared his throat and continued. "Well, yes, of course. But you must understand there are other issues as well. More practical issues, which suggest the punishment of God if things are not set aright. After all, it is in the best interest of all for Henry to be given the opportunity of a male heir. A man must have a son, and a king a prince to rule after him. It is a fact of this life God has given us. Henry would be grateful to you for such cooperation. He would allow you your dower rights if you would consent, and you would keep the high regard of the court. Continue to resist the will of the king, and there will be acrimony—even hostility—toward you. Scandal."

"Scandal about a wife who has been nothing but virtuous throughout her marriage?"

"No wife." Campeggio folded his hands in a manner that was matter-of-fact, as if his point were patently obvious, and anyone who didn't see it must be a fool. "Leviticus makes clear that a man cannot marry his brother's widow. You are Arthur's widow, and therefore within a degree of affinity forbidden for marriage by canon law. Surely you cannot wish for this to be brought to public scrutiny."

"Were it true, I imagine you might be correct. However, the thing is an evil lie. I was never Arthur's wife; I went to Henry a virgin. For that I have my maids to vouch, Estrella and Maria, who were there then, and know the truth of the matter. They will attest to that truth, as they did when the pope gave his dispensation." She nodded toward Estrella and Maria. "On their honor they will tell you I spent but seven nights with Arthur and at no time was he capable of consummating the marriage. The illness that ended him made it impossible for him to be any sort of husband to me." There was a slight hesitation before she added, "Nor to anyone else, for that." Then she went on, "He left me not a widow but the daughter of my father. Only Henry has made me a wife." Her gaze returned to the garden, and she repeated softly, "Only Henry."

"Nevertheless—"

"Furthermore, Cardinal Campeggio," her voice hardened again, "I have no vocation. God has not called me to the religious life. As a clergyman, I'm sure you must understand the importance of the calling. The Church never benefits from those who only attach themselves to it for convenience." There was a heavy pause, then she added, "Or for personal benefit."

The men hesitated to reply, then Wolsey opened his mouth

but Campeggio overrode him. "Your Majesty, your piety is well-known and appreciated by all. You are an example for all of England in your love of God and your diligent prayer. Surely a life of service to God would be pleasing to you. Indeed, it distresses me to hear you disparage the idea."

"My life is in service to God already. As you said, I stand as an example to my people, and to hide myself behind the walls of a convent would be to negate all I have done and prevent all I might do in the future. God cannot wish me to become a nun or to live a secular life among them. He brought me to England and gave me to Henry. He made me a mother, giving Henry and me both a daughter perfectly capable of reigning after him. Claims that God has made us childless for our alleged sin are thereby demonstrated to be patently untrue, merely by the existence of Mary. We are not childless." Her tone sharpened. "Though the Howards and the Boleyns would wish it so, God has not seen fit to oblige them. I would wonder at their own state of grace for that."

"Mary cannot succeed the king."

"I daresay she can."

"There has never been a female monarch in England."

The hardness in Catherine's voice turned brittle. "Then perhaps it is time there was. My mother reigned in her own right as queen in Castile, and with more success than many a king. And so did my sister, Joanna, after her."

Campeggio made a *harrumph* and set his hands on the table before him like a husband about to chastise his wife. Again he sounded as if he were talking to a child. "Your Majesty, the English are not like the Spanish. They are mired in custom, living in a cold, dreary land that does not provide the stimulation to intellect evident in more southern climes. Culture develops more slowly here than on the Continent." He indulged himself in a gentle smile. "Indeed, it's all we can do to bring them along within the community of Christendom, for they would hold us all back if they could."

Estrella took a glance at the Englishman Wolsey, but if he took exception to the abuse of his countrymen he showed it not a dot. Indeed, there seemed to be a smug little smile at the corners of his lips, though it was so tiny that he could have denied it if asked. He gazed upon Catherine with an expression that seemed to fully support every word uttered by his fellow cardinal. Chapuys glanced from one to the other, his expression discreetly amused.

Campeggio continued, "Were Mary to attempt to succeed her father, there would be insurrection led by those who would see an opportunity to gain the throne. Perhaps even a fully expressed civil war. Many would die. The country would suffer greatly for your persistence."

It was plain Catherine was moved by that. She paled and for a moment didn't speak. The clergymen waited as the words sank in. But then she drew a deep, slow breath and said, "I believe you are wrong. You're wrong that the English would refuse to follow a woman, and you're wrong that they are mired in pigheadedness. The English are my subjects; I've known them for more than two decades. They are a fine people, eager to grow in intellect and to take their place in the European community. Henry has struggled throughout his entire reign to show his kingdom to be as strong in wealth, intellect, and arms as any on the Continent. Most of the finest minds I've ever known were born and educated on this island. Far from being backward or stupid, they have shown themselves to be superior in some ways to many Italians I've known." Her tone was not pointed, but she paused to let that sink in for the Italian cardinal.

Wolsey honored the pause, then entered the fray and side-stepped that entire argument, abandoning it for another tack. "Please understand, Your Majesty, your resistance to retire-ment will have dire repercussions on the Church." Without waiting for Catherine to ask what those might be, he elabo-rated for her. "The king will not let this go. He has made that plain enough, though none of us ever needed to be told it. He means to have his way, and we all know him well enough to understand what that might entail. Surely you're aware the au-thority of the pope is already at risk. Lutheran sentiment is rampant, and Henry would find excellent support were he to declare the pope's authority in England at an end. By resisting his will, you give him no choice but to take matters into his own hands."

"I force nothing." Catherine's voice took on a quiet but deadly edge, like an assassin's dagger. "Henry's choices are to obey God or not, and I have naught to do with the matter. Those have always been his recourse, and the law of God has not changed."

"But you have a choice as well, Your Majesty. To save En-gland or destroy it."

Her gaze flickered, but she refrained from asking him to continue. He did in any case.

"If the king is forced—"

"*Chooses.*"

A short, impatient sigh escaped Wolsey. "If the king resorts to denying the authority of the pope, there will be terrible consequences for us all. Those who would promote heresy will rise against the true Church and attempt to destroy it.

There would be bloodshed. On your account. It would be on your head, and on your hands. Would you do such to your beloved English subjects?"

Estrella's eyes narrowed at the wily old man. He knew where to strike Catherine—he knew where her heart lay.

There was a long silence, then Catherine said, "I am an obedient wife. Always have I been loyal to my husband, and to the Church. I will obey Henry in all things that do not conflict with God's law. I can do no other. And so in this I have no choice but to stand firm, for there is but one truth. I am Henry's wife. To allow the lie would be as to say it myself, and I cannot. I am no whore, though you would have me known falsely as such. My daughter is no bastard. I have not lived nearly half my life in sin—"

"Unawares, Your Majesty."

A steely hardness came into Catherine's eyes, and her voice took on the edge of a Toledo sword. *"That would not be possible! And you know it!* I cannot possibly be mistaken about my own virginity when I went to Henry! And so, Cardinals Wolsey and Campeggio, I assure you there is no mistake. There is no error. I have not sinned in this, knowingly or otherwise. I did not go to Henry's bed without knowing for a certainty I was never Arthur's wife. Henry is my husband and I his wife. I did not casually enter my marriage; it was accomplished in complete compliance to canon law. The law of God. And though I am an obedient wife, as ever and as I ever shall be, I am first and foremost obedient to the law of God. I am Henry's wife. Were I to die for saying so, it would change nothing. Henry's wish for a son changes nothing. The ambitions of that Boleyn whore and her family change nothing. On my immortal soul I cannot, and will not, treat lie as truth."

"There will be a trial."

"And I will be vindicated."

"You cannot believe that, Your Majesty."

"I believe it with every shred of my soul. By every truth I have ever known. And by all the faith I have in God. I will not be moved."

The weariness Estrella had seen in Catherine earlier now seemed to have fallen from her and onto Campeggio. Even Wolsey, ordinarily impassive as a statue, had his lips pressed together and his eyes narrowed to slits.

"Might you take some time to consider your position?"

"I would have counsel to consider my position in the trial." She glanced around the room at the few trusted advisors at her disposal. "But I will never be moved to enter a convent."

There was a long silence. The two cardinals looked over at Chapuys, almost as if they were considering pleading for him to convince her for them, but everyone in the room knew he would not try even if he might have succeeded. Chapuys was one of Catherine's staunchest supporters, and would back her in whatever she decided. The glint in his eye suggested he might even be amused by their current discomfiture.

Campeggio sighed, and began to gather himself to leave. Wolsey also. The Italian said, "It is with heavy hearts we make our departure, Your Majesty. God help us all when the consequences of your decision come down on us."

"I have complete faith God will help us all, always." She said it in a tone that suggested she was fairly appalled a man in God's service, particularly such a highly placed cardinal, would not have realized that to begin with. "Good-bye. You may leave."

The cardinals withdrew, and the chamberlain followed them out, possibly to be certain they left the apartments in all due haste, by the sour look on his face.

Catherine went to the table to sit again, her weariness suddenly returned. She stared into the middle distance for a moment, then laid her face in her palms. There was no sobbing,
but Estrella thought the queen might have cried if not for the
presence of her advisors. Chapuys watched, patiently and
without comment, waiting for her to compose herself.

Soon she did, took a deep breath, and rested her hands in
her lap to look over at him. "There will be a trial," she said, her
voice level.

"Yes, there will be, I fear. We must find every document we
can in support of your case, and every witness who will attest
to your virginity at your marriage to Henry."

The queen nodded, and glanced over at Estrella and Maria.

Not long after that meeting, a letter came from Charles
that spoke of a newly discovered brief. On orders from the
emperor, Cardinal Quiñones had begun assembling information and documents, and among the papers of the late Dr. De
Puebla had been found a brief written by Pope Julius II, dated
the same as the bull of dispensation for the marriage. It also
dispensed for the marriage, but with different phrasing from
the bull. In it were enough differences to cast the document in
a light that did serious damage to the case on which the claim
of unlawful marriage was being built by Wolsey. Just as valid a
dispensation as the bull being attacked, the brief shifted the
case enough to make the attack mounted against the bull
worthless.

Henry's contingent would need to either discredit the document, or begin their research anew with a different attack.

Catherine was provided with counsel, among them her
confessor, Jorge de Athequa, and John Fisher, Bishop of
Rochester. The array of learned and enthusiastic defenders

were delighted to hear of this development, and set to work immediately constructing a defense centering on it.

Wolsey challenged the veracity of the brief, calling it a forgery. He wanted to see the original, and no copy of any sort would do. A paper was delivered to the queen, requesting she write to her nephew and ask him to send her the original of the brief.

Though some of Catherine's advisors recommended heeding the request, she ignored it and them. The queen knew her husband's court well and understood who was trustworthy and who was afraid of her husband. Bishop Fisher was among those who kept silent on the matter of relinquishing the original document, and so made his feelings clear. Catherine heeded that implicit advice and did not bow to Wolsey's pressure.

But then she was summoned by the royal counsel. By order of her husband, whom she had promised to obey in all things not under the purview of God, she was made to appear in private conference before the men trying to annul her marriage. She took Chapuys with her and was accompanied by only her two most trustworthy maids. The meeting was short and ugly. The queen was threatened with a charge of treason if she did not obey the wishes of Henry in sending for the original of the devastating papal brief. She was made to sit at the table in the middle of the room. Wolsey, Campeggio, and several others of Henry's advisors stood around her, no longer bearing their diplomatic demeanors appropriate when addressing the queen, and they seemed to be trying to make a point they no longer considered her queen. Their voices were hard, and they spoke more loudly than necessary.

They ordered her to write out a letter dictated to her, re-

questing of her nephew that he send the original brief immediately. Further, the charge of treason would be brought
against her in haste if she sent another letter to contradict
this one.

Treason. Estrella paled, as did Catherine. Everyone knew
what it meant to be convicted of that. A traitor's death was by
hanging and evisceration, then quartering. A noble, if lucky,
might receive mercy and be beheaded, but only if the king
were not made angry. Those who attracted the ire of His
Majesty suffered terribly. Worse than burning, for at the stake
there was always the chance of smothering quickly. A traitor's
death was not quick. The queen, without further ado, did as
she was told, for Henry, like his father, had shown in the past
he was not squeamish about executing those he perceived as a
threat. Catherine sat down to write out the letter Wolsey dictated to her. Estrella stood with her head ducked to hide the
flush of anger and hatred on her face. The queen's hand was
steady as she wrote, and she said nothing, but the color was
high in her cheeks, and her lips pressed tightly together. Estrella's mind flew to think of what might be done to prevent
this letter from reaching Charles.

But no sooner had the queen reached her apartments afterward than she sent for the Spanish ambassador by verbal
message.

It was a short wait before Don Iñigo Mendoza arrived in
the queen's gallery in disguise, striding in a hurry down the
long hallway, wearing a monk's robe with the hood well over
his face. Such discretion had become necessary, to protect
from retaliation those who would help the queen. His bare
feet slapped against the stone floor, a flaw in his disguise, for
his tender feet, accustomed to boots, might have given him
away to an alert observer. There at the far end of the gallery

he found her tucked away in an alcove, and the two had a hasty conversation before he strode away again on his mission. Estrella sat with Catherine in the alcove and asked what was planned.

"He's to get a message to Felipez. Cisco succeeded once before to thwart the king's assassins; I hope he can do it again. Charles will listen to him and will refrain from sending the brief."

The faithful Cisco Felipez departed on his mission in good time, but a fortnight later returned to London with a broken arm and a tale of failure for his queen. The letter dictated by Wolsey was sent, in the custody of one of Catherine's lesser chaplains, an Englishman named Thomas Abell. The man had been selected by Wolsey as loyal enough to the queen to be convincing to Charles, but as a subject of Henry he would surely understand where his true loyalties should lie. The only Spaniard on this journey was the interpreter, a gabby young fellow known to Estrella only as Montoya. No relation to herself, and thank God for that, for he was not only a commoner but also something of a ne'er do well, and not the sort she liked to call cousin. Less than an ideal messenger, he was the queen's only hope to communicate with Charles, and so he was entrusted.

Some time later, the interpreter returned to London and appeared at the queen's apartments as big and bold as anything, walking with a bit of a swagger that had Estrella gawking. Indiscreet, even prideful, he presented himself without any heed to what Henry might do to him for his friendliness to the queen. When he was admitted to the presence chamber and made his obeisance with all due grace, he then raised his head, looked up at her with a wide grin on his face, and said, "I have a tale to tell, Your Majesty."

"Do you indeed?"

"I believe you will be pleased to hear it."

Catherine had the room cleared of everyone except her two trusted maids and her two closest advisors. Then she said, "Proceed, Montoya. I pray your assessment of your own news will prove correct."

THE interpreter knew he was not the queen's first choice in a courier of her desperate message. Neither did he think she was wise in choosing him. Not Jose Montoya. He was no hero, and didn't want to be one. That was for stiff-necked caballeros and those who needed to impress the ladies with their valor. For Montoya a winning smile and an ability to discern a woman's needs were all it took to never be without pleasing, pliant company. He'd always been one to lie low in dangerous circumstances, for coming to the attention of that blustering, pompous English king was very often the worst thing that could happen to a man. Not much good for a woman, either, though Montoya sometimes thought he could have done with a bauble or two and might have let himself be fondled for it had the offer been made, even by that fat, pasty, *sucio* old king. But such an offer for Montoya's favors was unlikely—with this king at least—and so the queen's interpreter made a habit of wending his way in and out of court matters, acting only as a conduit and never as a force of any power. This assignment from the king's disfavored wife frightened him. All the long ride to Plymouth he kept one eye out to the rear, on the lookout for a king's assassin. Or worse, a simple official who might arrest him for torture and execution. A quick dagger through the heart would be far better than interrogation. But the first leg of the journey was uneventful, as was the crossing to France, and Montoya began to relax.

Once Montoya, Abell, and the Englishman's servant had landed safely in Le Havre, the journey to Castile was long and boring. The servant rode behind, and Montoya rode beside Abell, at his elbow in case any interpreting needed doing. Of course, they were still in France, and Abell spoke French well enough. Montoya wouldn't be much needed until they reached Spanish territory, and that suited him fine. To pass the time he chatted with Abell. *Thomas*, as he became known to the Spaniard over those days. The journey was some weeks along now, and there was little else to do to keep the mind occupied during the ride but to talk.

Abell was not terribly talkative. He seemed more interested in listening. That also suited Montoya. He talked of Spain and how happy he was to be seeing Castile again. When that ran thin, he tried to pry some gossip from Thomas. Any tidbit to give warning of which way the politics drifted was a help to a man who wished to steer clear of trouble. And that man would be Jose Montoya. But Abell was not talkative. Montoya wondered whether he knew much of anything at all about anything, he spoke so little. The interpreter concluded the fellow understood the nature of this journey and must be ashamed. Montoya would have been ashamed to betray his mistress. He would have done it if need be, and understood Abel's awkward position, but at least he would have been ashamed.

"Do you not feel a twinge about your purpose in delivering this letter, Thomas?"

Abell glanced sideways at him. "What do you mean?"

"You're chaplain to Queen Catherine. I should think you would be more loyal to the lamb entrusted to you than this."

Abell stared at him. "I cannot imagine what you are talking about."

What a dull wit this man was! Montoya glanced away at the French countryside for a moment, then said, "The queen. You know she wrote this letter under duress. She does not really want Charles to send the pope's brief."

Abell pulled up his horse, bringing his servant's horse to a halt behind him. Montoya drew his mount around and circled back to the other side of Abell, curious now what was going on with the Englishman. He glanced at the servant and switched to Latin, though it was not his strongest language. "You did not know?"

"Of course not. I don't even know the subject of this missive, and I'm astonished you do. I was told it was a highly private and personal communication between the queen and her nephew."

A cold sweat broke out on Montoya as he realized he may have made a horrible mistake. Now the Englishman was going to want to know why Montoya had been told what he had not. Montoya said, "Forget I said anything, then," and kicked his horse into a trot. Abell could catch up or not, he didn't care.

The courier did, and quickly. "Wait!" He gestured for his servant to hang back out of earshot, then admonished the Spaniard to pull up his horse. Montoya obliged and slowed to a walk, and Abell addressed him. "Don't say such a thing, then just drop it. Tell me what is happening."

"Do not mind me. Ignore me as you would Will Somer, for I know less than he."

"You are not the king's fool, Montoya. Near as I can tell, you're nobody's fool. Tell me."

Montoya nearly pleaded to let it drop. He had no desire at all to go into this. "I don't know what I'm talking about. I'm nothing but an interpreter; I hear what is said in one language, it goes in my ears, and out my mouth in another language. Nothing worth mentioning ever sticks in my head." He poked a finger against his forehead as if there were holes wide enough for it to go in.

"Nonsense. You know the queen's mind far better than I, and I wish to know it better. I wouldn't care to do anything that should give me a twinge of guilt, let alone that it should be done to the queen whom I respect. Tell me what she would have me do. I'm her chaplain, and have an obligation to her. If she would be harmed by my mission, it would weigh heavy on my soul."

Montoya looked over at the rather staid Englishman and wondered if that could be the truth. Then he realized that if Abell was not loyal to the queen, then Montoya himself was a dead man in any case. Abell would betray him to the king, and he would find himself in the Tower with the prisoners—or ghosts of prisoners—who inadvertently found themselves athwart the sitting monarch of England. Perhaps it would be best if he told of the queen's plight. Then he could observe Abell's behavior in Castile. Any furtiveness in Abell might tell Montoya whether he dared return to London at all. So he told of the meeting in which Queen Catherine had been threatened with execution. He watched Abell's face, but there was not a flicker of any sort of emotion as Montoya spoke. The clergyman took in the verbal message that was to be delivered to Charles, without a nod or a blink. When Montoya was finished, Abell was silent. Montoya had no idea what to make of that, as much in the dark as he was before he ever spoke.

The two continued to ride in silence, and Montoya gazed over at Abell in hopes of a reaction. There was none. His mind began to race, panic mounting as he became certain the

Englishman would betray him to King Henry. He glanced rearward to the servant still riding beyond earshot and wondered whether he should ride away immediately or wait until night and slip away into the darkness. Over the better part of that afternoon his mind tumbled with plans of how to get away and what to do with his life once he'd abandoned his post in the English court. It wouldn't be easy, but at least he would be alive, and death certainly wouldn't be preferable.

But as the sun descended and they approached a town where they would secure lodgings for the night, Abell said to his interpreter as if continuing a conversation they'd been carrying on all day, "I cannot let this thing happen to the queen."

Montoya glanced at him, wondered if he should reply, then ventured, "Indeed not." It came out sounding like a question.

"The king cannot be allowed to deny her virtue or the pope's authority."

"Certainly not." Cool relief washed over the Spaniard as he realized Abell had arrived at a conviction over the space of the afternoon. Apparently a firm one, by the tone of his voice.

"This letter cannot be delivered to Charles."

"The queen's message should be delivered." Montoya was happy to agree.

"More than that."

Montoya waited for Abell to go on, to elaborate on his idea, but was disappointed. Abell said nothing more for the evening and little more for the rest of the ride to Valladolid.

Once arrived in the palace of the Emperor Charles, Thomas Abell went to work in support of his queen, as industrious now as he'd ever before been stolid. He delivered the letter to Charles, and himself told the story of the meeting in which Catherine had been threatened. With his Spanish interpreter at his side, he described the situation in England, where Charles' aunt was nearly a prisoner in her apartments. He was adamant the brief, which was the most powerful document to damage the king's carefully wrought case, should never go near London, lest it accidentally-on-purpose go missing or be destroyed.

But rather, he drew up a document for Charles, stating in sensible terms why the original of the brief could not be sent. Well-thought-out and in Latin, it was a solid piece of work. Then he requested a properly attested, notarized copy of the original brief be drawn up to support the copy from De Puebla's files. Such a document would be as acceptable in a Church court as the original, and there would be nothing for Henry's counsel to say on that matter. For days he conferred with Charles, outlining what must be done to prevent the divorce. Then, when the notarized copy of the brief was ready, he packed it in his saddlebags and mounted up for the return trip to London.

Montoya returned with him, stunned at this turn of events and eager to tell his queen of how this mission turned from disaster to her salvation. All during the ride, he looked upon Thomas Abell and wondered if he could have been wrong about Englishmen in general. This one, at least, seemed to be as much a gentleman of honor as any caballero.

Eleven

1529

 THE brief was never declared a forgery. Though Henry struggled to be rid of the damaging document, it remained part of Catherine's defense and prevented him from invalidating the pope's dispensation. It was a tiny and temporary victory for Catherine.

Then, two years after Henry's announcement to his wife of his intention to set her aside, a court was called at Blackfriar's. Both king and queen were expected to appear as defendants to a charge that their marriage was invalid. Henry pretended the court was not his idea and feigned helplessness in the face of legalities. He fooled nobody but himself.

"Surely he can't believe he is forced into this," said Maria to her mistress as she and Estrella dressed her on the day the trial opened. It was mid-June, and though the sky was overcast today, the air was warm for England, and Catherine was donning a lightweight green overdress with little heavy decoration. The better for comfort on a temperate day, and the better to present herself in court as a virtuous wife. Estrella took a sharp silver pick to tug bits of the silk blouse through the myriad tiny slashes in the sleeves of the overdress.

"I assure you, he can. I'm certain my husband is sincere in his conviction the marriage is invalid."

Maria and Estrella peered at Catherine, who stood before her mirror to examine her costume for the day. The maids stood behind, ready to adjust anything that might come to their attention before the queen would proceed to the trial. It was an important day and a historical event, for it was the first time any monarch of England would appear in court in his own defense. Never mind the trial was encouraged by Henry, the commons of London were agog at the idea, and talk buzzed in the public houses of this turn of events. Judging the king and expecting compliance with findings seemed to imply the king was not the law in his land.

"But the trial is at his own request."

Catherine's voice betrayed no hint of rancor in this. "Exactly. And he is more than likely most proud of his self-sacrifice, in obedience with what he perceives as canon law. He is mistaken, of course, advised by men who love neither God nor the Church—nor Henry in all likelihood—and especially they do not love the pope. Lutheran heretics have poisoned his mind. He cannot help his error and will not even see it until his passion for this venture has waned. And it will, as his passions always do. As they do for most men."

"So we should forgive him, for he knows not what he does?"

That made Catherine smile, and she turned toward her maids. "Our savior was a wise man, Maria. It is good to follow his example."

"Of course, Your Majesty."

"And we must guide my beloved husband back onto the proper path. I believe today he will see his folly. He will see that what he is doing—or allowing to be done—is wrong. I feel it in my heart. Very strongly, I feel it in my heart."

Estrella glanced at Maria and hoped the queen was right. The maids fell silent on the matter as they continued to fuss with their silver picks and Catherine's blouse.

Catherine's position with Henry was of near helplessness. Though she had some excellent advice from her friend, Bishop John Fisher, there was still no counsel arrived from her nephew and she couldn't trust most of the men on the counsel assigned to her by the king. It seemed everyone on the Continent was holding still, holding their breaths, in hopes of this matter simply blowing over. Alas, the pope and the emperor knew too little about King Henry, whose stubbornness was so ironclad as to be incomprehensible to the more subtle and practical-minded Mediterranean men in the south. By their inaction, they were only making the situation worse, but there was no telling them that. Only those close to Henry knew the extent of his willingness to dig in his heels. Catherine was left to her own resources, and it was only her own intelligence and stubbornness that gave the maids hope.

Indeed, it was this stubbornness and singleness of purpose that made him vulnerable to the wiles of the Boleyn whore. Anne, by accounts, knew Henry well enough to not succumb to his advances too readily. Like everyone else in court, she'd seen how his interest in her sister had waned when Mary Boleyn was his paramour years before. In spite of the show Anne put on as his mistress, putting on airs and wearing his jewels, nobody could say the king had ever actually bedded her. He'd been panting after her for at least two years, ever at her in hopes of wearing down her resistance, as if it were a game. A conquest, like the hunting he'd so enjoyed in his youth or the jousting against his friends who'd usually let him win. He was the king. He never lost a contest in any significant or public way, and was certainly convinced it was only a matter of time before he would win this one. Now his fascination was as intense as it had been in the beginning, and showed no signs of waning. Some thought he may even have been enjoying the dance all along and didn't truly want to conclude it.

After a long silence while the women fussed and adjusted, Maria said, "They have no right to try you in this court."

"But they will do it in any case. I've protested it to the best of my ability, to no avail." Catherine turned and smoothed the already smooth skirt of her overdress.

"The judges are prejudiced. That is no trial."

"As I've pointed out in my protest."

"Is not the case still pending in Rome?" Estrella found herself confused by the legalities, wondering how there could be two trials for the same thing in two different places.

"Indeed it is, as I've said to Henry's court. And this is what truly alarms me; that Henry ignores the authority of Rome. This trial flies in the face of Church authority, and its very existence is abhorrent to me, regardless of what finding might result regarding me."

Estrella understood but still felt her own abhorrence toward the court had more to do with its threat to Catherine than to the Church. She wished the queen weren't so very selfless. A small part of her even wished her mistress had accepted retirement to a nunnery, where she could carry on her accustomed life in comfort provided by Henry, more or less as she always had in the past. There would have been peace then, and no need to defend Catherine's virtue before the world. That virtue should go unquestioned, for she felt her mistress was far superior to everyone she'd ever known for her faith and pious life. To allow anyone to point a finger at Catherine and call her "whore" was more than appalling, and Estrella wished for anything but to endure it. But whenever that thought rose, she banished it with shame. Catherine was right, that her own comfort was not the most important issue. Whatever hardship they would suffer for standing by her conviction was to the good, for the sake of the Church, as well as for truth and a clear conscience. Estrella saw that Catherine, for her very pious nature, had no choice but to resist.

In the great hall at Blackfriar's, Henry sat on a throne under a canopy, wearing his robes of state. He was resplendent in red silk, ermine, and bejeweled gold collar, his crown aglitter with gold and jewels. Beside him sat Wolsey and Campeggio, and beyond them sat Catherine. Defendants together, but not with common purpose. The floor was aswarm with officers of the court, bishops, and counselors. The clergymen glittered even more brightly than the king, wearing miters of gold and silk robes that shone in the light that streamed through tall windows. As if the very light were attracted by the concentration of England's wealth and power in one room and had come to dance with it.

Estrella watched Henry as the room prepared itself for what was to come. He gazed out over the gathering court with bland eyes that at first seemed to give nothing away, but occasionally a glint would rise in them. She was unable to tell whether it was anger or pride that lit them so but suspected it was pride. Perhaps even glee, for she thought he must be anticipating victory. And subsequently, conquest of his coy mistress. He might even at that moment be thinking of the first night he would spend with that mistress. In any case, he did not strike Estrella as a defendant vulnerable to the judgment of the court, and probably was not considering penitence once this would be over.

The king was called to the court, and he replied from where he sat, in all formality and proper protocol. Then the queen was called. Without reply, Catherine rose from her seat and made her way between and around the gathered men to where her husband sat on his throne. She moved without the least hurry, but with a stolid grace that made the room come to a halt and watch her proceed. There she knelt and looked up at her husband. One deep breath, and she spoke clearly, her voice ringing out over the assemblage in her slight Spanish accent.

"Sir, I beseech you for all the love that hath been between us, let me have justice and right, take of me some pity and compassion, for I am a poor woman and a stranger, born out of your dominion. I have here no assured friends, and much less indifferent counsel. I flee to you as to the head of justice within this realm."

Henry's eyes flickered once more, but this time Estrella saw no pride. Apprehension. The entire room saw the queen was not cowed, and Henry may have had some idea of what his wife was about to say. Surely he must have; he'd known Catherine as his wife for all of his adult life. They'd shared an intellectual relationship to a degree rare among spouses, and each knew the other's mind as intimately as a husband and wife would know each other's bodies. Surely Henry knew what was coming. But he said nothing.

Without faltering, the queen continued. "I take God and all the world to witness that I have been to you a true, humble, and obedient wife, ever comfortable to your will and pleasure. I loved all those whom you loved, only for your sake, whether

I had cause or no, and whether they were my friends or my enemies." Estrella shut her eyes for a moment, for this was untrue. Catherine had merely tolerated many courtiers, such as Wolsey, for the sake of her husband, and loved them only as a Christian loves a sinner. But when Estrella looked again, Catherine's gaze upon the king was as sincere as ever anyone's was. Perhaps she believed it.

The queen pressed toward her point. "This twenty years or more I have been your true wife, and by me you have had divers children, although it hath pleased God to call them from this world. And when you had me at the first, I take God to be my judge . . ." Tension filled the queen's voice as she stressed those words to Henry. Another flicker came over the king's face, and he stared at his wife. Something passed between them. An understanding of something nobody else could comprehend. He appeared to know what was to follow, and his eyes beseeched her to not continue. But she did. Relentless, she said the thing he would not have had her say. ". . . I was a true maid, without touch of man." The king's mouth opened as if he might interrupt, and she hurried to get the next words out. "And whether this be true or no, I put it to your conscience." The king's eyes narrowed, and his cheeks flushed. Catherine went on, "If there be any just cause by the law that you can allege against me, either of dishonesty or any other impediment, to banish and put me from you, I am well content to depart to my great shame and dishonor. And if there be none, then here I must lowly beseech you let me remain in my former estate and to receive justice at your princely hands."

The queen had just challenged the king to either admit she'd been a virgin on their wedding night or state before the world that he cuckolded his brother and lied about it for twenty years.

But the king did not reply. He only sat there, gazing at her with eyes that grew dull. Not a muscle moved, in body or face. Catherine waited, but it was useless. Henry would not oblige her with a statement.

She continued her speech, but nobody listened. Henry looked away finally. When she finished, she rose, curtsied, and turned to leave. With the same unfailing grace with which she'd approached her husband, she walked away from him through the gathering of clergy and lawyers. The formal summons of the crier calling her to her throne followed her out, but she did not respond to it. She made her way from the room, followed by her entourage.

Behind them could be heard Henry beginning his own formal speech to the court. He spoke of his sorrow at this necessity, his voice fading as the cluster of Catherine's people moved away from the room, until he could be heard no more.

Twelve

❧

1508

AFTER the death of Sir John Cranach, Estrella lapsed into a habit of moving through her days in quiet and uninvolved observation of all that went on around her. It wasn't that she'd given up hope, but anymore it was difficult to become excited about anything. The loss had not been of a great love, but she had hung her future on the marriage, and now there seemed to be nothing more for her. No possibility of love, nor comfort. No home. Not even the prospect of a bad marriage that would at least have been more respectable than withering on the vine, growing old and wrinkled in a position meant for young, unattached women. She began to understand that the world did not care what was right nor what was best. The world was neither glad nor unhappy this happened to her. It simply was, and would do to her what it would. She wondered why God had made it this way, but understood there was no recourse but to accept and go on. Each day she did so with neither joy nor sorrow but with a yawning emptiness.

The household of the princess was kept separate from most court events now, moved here and there among the king's many palaces and never given rooms of good quality. Sometimes not even of tolerable quality. Outbuildings, chambers over the stables, cramped quarters that were only provided if there was no other use for them and if nobody in Henry's court should be inconvenienced by Catherine's presence. Estrella found herself not caring where they lived, for that only brought frustration and longing for a better life. She'd been in England long enough now not to expect much from its cold weather and colder people.

Sir John's heirs—a brother and the brother's wife—tried to recover the ruby brooch he'd given her, calling it a wedding gift for a marriage that had never taken place, but a casual word from the king made them fall silent on the subject. Estrella felt little gratitude toward the king, and as little irritation at the brother's meanness. She pinned the brooch at her throat and moved through her days like a heavy barge on a wide river, slowly and with little response to those around her, everything an effort but nothing worth that effort in the end.

Catherine's struggles against Dr. De Puebla's seeming indifference to her situation increased as money became even more scarce and the princess incurred more debt to both her suite and the brokers to whom she pawned her dowry plate. Francesca's frustration grew, and her voice became louder, a constant refrain of dissent, insisting they all make a plea to Ferdinand to end their exile.

Though Ferdinand seemed oblivious to his daughter's

plight, a new ambassador was sent from Aragon to replace the ailing De Puebla: Don Gutierre Gomez de Fuensalida, Knight Commander of the Order of Membrilla. On his arrival, filled with energy but not particularly well equipped with diplomatic skill, he attempted to renegotiate the princess's dowry in the face of Henry's inclination to marry off the Prince of Wales to someone else. The new prospective Princess of Wales was young Eleanor of Ghent, the daughter of Philip and Joanna and niece to Princess Catherine. In his negotiation the ambassador was stunned to learn that Catherine had been pawning the plate she'd been told to not even use in her household seven years before. He was caught flat-footed, informed by Henry in the midst of a particularly difficult exchange. The plate was supposed to have been part of the dowry, and now there was even less offered by Ferdinand for the marriage of his daughter. Fuensalida's distress was plain for all to see.

The negotiations stalled amid the resulting uproar of bluff and squabble, badly handled by the inexperienced ambassador. Fuensalida then turned on Catherine and complained to her father, blaming her for his problems in solving the impasse.

Catherine's response to accusations of improvidence was silence. She'd done what had to be done to feed her household and did not see how it could have been otherwise accomplished. She had no use for opinions to the contrary. Fuensalida could chastise her all he wanted, but she was unmoved.

Estrella watched the wrangling, also unmoved, but deep inside she was desperate that something should happen. Anything, to solve this situation that had gone on so long and become so absurd. A hard core of desire knotted her gut, and she did not dare express it lest she explode in a fit of temper enough to destroy her standing in the household. She swallowed it, pretended it wasn't there, and sometimes she even believed it was gone. Often she awoke of a morning with her fingernails dug deep into the palms of her hands, and she would uncurl her fingers, knuckles aching from the clenching and little red marks in her skin.

Fuensalida's rows with the king became the talk of the palace, and Estrella once had even heard shouting outside Catherine's chambers. Catherine disliked the man's raucous behavior and sloppy negotiation tactics, and her lips pressed together whenever she heard his voice, no matter what he might be discussing at the time. The new ambassador was reckless in his dealings with the cold and calculating Henry, and he only served to annoy the king and his court of elderly Englishmen. The Spanish household had come to a shameful state in both finances and honor, and Estrella began to wonder if Francesca might be right, that it would be best for all of them to return to Spain. She began to listen to what her fellow maid had to say, and so did all the other girls. It seemed only Maria de Salinas and Catherine herself objected to the idea of petitioning Ferdinand to bring them all home.

One day in September Estrella awoke in the morning to the sound of shouting in the bailey a short distance from the disregarded buildings in which Catherine's household of nearly fifty people was quartered. She rose from bed and looked out and found carriages and packhorses crowded in the yard below. Men hurried back and forth, and voices carried a measure of fear. Her heart leapt to her throat, for though she'd never seen an invading army, she'd certainly heard stories. Everyone feared the approach of fighting men, and this mass of panicking people had all the signs of an evacuation. So near the king, the true horror was that the threat had come so close. Estrella hurried to Catherine's chamber.

The princess was also looking out, as her half-dozen maids hurried to dress her.

"What is happening?"

Several of the girls shrugged. "I don't know," said the princess. "Hurry, I must go to find out." They dressed her in her plainest outfit, the better to have her ready at speed, and then hurried into their own clothes as Catherine went with her confessor, Fray Diego Fernandez, to learn what was happening. The chamberlain hurried along behind them and caught up as he fastened his cloak. Estrella looked around for Fuensalida, but the ambassador was nowhere to be found; he was quartered with an Italian banker outside the palace and might not even know yet there was anything amiss.

Estrella returned to the maids' room, fairly leapt into a dress, and stuffed her disarrayed hair up into her most concealing coif. Then she hurried to the bailey, where she found Catherine arguing with Henry's head groom. He stood before her with the leads of two wagon horses in his fist. The animals were sensitive to the excitement of the people around them, and they tossed their heads and shifted their feet.

"You cannot leave us without horses," she was saying. Calm as ever, even with the fuss all around her, she did not betray alarm. Only confidence that this man would do his duty to his better.

"I most certainly can, Your Highness, and I shall. I must." The groom's manner was insolent, on par with the way Catherine had been treated by members of Henry's court for years. "The king has requested removal, and every horse is needed to fulfill his request. You'll have to find another way to transport yourselves."

"There is no other way." They certainly had no barge for the river.

"You have feet at the ends of your legs, do you not?"

"You would have me walk? With the threat of plague about? Do you suppose King Henry would take kindly to it if I were to die along the way?" Her tone was as regal as ever, in spite of the disrespect she was accorded.

"To be sure, Your Highness, King Henry has made it plain he would take kindly indeed to that very thing."

There was a long silence, and Catherine glared up at the man.

Finally, he said, "So, if you'll please excuse me, Your Highness, I have work that must be done, lest the king find fault with me." With that, and without leave from Catherine, he hauled the horses around and walked away to where a wagon was being loaded with household goods and crates.

Catherine watched him go. Estrella asked, "What is happening?"

The princess continued to watch the man with the horses retreat as she replied, "The court is abandoning the palace. There is a rumor of plague nearby. We're to be left without horses."

"Plague?" Estrella glanced around, afraid now of finding sick people about.

"There must be horses to be had, Your Highness," said Fray Diego, his demeanor calm and his voice soothing. Since his arrival from Spain last year, the confessor had become the rock on which Catherine rested her confidence. Fuensalida hated him for his youth and the influence he held over the princess. Catherine's religious bent had always brought her closer to her confessor than to anyone else, with the possible exception of Maria de Salinas.

"At what cost would we have them?"

"Your safety is paramount. You cannot stay here. I'll locate mounts and have them brought here. The household should begin to pack straightaway. Lightly, for there is no telling how many horses or what quality I might obtain." He bowed to the princess and took his leave to accomplish his mission.

Catherine and her maids watched him go. Estrella glanced around and noticed Francesca was not present, but that was no surprise. She was in the habit of visiting at the home of the ambassador's host, and was probably there now, with Fuensalida and the banker. No matter, for she was more likely to find transportation in that company than in the princess's. Fuensalida would make certain his friend escaped the sickness.

Those thoughts fled at sight of a horse approaching at a trot. Catherine turned to get on with the work of packing, and the rest went with her to her apartments, but Estrella lagged behind to watch the magnificent beast and its rider until they would pass. As he approached, she saw it was the Earl of Hartford, Piers Hilsey. She smiled at him, or rather at his glorious horse, and he wheeled his mount to approach her.

It was an enormous, black destrier. The stallion was young and appeared somewhat fractious, prancing and stepping lively, his long mane tossing with his nodding head, tail flying, and feathered fetlocks swirling about his black hooves. The earl drew him up beside Estrella and smiled down at her in return.

"I know who you are," he said cheerily as if nothing in the world could possibly be wrong. To look at him, one couldn't suspect there was illness anywhere in the world, let alone in this very palace. His cheeks glowed a rosy red, and his smile was filled with the healthiest teeth she'd ever seen.

"And I know who you are," she replied as cheerily. "Though you've absented yourself from the court thoroughly these past years."

"Not so thoroughly. I drop in occasionally, just to make certain the old king doesn't forget my name." He glanced off to the side and said in a slightly lowered voice, "Especially I don't wish the young prince to forget it."

"You like the prince?"

"He's a fine lad and will make a good king." Then Hartford shrugged and said, "In all good time." He said it in a very English inflection that meant "good time" should be soon, God willing. Then he spoke out again, "'Tis yourself who has avoided court."

"I avoid it as I avoid jewels and furs." She reached out to touch the soft, fuzzy muzzle of his mount. "And beautiful steeds like this one. Only because I have no choice. We have horses like this in Spain. My father's stable was large and filled with some of the finest animals in Aragon."

"I acquired him in Scotland, but I believe some of his line can be traced to Spain." Hartford patted the stallion's neck. "Do you like him? Of course you do, he matches your hair." He leaned a little toward her, "And your spirit, I think. I've seen it before."

"Have you?" She'd noticed his as well in the wedding tournament when she'd been only a girl, and liked what she'd seen, but would die before admitting it out loud.

"You enjoy the tournaments. I remember. I saw you in the stands, and for a moment I thought you were on the lookout for a champion. But I was mistaken, it seems, for nobody carried your token that day." Estrella wasn't entirely certain he wasn't teasing her, and had no reply. After a brief hesitation, he added, "And, in another context, I recall you dance with the grace of an angel." This he said with what appeared to be utter sincerity.

That took her entirely by surprise. Not only had he taken notice of whether she'd given a token at the tournament, he also must have watched her dancing the night of Catherine's wedding. What if he'd caught her looking at him? Might he have? Perhaps someone had told him she was staring? Pointed her out to him. Surely she had been staring, and now her face warmed. She kept her smile, though she no longer felt it. She replied in a tone of jest to make light in spite of her embarrassment, "You, señor, joust with the grace of an archangel."

That made him laugh. Then he straightened and said, "Well, we must move along. Wouldn't be good to be caught by the sleeping sickness, would it? Hurry with your packing, and perhaps I'll have another glimpse of you farther on."

"We've no horses. No way to get there. We might be forced to stay and brave out the plague."

Hartford's smile fell completely, and his brow furrowed. "No horses?"

"None."

He glanced around at the palace staff hurrying to load their masters' belongings onto wagons and packhorses. Then he said, "Where is your mistress quartered?"

Estrella turned and nodded toward the small building behind her. It had once been storage for the palace kitchen, so the rooms were large and cold. It crossed her mind that with winter approaching they would do well to find transportation onward just on that account.

Hartford said, "Go and pack. You shall have horses." A brief second as he calculated, then, "Five of them, and a wagon. Tell your mistress that."

"I will, my lord. And thank you."

Hilsey spurred and wheeled his mount, and the steed leapt away across the bailey, scattering a line of servants loading a wagon for the king.

The promised horses were brought within the hour: five

sturdy animals for wagon and pack, and a wagon large enough for luggage and some servants. Somewhat later Fray Diego was able to produce three saddle horses and a small carriage drawn by a pair of dun animals that were ailing and nobody wanted. There was some question as to whether the creatures would survive the journey, but they were what could be found. Even with the five provided by Hartford, most of Catherine's suite would have to walk, and the luggage would need to be minimal. The remainder of their belongings would have to be sent for later if they did not return to this palace soon. Meanwhile, the maids would have to live with even less than the meager usual.

Once they'd made ready to leave, Catherine and her maids squeezed into the carriage. The youngest rode outside with the driver, and the roof was heavy with trunks and boxes. Catherine looked out the window at the wagon and pack-horses provided by Hartford.

"Estrellita, you say you hadn't seen Hartford since the wedding?"

"No, Your Highness. Not from then until today. It was most remarkable that he even remembered me."

"If I recall him correctly, I must say it's hardly remarkable you remember him. That fellow is one of the more memorable men at court."

Maria de Salinas snorted a laugh. "I should say. The beauty of that one could launch a thousand and one ships." The young women all tittered at that, and even Catherine had a good chuckle.

Maria de Rojas said, "They say he's the most eligible man in Henry's court, with the exception of the Prince of Wales."

Catherine's voice took on a sharp edge. "The Prince of Wales is not eligible in the least. He's entirely spoken for."

The maid paled. "Yes, Your Highness. I only meant it in the strictest sense as he isn't yet married to you."

Estrella said, "So, in the sense that the prince is spoken for, Hartford would be the most eligible man in the kingdom, yes?"

"Oh, but such a chore to look at!" Maria de Salinas giggled. "One would have to close her eyes every time he came to her bed!"

A wave of laughter shook the carriage, and with a crack of the driver's whip and a jerk at the harness, the borrowed carriage of the princess rolled off toward their destination, leaving behind the disease and its danger. As the carriage bumped along the London streets, Estrella turned over in her mind again and again her conversation with the earl. It was a pleasant pastime. His smooth voice, the clean lines of his aristocratic face, his long-boned grace in the saddle. The knot in her belly seemed to loosen. Unravel. Relax. The relief was exquisite pleasure, and she sighed.

Their next quarters were rooms over the palace stables. The hearths were small, and the smell of horses that rose through the poorly constructed wooden floor was strong and constant. Catherine's staff set to cleaning the floors and walls as others brought the trunks and prepared to unpack. Catherine avoided the place until the work would be done and the rooms ready for occupation. Though the sun was well on its way to setting, she and her maids went to a nearby garden for a walk.

This palace was away from the center of London, but they were familiar with it for the court had made the progress many times over the past few years. Catherine's suite was never part of the court, but they always followed for the sake of support, as always alert for whatever advantage could be had.

Here the palace was occupied of a sudden, and there had

been little preparation for the king's presence. The fall season was taking its toll on the garden, and the grass was damp and strewn with dead leaves. It would be cleaned up soon, but just now it seemed wild. More like an English forest than a formal garden in the French style. The women strolled in silence, each with their own opinion of the day and its implications. And each keeping those thoughts to herself.

Then Catherine reached out, touched Maria de Salinas on the shoulder, and said softly, "Tag." With a giggle she picked up her skirts and hurried away from the maid.

The other women did likewise, and Maria turned a circle with a grin. "Oh, Your Highness! We haven't played this since we were girls!"

"But aren't we all still girls?" Catherine sidled a bit, and her head tilted as if she were indeed a child and not a woman of twenty-three.

Maria ran at her, and Catherine dodged and hurried away with a high squeal. The others scattered and ran, laughing as well. Maria chased, and they teased, coming close but not close enough to catch anyone. She dashed to catch Estrella, and when she missed and Estrella ran away with screaming laughter, Maria doubled over, laughing so hard she could barely breathe. Estrella danced on her toes, a lightness in her heart she hadn't felt in years.

Nobody noticed the cluster of men approaching from the palace. Possibly the men hadn't noticed the women, either. When Estrella looked up from the game, they were very near and headed in the direction of the mews where the king's hunting birds were housed. When she saw who led the group, she blurted in surprise, "The prince!"

The women's game came to a halt, and Catherine spun to see. It was the Prince of Wales, to be sure. The tall, athletic build was unmistakable. He was accompanied by four of his father's courtiers, all a bit older than him but each much younger than the king. Estrella saw the Earl of Hartford, and she stifled a smile. The tension inside her unwound just a bit more.

Catherine called out, "Ho! Young Prince, and my betrothed! Where are you off to?"

The cluster of men sauntered to a stop, each one casting a curious glance in their direction. Prince Henry appeared to finally notice the women. He seemed startled at first, but when he recognized Catherine his ruddy face broke into a smile. "Catherine, 'tis you." He started over at a jaunty walk, but paused when one of the courtiers leaned in to speak to him in a low voice. Henry listened for a moment, then scowled and said, "Nonsense! I go where I like and speak to whom I please." He strode toward the women, and his friends followed in likewise manner. He addressed Catherine. "I hadn't known you were among us still."

Catherine waited until Henry and his friends were close enough she didn't need to shout out, and said, "Always, Your Highness. On that you can depend." Then she addressed Hartford. "Thank you, lord, for your generous loan of horses for our trip. You've enabled me to be close to my intended, and that is no small favor."

"My pleasure entirely, Your Highness." Hartford gave a short bow, then glanced at Estrella. His gaze seemed to pierce her to the core, sending a shiver up her spine, and the smile she suppressed played over her lips. A bright one lit his eyes, and it struck her a bit breathless.

Henry glanced at Hartford, then said to Catherine, "Horses? You were forced to borrow horses?"

"Apparently in the confusion I and my household were overlooked for provisions of transportation. The removal of the court was terribly sudden; I'm certain it was unintentional. And all is well, as you can see by our presence and my cheerful ensemble. I'm sure you must have heard us laughing from quite a distance."

Henry's eyes narrowed, and he glanced toward the tall palace towers. They all knew better than to think the incident had been an accident, but even the prince didn't care to seem critical of the king. Instead he said, "I'm happy you've arrived safely. All is well with you, then, I presume?"

"Indeed. My servants are preparing our quarters at this moment. We've come out to enjoy the gardens for a time." Never mind that the pre-evening sky was slate gray, the ground soggy from the last rain, and the grass littered with wet leaves. Not to mention the damp, chilly air. Estrella pressed her slipper against the ground and it made a squelching sound. Hartford glanced down at the noise. Suddenly she wished the hem of her dress weren't worn ragged with age and soaked with the damp grass. Somewhere she needed to obtain some braid to cover that fuzzy, discolored edge.

Henry was saying to Catherine, "I'm glad, then. You and your maids are far too precious to us to lose you to the sickness. Had I known you were without horses I would certainly have provided them."

The fact was Prince Henry hadn't known, and couldn't have, for in recent years he'd been kept from any contact with Catherine. This was the first meeting between the two since the troubles between the king and Catherine's father had begun. Catherine's face shone with pleasure at seeing her fiancé, and her gaze was hard on him as if she were drinking in his visage. It was a pleasing one, and Catherine's joy danced in her eyes.

Henry's enjoyment of Catherine's company was also evident. He nearly gawked. A wide smile opened his face, and he stood with all the pride of a young man trying to impress a pretty girl. "We were just on our way to the mews to have a look at my birds. Would you care to come along?"

In her mind Estrella begged Catherine to say yes. The mews would be warm, and less smelly than the rooms to which they must return soon. And the company would at least be fresh. She glanced at Hartford, whose attention was on the princess for her reply.

"Indeed, Your Highness. We should adore it."

Henry puffed up like a peacock, grinned, and led the group toward the building where his father kept the raptors used for hunting small game. It was a rough stone outbuilding, large and roomy inside and the floor covered with sand. The inside walls were not limed, as was most of the interior of the palace. Perches ran from wall to wall, and several freestanding ones were against the far wall. A fire burned in a small hearth near a cabinet that held the tools of the falconer's and aus-tringer's work. Hoods, lures, bells, gauntlets, jesses, and leashes, and many ceramic jars of medicines filled it and lay atop it. There was an old beef joint, picked clean and dried out. It had been there awhile and smelled rancid.

Birds stood on their perches, mildly disturbed by the sud-den presence of so many people. They shifted their feet and eyed the newcomers carefully. Jesses dangled, a metal ring at the end of each, to which a leash was attached and secured to the perch. Many of the birds were sparrowhawks, but Estrella noted a Spanish lanner and Arabian saker among them.

Henry took a gauntlet from the cabinet and donned it, then went to the saker and took it onto his fist. "I'll be taking this one out in the morning."

" 'Tis a beautiful bird," said Catherine. And it was true. Except for a few dark feathers, the bird was almost entirely white and appeared as if dressed in ermine. Its bright eyes looked around at the gathered human nobility, and the creature seemed to know it was as noble as they.

More words were exchanged between prince and princess, but Estrella didn't hear them. Hartford had stepped behind her, and was now whispering into her ear, "No more beautiful than a certain Spanish bird, I should say."

Estrella whispered in return, "The lanner?"

"No."

Her head tilted slightly, and it took a moment for her to realize he meant her. There was a sweet fluttering in her belly as she replied, "You would style me a prisoner? A caged bird?"

"I see in you a proud and beautiful creature who is hindered and pines for freedom."

"Should you truly, then?"

He gave a frown of questioning.

"Say it, I mean."

Then he smiled and put his lips even closer to her ear. His voice lowered to such a quietness that she could hear his tongue on his teeth. "I would have you answer that. Would you hear me if I did?"

Her breath caught with the joy of hearing him. She couldn't reply, but only looked into his bright eyes with a hope that filled her until she thought she might burst.

But then he whispered, "You don't wish me to continue."

"I do."

Now he smiled. Then he returned his attention to Henry's boast of the last hunt he'd attended with his father, and the enormous crane his bird had brought down. Estrella's heart pounded in her chest, and she wished Hartford would say more, but he remained silent throughout the rest of their visit to the mews.

The sun was quite down by the time the party broke up. The men went their way, back to the palace proper where the bailey was lit with many braziers and torches, and the women returned to their rooms over the stables, fleeing gloom punctuated only by an occasional brazier throwing flames to the night air. Estrella stole glances at the earl as the men moved away, her heart skipping in her chest and a warm glow all through her. Her lips moved in a silent prayer he would speak to her again. Soon.

Thirteen

FRANCESCA de Carceres caught up with the suite the next day and made clear how unhappy she was she'd been given the least comfortable spot in the maids' chamber. Estrella had little sympathy. It was her own fault, as everyone would agree, for she had absented herself when the choosing took place, and the room was small and uncomfortable to begin with. Nobody there was living in luxury. But Francesca added her new discomfort to the list of grievances about their state. Now the complaint was that there wouldn't be such a competition for space near the tiny fire if they'd been given better apartments. A cluster of rooms over the stables was an insult, she said, and they shouldn't abide it. They should ask for more comfortable space.

Better still, they should ask to return to Spain. Surely they'd all waited long enough for Catherine's marriage. It would never happen. Anyone who thought Henry was likely to marry Catherine was a fool. She lay awake at night, talking to the Marias and Estrella about how old they were all getting and how they needed to look to their own lives after being strung along for so many years by their princess. Or she would mutter while repairing her worn clothing, bringing whoever might be near into her complaining sphere. She spoke constantly against Fray Diego, blaming him for Catherine's stubbornness in the face of harsh reality.

"She believes her prince will ride in on a white charger and save her."

"He may very well." Maria de Salinas was turning her best dress yet again, nimble fingers guiding the needle quickly and efficiently. The three of them, Maria, Francesca, and Estrella were huddled as close to the small fire in the hearth as they could get without setting their dresses alight. Cold weather was upon them, and as small as the rooms were, the fire was nevertheless inadequate. "I believe he has one."

"Not white, more of a gray," murmured Estrella. She'd been downstairs in the stable more than once since their arrival to admire Hartford's black destrier as well as some of the king's excellent horses.

"You both pay far too much attention to those French romances you read."

"I prefer the Malory," said Estrella. "He's English, and more authentic, I'm sure." Having been in this country as long as she had, she'd begun to think perhaps the English weren't so bad after all. "Besides, I think Catherine more fits the role of Rapunzel than Guinevere. Don't you think, Maria?" She and Maria exchanged glances and stifled smiles.

"We don't live in a faerie tale. We live in the real world where men are not shining white knights, and they rarely come to anyone's rescue."

"Had you seen Henry those weeks ago in the mews, you might think Catherine was right to stay."

"Maria de Rojas doesn't think so. She said he was only pretending interest in the marriage. I agree. I think he must be as false as any other prince with something to gain by keeping Catherine on his hook."

"Such as?"

"A negotiation tool for a contract with Eleanor. So long as there's a possibility of marrying Catherine, the king can obtain the best terms with the Habsburgs for Eleanor."

"And vice versa his negotiation with Catherine's father. King Henry may be only pursuing Eleanor in order to raise the price for Catherine."

"He won't agree to either of them," said Estrella. "He enjoys the position of power too much, watching the fathers of both women dance to his tune. He is jealous of Continental power, and he enjoys punishing Catherine for her father's behavior even more."

"We are hostages." It wasn't true in the strict sense that they couldn't go home to Spain if they were recalled, but Estrella considered the statement and thought there was some truth to it. The pity of it was that as hostages they were nearly worthless, for after all this time Ferdinand had made it clear he didn't care what King Henry did to them. It might well be that the English king intended for his son to marry Eleanor, and it wouldn't be long before the Spanish suite would be sent away for good.

Estrella thought about the words of Piers Hilsey the day they'd fled the sickness, and warm wishes of the things her own future might hold blossomed as Francesca spoke. They'd all long dreamed of having husbands so rich and powerful. And handsome. Oh, so handsome! Though a good ten years older than her, Hilsey was far and away the most comely courtier among the elderly cronies of the king. She'd not seen him in a fortnight, and now wondered whether he'd left the palace.

But he must still be nearby. Surely he wouldn't have left his magnificent horse behind.

Unless he'd given it to the king.

She sighed and glanced toward the window, then chastised herself for dwelling on him over such a short exchange. But it had been such a wonder to hear him say those things to her! Trapped among these women and old men for so long, the sound of an admiring man's voice so soft in her ear sent thrills all through her. She wished to hear that voice again, and thought she might go mad if she didn't.

Catherine entered the room, followed by the younger maids, and the three by the fire all stood to curtsy. The princess had fire in her eyes, and without preamble addressed Francesca. "What have you been telling Fuensalida?"

The pretty maid paled. "Only the truth, Your Highness."

"Fuensalida blames me for the loss of the plate." They'd all known that much, and Estrella wondered why Catherine was bringing it up now. "I've learned you are encouraging him in this."

"The ambassador draws his own conclusion, Your Majesty. I have no influen—"

"And now you've determined to slander my confessor."

"Slander?"

"You've told Fuensalida that Diego has been lying to me to convince me to stay here in England. My treasurer tells me your visits to Grimaldi's house were to speak poorly of me and my confessor. He has also reported to my father what you have said to him and Fuensalida."

"No, Your Highness. I visited Grimaldi because . . ." Francesca stopped herself and swallowed. Her eyes went wide. Estrella and Maria looked at her to know what she was about to say, and a suspicion rose in Estrella's mind. She visited Grimaldi himself? Not Fuensalida who was quartered there? What was there they had not known? Francesca continued on another tack. "Your Highness, you must admit Diego's words have influenced your decision to stay in England."

"My confessor's words have bolstered my confidence in the will of God. My confessor has provided strength of conviction, and the knowledge all will come about for the best. I know what is right, Francesca. Not you, nor anyone, can tell me what path to choose. Since the departure of Doña Elvira I have seen my own way through. Diego is guilty of nothing more than doing his duty, to guide me spiritually and to help me know the will of God."

"Your—"

"*Furthermore*, Francesca, it is not your place to decide what is best for me and my household." The anger was rising, and Catherine's temper began to make fissures in her usually calm demeanor. Her eyes were wide with fury and her knuckles white as her hands gripped each other. "Far better for Fray Diego to tell me what to do, for he at least has the ear of the almighty. You have neither knowledge of God's will nor understanding of mine. You know nothing but what your own heart desires, and that makes you the wrong voice to tell my household what is best for them, or for me, or for anyone else. You are a selfish, mean, immature girl, and I would have you out of my sight lest I put you out of my suite without penny or place to go."

"But—"

"Go!" Catherine waved a hand. "Leave this chamber!"

Francesca ducked her head, dropped her sewing onto her chair, and fled the room. She took refuge with the lower servants, and the other maids could hear her in there, weeping in small sniffles and sobs. Catherine turned and went to her own chamber in the other direction, leaving Maria and Estrella to pick up their own sewing and sit in silence. Neither dared speak.

Later that evening Francesca sneaked back into the maids' room while they readied for bed. She was silent and moved slowly, deliberately, as she undressed. Nobody else spoke, either. Francesca slipped into her bed, and they all lay there in silence, then as the fire in the hearth dwindled, in darkness and cold.

Estrella awoke the next morning to a comment from Maria de Salinas. "Well, it would appear Francesca has made up her mind finally."

The women all looked to Francesca's bed and found it empty. Her trunk was gone, as well. Though this wasn't much of a surprise, Estrella's mouth fell open in shock. Francesca had actually done the thing she'd talked about for several years. Estrella felt as if she'd been clouted in the belly. She hadn't realized how it might feel to lose one of their number, and looking at the empty bed now was like finding a gaping hole in the world. "Where did she go?"

"Grimaldi, the banker," said Maria de Rojas. "She told me he wants to marry her."

"That old man?"

"That rich Italian banker with no sons, you mean, who will leave her with his money before long. Then she can go where she likes, do what she pleases, and marry or not marry according to her prospects."

"He's not that old."

"Old enough, I think. Old enough to make it preferable to having no prospects at all."

"But she wanted to return to Spain."

Maria sighed and took on a tone as if talking to a child. "We will never go home. You heard Catherine yesterday. You know the princess as well as any of us. She won't ever give up. She'll stay until Henry is married, one way or another. And by then, regardless of who he marries, it will be too late for the rest of us." Her voice carried the bitterness of her own lost opportunity. "It could be that she was right. We should plead with the king to be returned home."

Maria de Salinas shook her head. "I would never marry a man who would take a wife against the wishes of her mistress. Only one without any sense of decency would do such a thing. There is no dowry, no family alliance, and he is getting a woman who has shown herself to be disloyal in the bargain. It cannot end well. Francesca is a foolish ninny."

Estrella remained silent, but fear spun in her gut. She set to dressing and let the others argue the pros and cons of staying or leaving.

Word quickly came that Francesca had indeed eloped with Grimaldi. Before returning to Catherine's apartments, she'd made arrangements with Fuensalida to meet her very late when the palace was asleep. He took her with him to the banker's house, and there the next day she was married to Grimaldi in private by a priest who was the Italian's friend. Francesca was gone from their lives, and Catherine never spoke of her again.

On the day they heard, Estrella went to the stables to be alone. She liked visiting the king's horses and missed the days as a girl when she would accompany her father on hunts, mounted on some of the finest steeds in Spain. A good horse was a joy to behold. Here she could let slip from her mind the pressures and ugly events of the day. Today many animals were away, but the black destrier belonging to the Earl of Hartford was in his stall and greeted her with a snort of familiarity and a pawing hoof in the straw. She reached out to pat the gleaming black face and sighed. "Such a beautiful animal you are!"

"Would you be speaking to the horse, or to me?"

Estrella's heart skipped, and she forced herself to composure as she turned to find the earl himself standing at the back of the stall, at one with the deep shadows, a bridle dangling from his hand. The piece of tack was heavy and terribly ornate, the leather adorned with many finely wrought bits of gold and silver. The man, on the other hand, was dressed casually and warmly, wearing rough buskins and heavy leather over linen rather than fine court shoes and delicate fabrics. He almost didn't seem himself, all bundled up for the cold weather outside, where snow was sprinkling in occasional flakes. Not a nobleman today, but a huntsman, and he brought to mind Sir John. Estrella shook the thought away and graced Hartford with a smile.

It appeared he'd only just arrived; his cheeks were still bloodred from the cold, and flakes were still melting on his velvet cap. In the stable, though, it was a bit warmer than outside, and Estrella was comfortable in her thin cloak.

"Are you an animal, then?"

A sly twinkle came to his eyes, and he hung the bridle on a wooden peg then stepped toward her. "I can be." One hand absently stroked the horse's neck. The movement was slow and sensual, and without thought as if it were another neck he wished to stroke so gently instead.

"All men can be, but not all men are."

"Could that be the voice of experience I hear? You know men so well?"

A hot flush spread over her cheeks. Her repartee was awfully rusty; she should never have been caught like that. Shame and irritation rose, and she blurted the thing that came to mind only because it was the sole thing she could think of that was remotely witty. "I only assume so about yourself."

"You assume too much. You know naught about me." His tone lost the light mischief of before. "Can you not believe I am entirely a gentleman? Could I be your champion and ride into battle with your token on my sleeve? Might I even rescue you from the dragon who oppresses your mistress?"

Silence fell. A smile played about his lips, but never quite broke over his face. He stepped closer and ducked under the horse's lead tied to the side of the stall. "Would you care to learn my heart and what it holds for you?"

"Indeed, señor, you do not know me either." Her heart began to trip over itself.

"The tragedy of my life, to be sure. For we should have met those years ago when we were so near to it. You should have given me your handkerchief to tie on my armor, and I would have ridden to the lists with your name on my lips."

She gazed at him, wishing she had the courage to tell him how close he'd come to that very thing, and of the irony that it was his very prowess in the lists that had prevented her from offering her token.

The mischief returned to his eyes, and he added, "And then I might have taken more prizes. It is on your head, señorita, that I did not."

She chuckled. Then from somewhere deep inside came a need to tell him what his words were doing to her. She reached down to her core and touched that need, and discovered the courage. She opened her mouth, hesitated, then said, "I would know you, every part of you, if I could."

The light in his eyes danced. His voice was husky when he spoke. "Perhaps 'tis time you were given the voice of experience you pretend so well?" He looked straight into her eyes, and it seemed he was searching hers for his answer.

Her heart pounded in her chest like a blacksmith's hammer on an anvil. It thudded in her ears and echoed into her toes. She wanted to shout to the heavens she would have him in an instant, but she only stood and stared at him.

Gently, he reached out and with his fingertips pressed her chin so that her mouth shut. Only then did she realize she'd been gaping at him. Her tongue touched her lips, and she said, "It might please me."

Now his smile broke, and his fine teeth showed. "I would ever so much wish to please my lady."

"My lord . . ."

He leaned down to kiss her. Never in her life had she been kissed like this. Sir John had been gentle, tentative. Hilsey claimed her mouth and invaded her, pressed her so that she could feel the day's stubble on his face. His tongue on hers. All the pent-up desire, stifled by the years in Catherine's service, now rose in her and filled her head so that it spun and screamed that she would die if she could not know this man in the ways he would teach her.

He whispered in her ear, "Would you learn more?"

Her reply was immediate. "Yes."

With another devastating kiss, he reached behind for the laces of her overdress. Her cloak dropped to the stone floor. As her dress loosened, she hardly knew where she was anymore. She slipped her arms around his neck and marveled at his broad shoulders that held her up as her knees weakened.

He pressed himself to her, and she found his excitement for her both alarming and exhilarating. Though she knew he needed no encouragement, a whimper escaped her, for she felt helpless in the face of what was happening. She knew this was wrong, that it was a sin, but it was also the most hopeful thing to happen to her in years. Her entire body throbbed with the beat of her heart, like a great drum. Asking him to stop was out of the question.

"Come," he whispered with barely a voice at all. He drew her down the row of stalls to an empty one piled high with fresh straw for a newcomer. There he loosened his doublet, then began to undress her.

That gave her pause, and she stayed his hand. "You're taking them all off?"

His lips pressed to her forehead, and he murmured into her skin, breathless, "Much better. You'll see. Fear not; I won't let anything bad happen to you."

Not much encouragement was necessary for her, either, and she acquiesced readily. In a trice he had her clothes dropped to the straw, and his own followed. Then he drew her down onto the straw, where she slipped into his arms and felt as if she'd spent her entire life waiting to be there. Longing for it, and for him. This man, and nobody else.

His skin was smooth and covered long, hard muscles. The scent of him was dark. Forbidding. Like him lurking in the shadows of the destrier's stall, it mingled with the earthy, musty straw. His mouth, wet and warm, played over her face, her neck, then took in a breast and made her gasp. All of existence went sideways, and when his hand slipped between her thighs to separate them with caresses, she knew nothing but that she would have him inside her in all his entirety if she could.

Then part of him was. Hard and sudden, he shoved all at once, then stopped for a moment. The pain was quick, but quickly became nothing more than distant soreness. Hilsey trembled. His eyes met hers in an astonishing moment of joy. As he moved, his eyes went half closed and sighs made her head spin. His trembling made her want more of him. The harder he pressed to her, the harder she moved to meet him, until he slammed against her with a cry that became several. His shoulders were solid under her hands. His belly rippled against hers, soon slick with sweat, and they were like two parts of one body. Then he held himself against her with a growl that descended into a groan, then finally a long, spent sigh. His face pressed to her neck, he murmured an oath he would never have said to her in public.

Far from taking offense, she agreed.

He lay beside her, both of them nearly covered in straw. Bits of it clung to his hair, and she picked some pieces off as he gazed at her.

"I'm a beast after all, you see." His smile held the same mischief as his eyes.

Her glance took in his naked body, a hearty and healthy long-boned frame. "I see more than I've seen of any other man and find you not at all beastly. Are all men as beautiful as you?"

He chuckled. "There are none to even compare. I assure you, my lady, you have enjoyed the best and most glorious to be found anywhere in Christendom." He nibbled her shoulder and made her giggle. "Islam as well, to be sure." Then he kissed it and murmured, "And so have I."

She turned her head to kiss him, and it was long and sweet. Then he pressed his cheek to her shoulder and said, "I would sleep, were it not too much risk."

The thought of curling up to sleep beside this man was a

pleasing enough thought that Estrella realized she would never actually have fallen asleep. Rather, she would have lain awake to enjoy every moment of it. She brushed a lock of his hair away from his forehead.

With a groan, he rose to his feet and reached down to help her up. "We mustn't tarry."

It was true. It would be most embarrassing for someone to wander into the stable and find them there. They helped each other on with their clothes, and it took what seemed forever to pick all the bits of straw from them. But finally each was arranged respectably, and it was time to return to their proper places within the king's domain.

Estrella didn't know what to say now. To thank him seemed less than ladylike under the circumstances. She wished to see him again, and wanted to know when. Even more, she first wanted to know what he desired.

"I would see you again," he said as he buckled the belt that held his dagger and purse. "Soon. Come to my chamber tomorrow evening at suppertime. We could eat privately."

Joy filled her. A private supper! "I would need to slip away unnoticed by my mistress." As casual as discipline had become in the Spanish household, Catherine and her advisors would still never countenance her being alone with the earl. Particularly so soon after Francesca's defection. She would have to make up something innocent and convincing.

"Tell her you've been invited to hear Mass with the king's court. She won't dare say no to that."

Estrella didn't like the idea of lying, particularly about worship, but she nodded and decided she'd think of something else.

"The chamber I occupy for this stay is the fourth from the entry to the residences. Through the alcove and down the short steps." Estrella knew the alcove, but not the steps, and at her puzzled look he said, "The king values me only slightly more than he does your mistress; I'm somewhat hidden away myself." She gave him a rueful smile to show she understood. "The steps are in the far corner, and they turn. You'll find them when you look for them." He brushed a bit of hair from her forehead and helped her tuck it up under her hood. "Adieu, my sweet Spanish bird," he said, then kissed her and went from the stable.

She watched him go, then slowly, feeling as if in a dream, went toward the stairs that would take her to Catherine's apartments. She relished the soreness inside her, and her bruised thighs that reminded her of where her lover had been, and turned over in her mind again and again what had just happened to her.

Fourteen

✣

I T was a struggle for Estrella to pretend in front of her fellow maids. In the uproar over Francesca that day the rest of Catherine's servants went largely unnoticed, but for Estrella it was an effort to not shout for joy to her friends about her new discovery. All that kept her from it was knowing how Catherine would feel. That her maid had committed such a sin, no matter how pleasing or filled with hope, would surely have caused the princess to mourn Estrella's behavior and condemn it. No, Catherine would never understand Estrella's need for Hilsey and what he could offer, today and in the future. Estrella kept the news to herself and had to struggle to not smile too much, for she wanted to tell all the girls how wonderful it was, what they'd been missing. But she didn't dare, and kept her face as expressionless as possible.

Nevertheless, all through the evening Maria de Salinas stole glances at her. Estrella said nothing and concentrated on

Catherine's voice as she read aloud to the maids, but was certain Maria could see there was something different about her. Estrella certainly felt different. More alive. As if her entire life and person had changed, and it was for the better. It would be difficult to keep Maria from finding out for certain what had happened, but especially Estrella needed to keep her from finding out who the man was. This new possibility was too important to allow anyone to interfere, even with the best of intentions.

While undressing for bed, Maria whispered to Estrella, "You have straw on your shift."

Panic seized Estrella, and she reached around behind to snatch at her back. Maria calmly picked the betraying bit of stuff from her clothes, then presented it to her. She whispered again, "Who is he?"

"Who is who?"

"Very well, don't tell me his name. But do not expect me to believe you were alone when you threw off your clothes to lie in the stable straw. You must take more care than to sport debris on your linens if you are to keep such a secret."

"I have no secret."

"Not anymore, for a certainty. Pray Catherine doesn't learn of your fall."

Estrella sighed and turned to look Maria in the eye. "You won't tell, will you?"

"Never. Unless she asks me, for I cannot lie to my mistress. But if you're smart, you'll either marry quickly or tell the gentleman good-bye. The longer this goes on, the better will be the chance you will be caught and your reputation ruined. Then he will never marry you, and Catherine will have you sent back to Spain in shame."

"He will marry me, I'm sure of it. I can see it in his eyes he wishes it."

Maria smiled. "For your sake, I hope so. And I hope he is worth the risk you are taking."

"Oh, he is!" Estrella wanted to blurt it all, to tell who he was and that Hilsey was worth any risk there might be in encouraging him to need and want her, but she bit her lip and said nothing further. The giddy heat of affection tickled her insides and grew like a freshly kindled flame in an open hearth. Too much unfriendly air, and it might go out. So she kept her mouth shut to protect the lovely warmth and light Hilsey had brought to her life so suddenly.

"Good," was all that Maria said, and the maids went to their respective beds.

The following afternoon Estrella invented a tale for Catherine and the chamberlain, that she'd been requested to teach the lute to the daughter of one of Henry's courtiers. She neglected to mention a name, in case anyone should go looking for her, and nobody asked. When time to meet Hilsey approached, she was so excited her fingers trembled as she tied her cloak around her neck. She barely remembered to take the lute with her, and hurried from the rooms over the stables with the instrument under one arm.

The route to Hilsey's room was meandering, taking a tortuous path through rooms and corridors, but she remembered what he'd told her and knew where she was going. Through the alcove among the residences and down the steps. This part of the castle was old and dank, dating back to the time of Edward I. Over the centuries it had been gradually surrounded by newer stone, tucked into the midst of structures that had been added in more recent times. The walls here were riddled with damp spots, and the smell of earth was strong. Far better, she thought, than the sharp odor of sweaty horses and manure. She considered wet stone an essentially English smell, and found she rather liked it. Piers was English, and so everything English became good in her eyes.

Before the door at the bottom of the steps, where the passage came to an abrupt halt, she knocked.

A brief moment later Hilsey answered, and that bright smile splashed across his face. "My dear Spanish bird," he whispered, and stepped back to allow her entrance. He was dressed informally, in simple hose and linen shirt belted with a gold chain. The ties at the neck were loosened, and most of his chest bared where curly, dark hair lay beneath. Estrella longed to reach out and touch it, but refrained and looked around the room instead.

The chamber was remote, but not small for it, and well furnished with a large, carved bed and stylish chairs by a spacious table near the brightly flaming hearth. The quality of the furniture and the newness of the several wall hangings made more sharp her awareness of the poverty of her own circumstances. Hilsey may not have been the king's favorite, but he was nevertheless treated with far more respect than the woman who was in theory the king's future daughter-in-law. When the old man passed and the prince succeeded, the earl would be treated with even more respect, to be sure. Certainly there would be even better quarters for him among courtiers in the future.

She set her lute on the floor and removed her cloak to hand to Hilsey, for there was no butler to take it. And no squire to serve them, either. They were quite alone.

"I've given leave to my servants for the evening. We'll not be disturbed." He leaned down to press a light kiss to her mouth. He nodded toward the lute. "Have you come to serenade me?"

"I could, if you wish it."

He leaned in ever so slightly and his voice went soft. "I can think of only one thing I'd rather have more."

"Whatever my lord desires, he shall have." Her lips formed a coy smile though she raised her chin so he could touch his mouth again briefly to hers, then he leaned back to look into her face.

The spark in his eyes nearly made her laugh out loud. She loved that he enjoyed her. He gestured toward the table.

It was set with silver all around, the food arranged in a delightful presentation on a platter in the middle. Estrella warmed to the memories it brought of the king's court when she and the rest of Catherine's people had been welcome there. Those had been joyous days, when she'd been maid to the Princess of Wales and her company had been sought by nearly everyone. Hilsey's desire to know her was relief she didn't care to admit even to herself, for it would have made her feel pathetic. More than anything, she wanted to not feel pathetic anymore.

So she turned to Hilsey with a smile and kissed him again. "I've missed you terribly this day."

He laughed and stepped close to murmur near her ear. "An entire day. *Pobrecita*. Then I shall make up for my thoughtless absence from your life and your person. But first let me fill you with food before I fill you with the other." He nodded toward the table and the hearth. "Do sit, before it becomes cold."

The silver plate held the heat from the kitchen, and the food was quite tasty. Hilsey talked to her of court gossip, a subject that held Estrella's interest like the talons of a raptor. Her hunger for stories of the wealthy and powerful people among whom she lived but about whom she rarely heard was sharp, whetted by her life spent always on the fringes of excitement but never involved in it. Piers updated her on the lives of people she'd known briefly during Catherine's marriage to Arthur and no longer knew in her isolation, and she lost herself in the stories of intrigue, affairs between people she'd thought would never have become involved with each other, and news from the Continent and from Scotland.

Eventually, though, conversation slowed as their repast settled, and a sense of laziness crept in. Piers lounged back on his chair, leaning on the arm of it, and gazed at her as he spoke with a wistful smile. Slowly the talk petered out, and he only gazed at her. The look in his eye was of hunger, a yearning for her that made her shiver. It was in such earnest she couldn't help but return it. Then he sat up and took her hand to hold it. Just to hold it for a moment, then he turned it over to the palm and stroked it. "Such lovely hands. The hands of a true lady."

She knew that, but it had been a long time since anyone had said it to her. Or anything like it. She put her other hand over his and smoothed down the hairs on the back of it. His hands were long and finely made, but strong. There were calluses where the reins touched, and nowhere else, leaving the rest of his skin smooth and pale. They were the hands of a nobleman and a knight.

He stood and drew her to her feet, then guided her to the bed.

Unlike before, tonight he was careful and tender when he touched her. Gentle, and she found herself surrendering further to him than she'd ever imagined possible. With the surrender came a moment of ecstasy that caught her by surprise and embarrassed her terribly, but it only made him chuckle. He continued on, making the thing happen twice more, and she thought it would never end. It was almost a relief when he took his own satisfaction and collapsed onto the bed beside her.

Deep in the feather mattress, they lay in silence to regain themselves. When she could speak again, she said, "Had I known how wonderful this could be, I might not have waited so long to try it."

"You were waiting for me."

"I would have sought you out." That made him laugh, but she knew it was true. She remembered how he'd caught her eye those years ago, and now wished she'd been more bold as a girl. This was too wonderful to have wasted so much time. Her fingers played over the line of dark hair that started wide at his chest and narrowed as it made its way down his belly to regions that fascinated her. "I would have given you my handkerchief to carry into the lists."

A chuckle rumbled in his chest, and he kissed her. Then he nodded toward the instrument propped against the foot of the bed. "Play your lute for me."

She saw he was serious. "Could you bear to hear such a poor player?"

"You play for your fellow maids, do you not? You play for Catherine, who surely must know good music when she hears it."

"I am what there is for them. We've no minstrels in our apartments, so we make do. You, however, hear the king's musicians every day and must be quite spoiled by their skill."

"I would enjoy hearing you for the sake that it would be you, who are so dear to me. No minstrel can give me that, no matter how skilled."

Estrella's heart warmed, and when Piers reached to the floor for her lute to hand it to her, she sat up on the edge of the bed and took it onto her lap. Slowly, for it made her nervous to play for the earl, she began to pluck out some Spanish tunes from her childhood. He lay back on the stack of pillows and listened with a dreamy look, gazing into her face so that a thrill skittered through her whenever she glanced his way.

"I can't understand a word you're singing, my dear Spanish bird, but it's very pretty." He reached over to tuck her loosened hair behind her ear so it was no longer covering her face as her head bent over the instrument.

She paused. "You don't speak any Spanish?"

"A word or two. Maybe three, but not nearly enough for conversation. I've always made do with French or Latin, and I thank God your English is as fluent as my Spanish is not."

A sudden insecurity about her accent surged. "I've done my best to learn the language of my adopted country. I hope my accent isn't too awfully unpleasant."

"It's delightful. Musical. A pleasure to my hearing." Piers was so different from Sir John! Unlike the huntsman who was far more sure of himself stalking animals than entertaining women, Piers lavished her with attention that was warm and comforting, and above all, self-possessed. John had been like a wide-eyed boy, thrilled to have found a gift and eager to open it. Piers had opened the gift, and was now enjoying it with a calm that was a sign of his fine breeding. His manner was as if she were his due, but he was fully appreciating her nevertheless. There was affection in that gaze, she could see, and she was glad to return it.

When Estrella returned to the rooms over the stables, nobody in Catherine's suite questioned where she'd been that evening, though it was quite late. Neither did anybody question in subsequent days, when she returned to the palace proper on the pretext of lessons for an unnamed noble's daughter. It appeared the household was too intensely involved in their own plight to care much where she went or with whom. Estrella even suspected she might not even be prevented from going if she were to confess she was visiting Hilsey's bedchamber. The desperation among Catherine's suite was like a physical thing in the air. One could taste the fear.

Only Catherine seemed free of it. She moved through her days like a barge floating gently downriver, carrying the weight of everyone's needs and wants so placidly there was nary a ripple. Estrella, beginning to see things from the outside now that she was hopeful for a bright future, knew that if the princess would achieve what she sought, it would be because of the peace she carried with her everywhere. Estrella longed for some of that peace.

Christmas approached, and the weather turned icy. Estrella was glad for the days in the warmth of Piers' chamber and company. The suppers were welcome as well. On days when she ate with the Spanish household she often gagged at the terrible quality of sustenance provided, and wondered how she'd ever tolerated the strong fish and stale bread. She longed for the day when Piers would make his proposal, so she could marry him and be done with this. In the meantime, though, she made the most of the pleasant times with him wrapped in his arms as in a cocoon of warmth.

One evening in December they lay entwined, deep in the castle with the fire in the hearth dwindling to coals. Some of the candles had guttered, but there were many still alive and throwing dancing shadows across Piers' face. His eyes drooped closed, and he appeared on the verge of sleep.

Estrella snuggled her face under his arm, where it was warm and musky. The hair there tickled her nose. She seemed to tickle him as well, for his shoulder shrugged and he emitted a chuckle that was almost a giggle. Sleepily, he whispered, "I will always love you, *mi pájara d'España*."

Equally as sleepy, she murmured, "Will you even after we're married?"

He chuckled as if she'd made a joke, then went silent. And very still. He was holding his breath.

A coldness crept over her, and the silence went on. Finally she said, "Will you?"

He drew a deep breath, cleared his throat, then said, fully alert now, "You know I can't marry you. Surely you must."

"I do not." Her chest tightened, and it was hard to breathe. "Nobody told you?"

"Told me what?" She disengaged herself from his arm, her body tensing, not yet knowing how to respond. "And how should anyone know to tell me we can't be married? You've kept my visits so secret nobody could know it might interest me. Why can you not marry me?" Her voice raised in pitch as her throat tightened.

"Estrella, it's common knowledge that I'm betrothed to Elizabeth Howard."

Estrella gave him a quizzical look, uncomprehending, for the daughter of the Duke of Norfolk was married.

Piers said helpfully, "Beth Howard, the duke's niece."

Now an image came, of a painfully thin woman who had been widowed twice already and had two daughters. She was close to Piers' age but looked much older. The woman had a reputation for piety but not for intelligence, and talked far too much for someone with so little mind and no talent for any womanly skill to speak of, not even music or embroidery. But with a rich dowry and the growing influence of her uncle, she would make Piers a perfect wife. Horror of realization hollowed Estrella's gut.

She sat up and moved away from him on the bed. He reached for her hand to keep her there. "Don't, please."

"I thought . . ." She couldn't say it. The pain made her gasp. She tried to wrest her hand from his, but he held it until she gave up and only stared at his fingers gripping her wrist. Once again the future crumbled to dust before her eyes. The rescue she'd so needed turned out to be only illusion, this time an intentional ruse. Suddenly she needed to cover herself, and she yanked her hand free, then went to draw her shift over her head.

He slipped from the bed and pulled his linen shirt over his head. Then he reached for her hand again. "My dear Spanish—"

"Do not call me that anymore!" Her hand retreated from his and curled near her shoulder as she stared at the floor. Tears rose, and she swallowed them.

Piers stepped back. "Come, Estrella. *Estrellita*. You must understand there was no chance of us marrying. Beth brings lands and cash, not to mention the alliance with her family. Her uncle is the Duke of Norfolk. What can you offer me to compare with that?"

She could only stand there, knowing he was right. There was nothing for her to offer that would move him to marry her. She was a penniless Spanish maid of honor to an ill-connected and debt-ridden princess. At a loss for any coherent reply, she told him something she knew was meaningless. "I love you."

"And I love you. More than I can say. These past months have been a joy to me, and I would have that joy continue forever. But love has nothing to do with marriage."

"It could." It had to, if she were ever to marry.

"It never has, and thinking otherwise has been the destruction of many folk who might have been happy in their lives." Irritation tightened his voice, and he bit it back with teeth at his lower lip. "As much as I care for you, I can't let our love stand in the way of the advantages Elizabeth could bring me. And my family. Were I to marry you, my standing in His Majesty's court would vanish. Utterly. I must look to the welfare of my brothers, who could turn athwart me if I did not. Not to mention I must consider the futures of any children I might have."

The painful truth clenched her body. It crumpled her like a bit of paper so she had to kneel on the floor. Bitterness overwhelmed her. "You cannot love me; that is a lie. You hid me because you were ashamed of me."

"No. I kept our meetings secret, so to protect your reputation. So you could marry someone else if you wished. Though losing you to another would gut me entirely, I want you to be happy and won't destroy whatever chance you might have at a good marriage I can't provide."

She looked up at him, and now the tears came. "You would let me go?" A sob shook her. That he would take such care for the sake of being rid of her cut her to the core. The pain was monstrous.

He came to kneel before her, and held her shoulders. "If you wished it. Only then. If it could make you happy, I would set myself on fire."

"But you wouldn't marry me."

He didn't reply to that, but only looked at her with pain in his eyes. She knew the way of the world, and understood that his dynastic responsibility was as burdensome as Catherine's or Henry's.

"If I'm pregnant?"

"I would acknowledge it, of course. If you would continue as my mistress—"

"No."

"But—"

"No." Another sob erupted, as she realized what she'd become: the very sort of whore she'd looked upon with contempt all her life. The woman her priests had warned about, defiled and unclean. *Used*. She stood and hugged herself. Piers stood also and tried to lay a palm aside her face, but she fended it and stepped back. "I'm not a whore. I won't be known in that way. I do wish to marry, and for my children to be legitimate. I am the daughter of a duke." Her eyes narrowed at him. "The *daughter*."

"The daughter of a duke with no influence in England. To be sure, the alliance would be a liability."

That cut her again, and she flinched. He didn't seem to notice, or perhaps just not to care, and his lips pressed together into a straight line. Her mind cast about for a riposte, and grasped at a straw. "My mistress will be the Princess of Wales. One day, Queen of England."

"No, she won't. You know it as well as I. That is why you are here."

Again his steel found her heart, and she gasped. "I am here out of love for you."

Hope lit his eyes. "Then stay for it, and forgo marriage. I assure you you'll be the more loved."

Caught hard between what she so desperately wanted and what she knew she must do, she cringed with the overwhelming pain. Her shoulders clenched and drew in. It was hard to breathe. There was but one choice for her, for she couldn't live with herself to become the hated wanton. She couldn't defy the standard of faith she'd lived by all her life. She said, "No, Piers. It is not for me to live that way. I cannot allow you to ask me to do to my family what you will not do to yours."

He let his hands drop to his sides. They gazed at each other, and she blinked the tears from her eyes to find the pain in his. She continued, "You should have known I could not."

For a moment he considered that. Anger clouded his eyes, then they cleared as he brought himself under control. Slowly, he nodded. She was as right as he had been. He started to speak, then closed his mouth. But then he opened it again and said, "I don't love her."

"As you said, love matters for nothing."

"Not for nothing."

"*Less* than nothing," she snapped in sudden anger and full realization, "for it has led me to commit a sin I once held unthinkable."

"You would tell me good-bye, then?" His voice was thick with emotion, but she couldn't tell what sort, whether anger or grief.

She turned away from him and attempted to dress without help. The outer garment was heavy and difficult to manage. "I would tell you far more than that, but I wish to do no more damage to my soul than I already have."

"Estrellita—"

"Do not speak to me." She wrestled with the threadbare silk, and one seam began to pull away in the aging fabric.

"You can't—"

"*I said, do not speak to me!*"

He fell silent, then stepped in to help her straighten her

dress and tighten her laces. At first she tried to fend him and do it herself, but it was no use. She needed him to arrange her sufficiently to keep others from suspecting where she'd been. She held still enough for him to secure her overdress, then donned her cloak. She saw once again its ragged appearance, and shame reddened her to her chest. Then she picked up her lute and left the chamber without looking back.

Fifteen

1533

"THE child is a princess!"

Estrella had just run from the drawbridge below with the news, and now stood in Catherine's presence chamber, struggling to catch her breath. Age was creeping up on her; she should know better than to run up stairs these days.

Catherine, no longer called "queen" by anyone but her own servants since the coronation of Henry's new wife, now resided at the palace of Buckden in Huntingdonshire. For all intents she was a prisoner, in the custody of her new chamberlain, Lord Mountjoy. She wasn't allowed to see her daughter and was reduced to a quarter of the allowance she'd once had for her support. The number of maids was down to eight, the same number she'd had during the years in her youth waiting for Henry to marry her.

Buckden was comfortable enough in summer, but now

that winter was on its way the cold and dankness of the place was becoming apparent. The accommodations were far below the standard by which the queen had lived since her marriage to the king. The redbrick episcopal palace had been chosen by Henry for its remoteness for the task of hiding away his discarded wife, so most of his subjects couldn't observe the way he was treating their queen. Though Maria de Salinas was no longer one of Catherine's maids, among the household were Francisco Felipez and Thomas Abell. The latter was one of her staunchest supporters and had been to the Tower of London for his defense of the queen.

Word of the gender of Anne's baby was delivered in a hoarse whisper that was half horrified and half exultant. Estrella then whispered, "Your Majesty," for Catherine's servants were constrained to call her "dowager," but the most loyal were stubborn in their insistence on using the accustomed address. Indeed, the queen would not acknowledge any other. The young maid who had been reading aloud from Malory sat silent, waiting for the signal to continue. They all watched Catherine for her reaction.

Catherine, in a large chair near the fire, betrayed no expression and continued with her embroidery of a silken sleeve, as if the matter were not one of life or death for herself and her daughter. The Great Whore, that Boleyn woman, had just given birth to a girl and had failed to give Henry the male heir he'd so expected. The one they'd all expected. The one Henry had thrown over his marriage for, declared his wife a whore for, and had made his daughter illegitimate for. Estrella could only imagine the rage of the king and felt a surge of righteous satisfaction that the Boleyn woman had received justice from God.

After a very still moment, Catherine let out a long, slow breath. She'd been holding it. Many years ago while in the service of the queen, Estrella had come to realize this was Catherine's way of keeping herself from reacting badly. If she didn't breathe, she couldn't say anything unseemly. The tactic always seemed successful, for it kept her from saying anything at all in her first moments of reaction. Now, in the small room that served as her presence chamber, surrounded by her household of advisors and servants, she maintained her aplomb, though they all knew she must be terribly relieved. Perhaps even pleased, though Estrella doubted Catherine would indulge in so unchristian a thought as to take pleasure in another's misfortune.

Instead the queen asked, "How has the king reacted to this news?"

"I'm told he is not happy."

"I daresay," said the queen. "And I'm afraid it bodes ill for those who support me, for Henry will make his displeasure known and felt by everyone within his reach. Chapuys should beware."

"But what of the whore?"

Catherine looked over at Estrella. "What of her? She will receive her due, as will everyone in the end. In addition, Henry has already chosen her replacement."

The room fell silent at this revelation. "What have you heard?" asked Estrella.

"Nothing. But I know Henry. He's tasted the forbidden fruit he pursued these past many years, and now found it wanting. His interest must wane for her as it has for nearly every other thing that has held his passion, particularly now that she has produced a daughter. The king will not remain loyal to someone who has betrayed him so terribly as to deny him his heir. Also, I know the intriguers who have been whispering in his ear for the past twenty years. Anne has caused them too much grief for them to let her be. She's been far too arrogant to certain men for them to let this go by without taking advantage. They have no love for her, nor for her grasping and ambitious relatives. She's not endeared herself to Archbishop Cranmer any more than she did to Wolsey. She's not endeared herself to anyone, and anymore not even to Henry."

Estrella said, "If the imperial ambassador were to say the word to those in the north who would come to your defense, Henry would be forced to take you back. Charles also would raise men for you. You've shown your ability to rule in wartime; after your victory at Flodden they'll follow you in complete faith."

Catherine made a disparaging noise in the back of her throat. It wasn't terribly regal, but was most expressive. "I had nothing to do with the victory in the north. Chapuys has already been told I won't lend my support to rebellion. I won't have the blood of good people on my hands."

"If you had allowed Charles and the pope to take up arms when the king married that whore in January, the problem would have been solved by now."

Catherine set her sewing in her lap and looked up at Estrella. "And how many dead, Lita? What destruction? In addition, I would have proven myself a disobedient wife, whom Henry would have been right to set aside. How can I claim before God my position and my right if I behave as if it weren't true? How could I call myself Henry's wife and the queen of this realm if I call men to arms against him?"

"What is the difference now, Your Majesty? You are held prisoner, and Mary is a hostage in the shadow of the gallows. Henry doesn't allow you even the slightest acknowledgment of your marriage to him, nor does he allow you to live like a human, let alone a queen. He threatens the life of your daughter. *His* daughter. What sort of husband does such a thing? How can you obey such a husband? What does it matter if you do or do not?"

Catherine raised her chin, and her voice took on the dark tone of deep offense. "It matters that I do my duty to my husband, because I *am* his wife. No matter what anyone might say on the matter, nor what they might do to me, I am still his wife. That is God's law, and I will obey it even before I obey the law of my husband. Even less than obeying an unjust husband, I will not bend to mere temporal pressures and obey men who are neither my husband nor my God, to take up arms against the man who is and always shall be my husband."

Exasperation made Estrella sigh. "But Henry has remarried."

Catherine's attention returned to her work. "He is a bigamist, and I fear for his soul. My poor husband has been led astray by Lutherans who will destroy the Church in their zeal to bring down the pope." She tugged too hard on the thread in her hands and had to smooth out a pucker with her thumbnail. "He would never have done this thing if not for the evil of the men surrounding him. They want to usurp the pope's authority. It's all a question of temporal power to them. They've blinded Henry to the consequences to his soul, for they've lost their own."

"Forcing Henry to take you back would have prevented it."

Again Catherine looked up at Estrella, wrath gathering in her eyes. "I will not countenance war on my behalf! I cannot do it to my subjects, nor to my husband, nor to my God! It would defeat my purpose here on earth."

"You are too unselfish."

"On the contrary, I am quite selfish, for it is my own soul

that would be destroyed, were I to succumb to the temptation before me."

Estrella acquiesced, her heart heavy that Catherine's fate seemed sealed. She saw how the local villagers loved her, how they brought their queen things they couldn't afford to give, and cheered her whenever she made appearances in public. All of Catherine's household, as well as the court in London, knew the entire country would rise up and bring the king to his senses if Catherine willed it. Especially the king knew it, and Chapuys made it no secret to the household he was keeping the king on tenterhooks regarding Catherine's refusal to support an uprising. Who knew what humiliations Henry might visit on the household if he knew there would be no reprisal from Catherine's supporters?

There was a visit from the imperial ambassador not long after that made it apparent the situation was becoming critical. Henry's reaction to the birth of Princess Elizabeth was terror against all who might oppose him in his struggle to rid himself of his first wife. Chapuys came with word that Mary's life was more endangered than ever.

Catherine sat in her chair by the fire in her presence chamber and gestured for her visitor to take a seat nearby. At mention of Mary she would have the conversation more private than a formal audience. Estrella, standing by to serve, could barely hear the murmuring.

"Tell me, is my daughter well? Has she been hurt in any way?"

"She's alive and healthy, Your Majesty, but unhappy. She's threatened with conviction of treason, for she has declined to sign the act removing her from the succession."

Catherine only stared at the floor, silent. They all knew

she'd resigned herself to her own execution and had advised Mary to do the same. They all hoped Henry would stay his hand in this, not out of love for his daughter but because he was afraid of repercussions from the religious conservative nobles in the north. But they also knew Henry would do whatever it took to maintain his authority in the kingdom. They knew he had it in him to execute Mary.

Chapuys shook his head. "No, not execution. Not yet, in any case. But if she continues to refuse, he will be able to make a case against her the nobles will find acceptable, and he will send her to the tower. You know he will, and he will be able to show cause."

Catherine paled.

The ambassador continued, "Furthermore, there is the likelihood of assassination, for her new guardian is Anne Boleyn's aunt. Mary could be poisoned, and nothing might be proven. She is at the mercy of the king. It is not safe for her."

The queen's gaze was steady on Chapuys's face, and her voice dull. "You want me to ask the nobles in the north to rise against my husband." It was a statement, for they all knew what was desired by most of Catherine's supporters. They all knew the populace would rise with them, as well.

" 'Tis the only way, Your Majesty."

"You know my feelings on the matter."

"Indeed, but the situation has worsened, and the lives of Mary and yourself are at stake. Thwarted for so long, the king is now frantic to be rid of you both so that he can also be rid of his new wife and her unfortunate daughter. So long as you remain alive, he cannot do away with the Boleyn woman without having to take you back as queen."

Catherine nodded slowly. Everyone knew that her own existence was the only reason Anne was still queen. But she said,

"I will not countenance rebellion against my husband. Were one to erupt spontaneously, I would condemn it. And that is all I will say on the matter."

And that was all she did say. Though he stayed several more days, Chapuys left unsatisfied.

Two months later, in November, news came to Buckden that a Kentish nun, two monks, two priests, and a friar would be sentenced for treason. The nun, known as the Holy Maid of Kent, had prophesied the death of the king for defying the pope in his attempt to divorce Catherine. The others had declined to sign the Act of Succession, which declared Henry's marriage to Catherine null, Mary illegitimate, and the pope without authority in England.

At the same time came word that there was talk in Parliament to declare Catherine a traitor. Terror struck the household as the possibility of execution for their mistress loomed like a graveyard shadow. Estrella prayed against it. In her chamber, by the light of a single candle, she beseeched God to spare the queen and make Henry see his error. In private moments with the queen she tried to convince Catherine to agree to the ideas Chapuys had for raising the people of England in rebellion. Still Catherine would not consider allowing war in her name. She stood firm in her conviction that death with a clean conscience was preferable to losing her soul and finding herself eternally damned.

Estrella found herself thinking hard about that conviction, knowing her mistress was right and wishing she weren't. That Catherine would rather die than commit such a sin—one that would have had more impact on others than on herself—made Estrella think back on the sins of her own life. She thought of Hilsey, and how she'd believed her love for him would save her. And how terribly wrong she had been to believe that. Anymore she wasn't certain from what she'd needed saving. Looking at Catherine, calm in the moments when she wasn't being harassed by emissaries from her husband still urging her to enter a convent, she began to wonder if perhaps the queen knew a secret of life she didn't.

In December Henry sent Charles Brandon, the Duke of Suffolk, to badger his wife yet again in an attempt to convince her to retire gracefully and stop causing him trouble. Often he sent men to repeat his offer to support her in a convent if she would be so good as to declare herself never married and her daughter illegitimate, and the pope without authority. These emissaries were not gentle.

That day Catherine received Suffolk in her presence chamber, having made him wait a suitable amount of time while she dressed herself appropriately for the formal visit. Her wardrobe was not what it had once been, but she retained enough quality furs, silks, and jewels to at least appear the queen for the moment, though Suffolk didn't consider her one. She sat before the fire on a raised chair, and gazed blandly at him as he entered with his entourage. He'd arrived at the residence with a full military contingent, and guardsmen were posted about the musty old palace. Those of higher rank, earls and better, accompanied him to the presence chamber, flanking him as if men-at-arms confronting an enemy on the field.

Catherine's household was present in its entirety; the maids were arrayed to the side, and her advisors stood nearby in a loose cluster. They took their cue from their queen and appeared comfortable, at home and relaxed. Calm. Immovable.

Certainly it was a lie. The guard outside was a rude enough threat, but Henry's representatives made everyone in the household nervous. Starting at every sound. Estrella's hands gripped each other to hide the trembling. These ugly visits never brought good news, and Suffolk was a weightier menace than most, for until recently he'd been married to the king's sister.

Estrella's heart skipped, as it always did whenever such people came to call, but today it was because among Suffolk's entourage was the Earl of Hartford. Hilsey gazed steadily at her from across the room, and whenever she stole a glance at him she found him still looking at her. She looked away. His wife, Beth Howard, was still alive and he had three sons with her. Being a Howard, and cousin to Anne Boleyn as well as cousin to the current Duke of Norfolk, the alliance made Hartford a likely tool for this episode of bullying the queen. Estrella couldn't tell by his face how he felt about being there, but wished he would stare elsewhere. Seeing him again was stirring memories she'd kept long buried. Joyous memories that had become shameful, and they wrung her heart into a twisted, bloodless knot.

The duke began the interview by repeating the offer of support befitting a queen if the dowager princess would agree to go to a convent. In addition she would be required to acknowledge Archbishop Cranmer's decree that her marriage to Arthur had been consummated, that her marriage to Henry was invalid, and that the pope's dispensation allowing her marriage to Henry was without authority.

Catherine's eyes narrowed, her lips pressed together, and she said nothing. Suffolk waited and shifted his feet impatiently, but he should have known she would not reply. Estrella had to clear her throat during the silence, and it sounded horribly loud in the room. Suffolk glanced at her, and she looked away.

Finally he said, "You would be well advised to consider this generous offer. You should not wish to incur the king's displeasure."

Catherine exploded in vehemence, "Even more, I do not wish to incur the displeasure of the Lord our God. Nor do I wish to destroy my own honor, nor that of my daughter. Nor that of my husband, and that is exactly what I am being asked to do. To lie for the sake of my husband's . . . *pleasure*."

Estrella nearly laughed and turned it into a cough. Suffolk glanced at her again, and she kept her gaze on the floor. Hartford was still staring at her. If she looked at him she knew she couldn't bear it.

Her mistress continued as if there had been no sound from the maid. "I would die a thousand deaths before I would sully my reputation, dirty my soul, and lie before God. I am a virtuous wife, and to even suggest otherwise would be a lie. I do not lie."

Suffolk's voice hardened and rose in volume. "If you will not go to a convent, then you must be removed to another residence. The king offers you Fotheringay."

Several of the maids gasped.

"No!" The queen's eyes were wide, and her voice carried the horror she felt for that place. Fotheringay was a diseased place for its dampness, and would be a danger to them all if they were forced to go. "You cannot be serious! He knows I despise it! There is malaria in it; I would fear for my life!"

Surely she would also fear death by the hand of an assassin. Anything at all could happen in a residence so far removed from common habitation, and there would be nobody to say what had actually transpired.

"Somersham, then." He said it with an air of generosity, as if it were a compromise, though it wasn't.

"Absolutely not. I would take my death from the dampness. My arthritis is unbearable here; I could be a cripple in that place. I would only go if I were dragged by force, for to go willingly would be suicide and therefore against the law of God. Neither residence is acceptable, and Henry knows it. He only wishes me to be out of sight of my subjects who love me."

"I can force you to go."

"You would murder your queen? For it would be murder, I assure you. Regicide in the plainest form."

"You are no queen."

"I am the wife of your king, and no man on earth, except the pope, has the power to say otherwise. You commit heresy by suggesting it."

With unmistakable relish he replied, "Anne is the queen."

That made Catherine blanch for the first time, and her voice tightened. "She is a fool, and a heretic, and a whore."

Suffolk's face reddened, and his voice rose further. "Perhaps your isolation in this remote village with your servants has deluded you, Princess. You think you are queen because they still address you as such." He nodded toward the maids. "Because of that, the king has also sent me to administer an oath to them."

"What oath?"

"That they will address you only as dowager princess."

"Nonsense! My household is loyal to me, and they address me by my proper title."

"Your title is Dowager Princess of Wales! You will come with me to Somersham, and your household will submit to the oath!"

"I will not have my servants call me any other but 'queen'!"

Now the duke was shouting, red-faced, and his hands were clenched at his sides. "You have no standing at court, *Highness*, and you must obey the word of the king! Order your suite to take the oath, or there will be repercussions!"

Without another word, Catherine rose from her seat and strode into her bedchamber while Suffolk shouted after her, following as he did so.

"Have your belongings packed, *Highness*, for I am taking you and your servants to Somersham today!"

The heavy, iron-studded door of the bedchamber slammed shut in his face. The bolt inside fell to with a solid *thunk*. Suffolk slapped his palm against it, then hit it with his gloved fist, shouting at her to come out and obey the king's orders, but his bellowing was met only with silence.

Catherine's maids stayed where they were, taking glances at each other, not entirely certain what to do now. Suffolk went on shouting for a bit, then fell silent when he finally realized she was more stubborn than he. He spun, and glared at the assembled household, each boggled by his behavior.

"You!" he shouted at Felipez, and strode toward him. Hand on hip and chest forward so Cisco would know who was in control, Suffolk said, "You will swear an oath to never address Catherine as queen!"

Cisco blinked and said mildly, his English still heavily accented after so many years in England, "I will not."

"I order it, by authority of the King of England!"

"I cannot address my mistress by anything other than her rightful title, and that is Queen of England."

Knots of muscle stood out on Suffolk's jaw, and he glared at the retainer with keen hatred. Then he turned to Thomas Abell and repeated the order to take the oath. Abell replied as Cisco had, nearly word for word. Then he added, "To expect me to do otherwise is foolhardy, for I am a pious man and will not violate the law of God."

"You would go to the Tower again, Thomas?"

Abell nodded. "I'm no heretic, Your Grace."

"You may not come out this time, you understand that."

The terror showed in Abell's eyes, but he stood firm. He was willing to brave the Tower again for the sake of his principles and his queen. "I understand completely."

Suffolk emitted a noise of frustration, then turned to the next of Catherine's suite. One by one he ordered each to take the oath, and every one of them refused. He threatened imprisonment and execution. He threatened the families of those in the household who were English, but to no avail. Not one of Catherine's servants would swear to call her princess dowager.

By the time he came to Estrella, his face was red and his eyes bloodshot. He fairly spat the order into her face, and she blinked. Calmly she wiped the splatter from her nose and said, "I cannot. I will not. Catherine is my queen."

Having failed to move even one of them, Suffolk then had his men take them all to the porter's ward and lock them in. They all filed into the damp, cramped space and found seats in which to settle themselves, gazing around at each other in subdued silence. Nobody knew what might happen next. There they stayed. Nobody spoke, for nobody wanted to give Suffolk any ideas.

Throughout the afternoon they could hear the duke in the other part of the castle periodically pounding on the queen's bedchamber door and shouting at her to come out. There was never a response from inside that room. The servants sat in their makeshift prison cell until sunset, when Suffolk relented and allowed them leave to attend to needs. Also, in a show of generosity, he allowed the physician, apothecary, and confessor—all Spaniards—to enter Catherine's bedchamber.

They disappeared into the room, and no sound was heard from it thereafter though the duke shouted some more at the door in an effort to budge her.

The cooks were ordered to prepare food for Suffolk's contingent, but none was offered to Catherine's suite. When the household realized their complaints to Suffolk were being related verbatim to Catherine to pressure her, they went silent and accepted there would be no food that evening. Instead, they complained to each other of the duke's cruelty.

Estrella sat in the presence chamber to watch the door in case something should happen or her mistress should need her for anything. Her stomach growled as she watched Suffolk shout at the bedchamber door every so often, pacing back and forth before it, grumbling to the nobles clustered nearby. Hartford was currently absent, and she was loath to wander about the halls for fear of encountering him alone. The onlookers to the spectacle presented by Suffolk dwindled as the men went to their suppers, until only the duke remained, still thwarted by the woman inside the locked chamber. Finally he went to his own supper, though he'd been called long before and it was more than likely cold by now. Estrella rose to lay a fresh log on the hearth, for the night was cold and it appeared she would be there a while.

The Earl of Hartford stepped into the room with a plate of beef and a napkin. He stood near the doorway, hesitating as if hoping for an invitation to approach. She glanced at him, finished her task calmly though a shiver of apprehension skittered up her spine, then she sat on a chair to stare at the fire. Hilsey watched her for a moment, then moved another chair to sit near her.

He held out the plate. "I brought you this."

She glanced at it, then at his face. Unlike herself, his beauty had not waned this past decade and a half—not that she could see. He was in his fifties now but was still as bright of eye and ruddy of cheek as ever. His silver hair glinted in the flicker of the firelight. She murmured, "Always wanting to feed me. And then afterward?"

A shadow fell over his eyes. "That's hardly fair."

Her gaze returned to the fire. "Life is unfair. You taught me that."

"I never stopped loving you."

Her heart sickened. "You no longer know me. If you ever did."

"Can you not believe my affection is genuine?"

Knowing it was a mistake, she turned to look at him again. To look into those eyes that had captured her heart so long ago and now made her yearn for the all too brief time when they'd also given her hope. The affection was there. Unmistakable in his frank gaze. Her throat began to close, and she cleared it. "Yes. I do believe it's genuine. But it's not enough. I was married to Whitby for fifteen years, and what he taught me is that, though affection from him would have been a lovely thing, love alone would not have been enough."

Hilsey was silent, gazing at her for a very long moment. Then he offered the plate again. "Take this before it grows cold. We've been here all day, and I know you haven't eaten anything. You must be ravenous."

Estrella looked at it, then at the earl. The smell of the food was most enticing. Her better self didn't want any of it, but the base need in her was very hungry and she found it impossible to resist. She reached out and picked up a thick slab of the meat, then took a bite and watched the fire as she chewed. Hilsey attempted to engage her in conversation, but she ignored him as best she could, answering only in single words or sideways glances. Finally, after she rejected his urging to take more than the one piece of meat, he gave up, stood, and bade her good night. When she turned to see him go, she found the plate and napkin sitting on his chair. She reached over to wipe her fingers on the napkin, then rose from her seat and retired to her chamber, leaving the plate.

The next morning Suffolk returned to pound at Catherine's door but of course achieved nothing. He and his cohorts went to the great hall and put their heads together to know what to do but produced nothing more than shouting and recrimination amongst themselves. They came away from their meeting as confounded as when they'd gone in.

The queen's servants were now being fed and had been given a breakfast of bread and fish. The men who had been allowed into the bedchamber emerged to eat, and Estrella was allowed in with a breakfast tray for her mistress. She found Catherine sitting by a window that commanded a view of the village street below. Her shoulders were slumped in despair, and tears stood in her eyes as she gazed out on Buckden Village. Estrella set the tray with the plate, cup, and knife on a table near the bed, then went to see what had caught the queen's attention.

The street was far more crowded than usual, dotted here and there with village men who happened to be bearing large knives, hooks, and various other tools with points and sharp edges. They stood casually, without overt threat in their demeanor, but it was plain their focus was on the guard placed yesterday outside the queen's residence, and their demeanor was not friendly. Some gazed upward toward the tower, the way villagers often did when hoping for a glimpse of the queen, but today it was with a sense of concern rather than merely a pleasant pastime inspired by curiosity. Suffolk now faced a brewing rebellion from villagers who would protect their queen from him. A sigh of relief escaped Estrella, for she knew the duke would not harm Catherine here before the villagers. She would not be taken by force, for those men down below would not allow it.

But when Catherine heard that sigh, she said, "No, Lita, this is not our salvation. If the village men rise against the duke's guard, they will die. Many guardsmen will die as well, and I cannot countenance their blood on my soul."

"What will you do, then? If you order them to stand down, Suffolk will take you to Somersham by force." She laid her hands on the queen's shoulders, where so much weight already rested.

The queen thought. It seemed minutes before she spoke, and when she did it was with the frail voice of someone truly lost. "I don't know. God help me, I don't know."

The duke sent a courier with a letter to the king, asking what should be done about Catherine at this juncture. For five days Suffolk awaited orders from Henry in London regarding the standoff. The villagers maintained their unobtrusive watch on the residence and the duke's guard. Catherine remained in her bedchamber, unwilling to allow herself to be taken to her death in a more remote residence. Estrella avoided contact with Hilsey, and declined to speak to him or even look at him when he was in the room.

On the fifth day, frustrated at the lack of reply from London, Suffolk finally gave up waiting and took action. With an air of determination that he should not be hindered, he ordered his guard to remove the furnishings from all parts of the tower accessible to them. The corridors and chambers of Buckden Palace came alive with Suffolk's contingent of men as they hurried to obey, each one glad to be doing something at last. They made haste to pack Catherine's things and loaded them onto mules in the courtyard.

The interest of the villagers perked as they watched the guards scurrying out with their loads of furniture and wall hangings, then back in for more. Estrella watched the loading in the courtyard from the window in the presence chamber. It was an efficient crew. Nobody lollygagged, and every piece of plate, every rolled tapestry, every stick of furniture found a place on the pack train. It was like watching ants carry bits of food into a tiny hole atop a hill. That day the residence was stripped nearly bare.

Suffolk and his personal escort barged into the presence chamber. Estrella started and turned, took a single step backward toward the window curtain, and hoped she would blend in with the fabric colored similarly to her dress. She watched the men from a discreet distance. With his nobles at heel, the duke strode across to pound on the bedchamber door some more. The men hung back, wearing bland expressions and appearing to know this was a fool's mission.

"Princess Dowager!"

Of course there was no reply to that. It was a wonder he even wasted breath to address her that way.

He continued, everybody in the room knowing the duke could wait forever and not hear an answer, "I've begun to load your furnishings. A litter is being prepared for you. When it is ready, I will have my men break down this door and take you to it. You will be carried, tied and gagged if necessary, to Somersham." His voice was hard, angry that he'd been brought to this. The scowl on his face had been there for days.

Then, for the first time since her retreat to that chamber, Catherine spoke to Suffolk. "Do what you must. Take me by force, but by God I will not go willingly. Break down the door and let it be heard in the street below. Carry me to the litter, bound and gagged, and then haul me through Buckden like a quarry about to be unmade. If that is your duty, then do it. I cannot stop you."

Estrella and everyone else present knew Suffolk would indeed be stopped were he to try such a thing. Not by Catherine but by the angry villagers. So did Catherine know it. Estrella watched the duke's face carefully as it grew a deep red. He turned away from the door in utter frustration. The queen had banked on his reluctance to let his outnumbered contingent be attacked and possibly destroyed by common locals bearing farm tools. She succeeded.

He made a long growl and strode out of the room, shouting orders to his men as he left. They were to begin arresting the household, the servants to be taken to London and to the tower. A shock of terror stuck Estrella's feet to the floor.

Hilsey, at the rear of the group, halted just inside the chamber and looked over at her. The others followed Suffolk, but Hilsey lagged behind. Estrella was caught. Eyes wide and heart pounding, she waited for him to order her from the room. Then he would take her away to prison. Possibly to be executed, if the situation became bad enough. Her refusal to take an oath on the order of the king could be called treason if Henry wished it.

But instead of arresting her, Hilsey nodded toward Catherine's bedchamber. Then, with only one quick glance back at her, he hurried after the duke and let her be.

Estrella stared after him, stunned. Then she grabbed her skirts in her fists, hurried to take the advice while it was still good, and knocked on Catherine's door to be admitted. She called out to make haste opening the door, and one of the maids attending the queen let her in. Quickly she laid the bolt across the door, lest any of Suffolk's men take advantage of this moment.

Catherine was sitting on the edge of the bed. She stood and asked, "What is he doing now?"

"Making arrests, Your Majesty. He intends to take someone away today, to save himself too much embarrassment."

Catherine sighed and went to the window to look out on the courtyard. There was much shouting going on below and throughout the residence. A few minutes later small clusters of men began to emerge in the courtyard below. One of them had a woman at its center, held roughly by one arm in the grip of a guardsman.

"Oh, no. They've taken Margaret."

The queen sat in the chair behind her, no longer looking. Margaret was the youngest of her maids.

"She should have run and hid," said Estrella.

Others emerged. A cook. The apothecary, De Soto. Then they brought out the one man she had known they would search down for very public arrest. Estrella gasped nevertheless.

"Your Majesty, they've taken Thomas Abell."

Catherine put her hands over her face and began a murmur they all knew was a prayer for the safety of the man who had championed her for so many years, in print and in deed. Estrella began to pray for the safety of others in the suite who might have a chance at escape. For Thomas had been to the Tower before, arrested for having written a book in support of the queen's case, and his chances of emerging alive a second time were terribly slim.

Once the arrests were made and the captives tied and loaded onto horses, the duke gathered his men and most of the guard, leaving only a token number of men-at-arms to watch the residence. Then the contingent made its way through the gathered villagers and off down the road toward London. The men in the street with axes and hooks watched them go, uneasy. But since Suffolk didn't have the queen, nobody raised a weapon against him. Then, when the duke and his prisoners were away, the villagers dispersed and returned to their homes.

Catherine sat by the window for a long time with tears in her eyes. She had made her stand to not be removed to a place where she could be killed, but there were casualties and that broke her heart.

Sixteen

❧

1534–1535

WITH the already small household reduced by nearly half, and most of the rooms in the Buckden residence stripped bare, Catherine's servants had to struggle to make their lives where they'd been left. Though there were fewer people to support now, there were still fewer beds than people and the bare stone rooms were cold and hard. Workloads shifted to accommodate, and Estrella found herself doing tasks she'd never in her life considered attempting. It was terribly awkward and demeaning, but she looked toward her mistress and knew her service was needed and appreciated. She believed Catherine was the true queen and was honored to wait on her.

All the remaining servants and advisors felt keenly the absence of their comrades in the way soldiers missed friends who had fallen in battle. They wished for word from London of the fates of those arrested, and when it came it was not heartening.

All the ones taken that day of Suffolk's departure had been imprisoned in the Tower of London, there to await judgment. Or not, perhaps. There was no telling whether anyone would ever actually be tried, or sentenced if they were tried. In a sense, delay of judgment was a blessing. Given Henry's mood and his recent threats of treason conviction for the woman who had been his wife for over two decades, nobody was eager for judgment from the increasingly despotic administration and the possibility of being hung, gutted, and quartered as a traitor. Imprisonment without trial was to be preferred.

The incarcerated nun from Kent was still held in the Tower without trial, for there was inadequate evidence against her for a conviction. Even so, arrests continued among those who had come in contact with the self-styled seer who had been so indiscreet as to predict the death of the king, and many who had opposed Henry in his attempt to discard his wife along with the authority of the pope were imprisoned on the basis of merely having spoken to the nun. Bishop John Fisher and Sir Thomas More, longtime friends of Catherine's, were both arrested for their resistance to the king and to the divorce.

Then, in late April, Chapuys brought news the nun and three monks had been executed without trial. The monks had refused to sign the Oath of Succession stating the invalidity of Catherine's marriage, the illegitimacy of Princess Mary, and denying the authority of the pope. In the tradition begun by Edward I two centuries before, while the monks watched and waited their turn, the nun was hung till nearly unconscious, was gutted and her entrails burned before her eyes, then finally beheaded and her body quartered. Each of the three monks met his death in the same manner, one by one, as the remaining looked on. The severed heads were then displayed on the bridge across the Thames for all to see and take as example.

Plenty of Londoners came to gawk, most of them commoners with nothing better to do, but many were nobles with a dear stake in the outcome of this controversy. Each man had to reconcile his religious convictions with the knowledge of what happened to those whose beliefs were contrary to the king's. Onlookers of every stripe gathered in silent clusters, feet shifting uncomfortably or planted firmly in self-righteous affirmation, and gazed up at the rotting, discolored heads, then looked to one another to see who might be next to face the choice everyone was now being asked to make. No matter who, they each looked to the other as if to ask, "Do *you* support the pope, and therefore the queen? Would *you* die for your faith?"

Shortly after, for the same refusal to sign the oath, three more monks were chained to stakes and left to die slowly over several days. The city tensed at sight of the condemned, who gave so much the impression of crucifixion that it was impossible to not think of the three crosses on Calvary. Once again Londoners looked to each other with questions in their eyes.

During this time Catherine and her reduced household were removed to a drier residence at Kimbolton. There the queen secluded herself deep within her few personal chambers, away from and out of sight of the king's guard who kept her prisoner. Insulated by her servants from contact with her captors, she maintained her household in regal manner if not richness or style, refusing to acknowledge the presence of anyone who did not address her in the proper manner. For Estrella it was comforting to be part of the small pocket of Catherine's court. It was nevertheless a more orderly existence than they'd had at Buckden, where there had been a mix of those who obeyed the king and those who were loyal to the queen. At Kimbolton the days were sedate, spiritual, and everyone lived by the protocols they'd observed during their time in Henry's court. And they all knew it was the beginning of the end.

Physically the queen was beginning to fail. Day to day, the strain on her showed in her haggard face and thinning body. Little by little Estrella watched her longtime friend and mistress weaken, though her spirit stayed firm in her conviction that her course was the right one. The Catherine inside the failing body was not weak at all.

Not long after their arrival in Kimbolton, a message came from the king. The courier was allowed into the residence, but Catherine refused to allow him to approach her. Instead, he was escorted by the sergeant of the guard to the vicinity of the queen's apartments, then the missive was carried by the hand of one of Catherine's maids to the privy chamber. The young woman hurried up the stairs to the queen, where Estrella was brushing Catherine's hair. There was no longer a mirror to use, so she had to trust her grooming to her servants without observation. Estrella brushed the graying reddish hair slowly and gently, for it had a calming effect on Her Majesty. In these times they all needed as much calm as could be had.

But the room erupted in concern when the maid sent for the message entered with it and announced it was from the king. Catherine stared at it as if it were a snake she would crush with a blow from a fire poker. The maid held it out before her, and nobody in the room wished to touch it.

"What do you suppose he wants?" asked Estrella.

"We know what he wants. What we don't know is how he's going about demanding it this time."

"You've nothing left for him to take, Your Majesty."

Catherine sighed. "Indeed. There is some comfort in that. Though I imagine the whore still wants my baptism robe."

She nodded toward the maid. "Open it and see what it says so I can tell him no."

The young lady broke the seal and unfolded the single sheet. The message had but one sentence to it, which she read aloud. "Under no circumstances will you give audience to Eustache Chapuys."

Catherine stared at the letter, thinking. Estrella said, "Why would he tell you this? The sergeant of the guard already has orders to admit only those with passport from the king. Especially he would hesitate to admit Chapuys, who has been denied permission more than once since we've been here."

The queen said, "Henry must have reason to believe there is a possibility of an audience, and so has directed his order to me instead of the guard."

The maid who delivered the message piped up. "The king's messenger has told me that the ambassador is making a pilgrimage to Our Lady of Walsingham, and it is known he intends to make a stop here. He's accompanied by his suite, Spanish merchants, and many others. They say it's an enormous procession, all dressed in fresh livery and looking terribly festive, raising a great sound of drums and trumpets the entire way. Everyone in the kingdom must know he's on his way here, and so they will know if he is refused. He was told to turn back, but has not obeyed the order."

That certainly explained the cryptic message, and Catherine nodded understanding.

"Will you see him?" Estrella asked the queen.

Catherine looked up at her maid. "Certainly not. To violate a directive from my husband would be the very sort of disobedience I've sworn against since the day I married him." She waved a hand at the maid who had brought the message. "Isabel, bring pen and paper and write for me." The maid hurried to obey, then sat at a table to write what Catherine dictated.

It was a letter to Chapuys, telling him she would not see him, and that he should return to London. She sent the message on to the approaching procession with Cisco Felipez. The faithful former page leapt onto his horse and rode off down the road toward London.

They all thought that would be the end of that, but the next day brought the approach of a group detached from the ambassador's pilgrimage. One of the maids spotted them from the window of Catherine's bedchamber and cried out to the queen, "Oh, look! They've come after all!" It was a lively procession, of beautiful horses and beautifully decked-out horsemen, acrobats and hangers-on walking alongside and behind. Like a carnival coming to entertain the queen.

Catherine rose from her chair with no small effort and made her slow way to the window to look out. Estrella asked, "Is it the ambassador? Is he with them?"

After a long look, the queen said, "No. I don't see him."

Estrella went to take a look for herself. There was quite a crowd of Spaniards on horseback gathered at the moat. Gentlemen and youths, merchants, musicians, and knights. When they saw the queen in her window they all lifted their voices and began singing in Spanish to her. The music was loud and gay, a festive celebration of their pilgrimage, then with the next song it turned gentle. Contemplative. Then it was lively again, and the queen waved her appreciation to them with a red kerchief. Their response was to take turns showing off the talents of their exquisitely trained horses, putting on a show of prancing and leaps by the edge of the moat.

"Oh!" cried Estrella. "The capriole!" One of the stallions

kicked out his hind legs, his front legs curled high, and landed in place without disturbing his rider. Some executed the passage, and courbette as well, both very difficult maneuvers for a horse. To rise on his hind legs, then leap and land on the same legs before resting again on all fours took great training and skill in both horse and rider. She applauded. All the windows in the queen's apartments were filled with people applauding the fine riding.

Next the riders formed a half circle by the edge of the moat, and a single man leapt from his horse to make his way to the center of it, turning cartwheels and backflips. There he engaged in comic acrobatics, throwing himself this way and that, always seeming on the verge of hurting himself but ever catching his own fall just before disaster.

Catherine made a sound that was nearly a cooing. "Oh, it's the ambassador's fool!" She applauded him with a delighted smile. "Isn't he an amusing fellow! I always did enjoy him in London." Her voice held a note of pleasure Estrella hadn't heard in a long time. It warmed her heart to see Catherine so enjoying the show.

Then in the midst of a double flip, the acrobat tossed something over the wall, a small, dark object that landed in the courtyard commanded by the queen's apartments.

"Isabel," said the queen, her voice suddenly alert and urgent. "Run. Hurry and find that casket before the guard reaches it."

The maid snatched up her skirts to speed on her errand, and the queen continued to wave from her window as if nothing had happened. Estrella watched the scene below. They could see the thing that had been thrown, a dark bit in a narrow corner where wall met tower. It appeared to be a wooden box. But all the attention was on the fool now, for he'd fallen into the moat and was being fished out by his Spanish comrades. From the windows of the castle the Spaniards of Catherine's household bantered with the caballeros below in their native tongue, and the guard by the drawbridge was focused on making certain the fool did not try to swim across to the castle side of the moat.

"Is the queen well?" shouted one of the horsemen in Spanish while this was going on.

Estrella looked to Catherine, who gestured that she should reply for her, so Estrella did. "Well enough. She misses her daughter."

"Princess Mary is alive, well, and wary. She fears her father and takes great care for her own safety. She will continue in safety, I think." Then the Spanish gentleman, a friend of Chapuys's shouted, "Is the queen allowed visitors?"

"Yes. It is only the ambassador the king fears." She laughed and added, "And his messengers."

The don also laughed. "Sometimes the king acts wisely." That made even Catherine chuckle. He continued, "The ambassador sends his regards and hopes to visit the queen when her husband is better disposed to allow it." There was a pause, and he added, "Soon."

Estrella declared her own desire for such a visit and waved as the caballeros were called away from the moat and made their way back to the road by which they'd come.

The mood in the queen's apartments was much lighter now. Catherine pressed her fingers to her lips and murmured, "Mary is well." Estrella's heart lifted for the sake of her friend, for she knew how she had treasured her own children when they were alive. That Mary had not been executed—yet—was good news indeed. Nor had she been poisoned, and that was an even greater fear, for it was more likely.

Isabel burst into the room with the small box Chapuys's
fool had thrown over the wall and presented it to Catherine.
The queen opened it as she took a seat in her large, well-
cushioned chair. Inside was a letter, which was no surprise to
anyone in the room. It was from the ambassador, again no surprise. The note said simply, "Expect a visit from a Spanish
merchant named Mendez."

Catherine gazed at the single sentence thoughtfully, then
folded the paper and went to place it on the fire. Once it
burned, she poked the ashes with the iron rod hung by the
hearth until they were dust.

The countryside all watched the ambassador retreat to
London, having been refused admittance to see the queen.
Over the next days the household settled back down to its sedate daily routine. There were messages from Chapuys, but
since all such messages were read by the castle guard he
trusted little to paper, or even to the memory of his messenger, and so information continued to be sketchy and only what
could safely be written down.

Months passed, and the queen kept vigil from her window
whenever she wasn't praying with her chaplain. Rarely was
she seen without her rosary entwined in her fingers, whether
she was reciting or just taking comfort from the beads. Summer became fall, then another winter as the matter of her
marriage dragged on and the king's persecution of the Church
escalated. Throughout the kingdom, monasteries were dis-
banded and plundered, their cash wealth and land claimed by
the Crown, and that did not set well with the nobility.

In the summer of 1535 a single rider came to the drawbridge at Kimbolton. It was at sunset, late in the evening,
when summer twilight was long and the sun wended its way
to the horizon in a leisurely manner, in no hurry to set. Word

came from the guard her visitor was one Don Miguel Mendez, a Castilian merchant of London. Estrella had nearly forgotten the note from Chapuys, but Catherine never hesitated at hearing the visitor's name. She relayed back to the guard that Señor Mendez would be permitted an audience even this late in the day, and she requested Estrella to ready her to emerge to the presence chamber. The maid wondered aloud why it had taken so terribly long for Mendez to make his appearance, but Catherine did not reply.

She settled into her chair, and Mendez was immediately escorted into the room. The merchant was still dirty and in disarray from his long, hurried ride, but his attire was new. In fact, it was a bit too new. And more fine than one might expect from the merchant class. As Mendez knelt before the queen and looked up at her, Estrella nearly laughed out loud. For beneath a wig of long, dark hair and a hat too large to be stylish, was the worn face of Eustache Chapuys.

"Good evening, my special friend," said Catherine with a smile.

"Greetings to Your Majesty," he replied.

The queen gestured for a chair to be brought, and he took the seat next to her. "Have you seen Mary?" she asked eagerly.

"Last I saw the princess, three days ago, she was ill but recovering. These terrible times have not worn well on her, and her health is frail. But she lives and is in no danger by that account just now."

"Was she poisoned?"

"There is no telling, Your Majesty. At any rate, nobody has been charged with an attempt on her life."

"There wouldn't be anyone charged in any case, to be sure."

The ambassador's eyes sparked with interest at that. "Am I

to understand you have finally begun to consider the culpability of your husband in these affairs?"

The queen sat up and raised her chin. "I still believe he is being misled, and that were it not for the evil company he keeps he would be as loving a husband and father as any man in the kingdom."

Chapuys's eyes closed for a moment, and he nodded as if to himself. The moment of false hope that Catherine would turn blame on Henry passed. Then he said, "You may change your mind when you hear the news I bring from London."

The queen eyed him and waited for him to continue.

"Your Majesty, it grieves me to report that your two friends, Bishop John Fisher and Sir Thomas More, have both been executed for treason."

That news took Estrella by surprise. It felt as if she'd been clouted in the stomach. John Fisher, Bishop of Rochester, had been the only man in Henry's court to support Catherine's case in the Blackfriars hearing. Catherine's countenance paled, and she gripped the arms of her chair hard. Chapuys knelt before her and took her hand, his own grief etched on his face. Estrella and the other two maids turned away and struggled to pull themselves together while Catherine wept with one hand over her face. Estrella thought of the many days her mistress had spent in lively conversation with More on religious matters and the New Learning. They'd both been excited by the idea of independent study of scripture and the dissemination of knowledge to everyone, not just to select intellectuals. It had been a lively, productive friendship, and now Thomas was dead.

Chapuys continued, "The bishop had begged to not be gutted, that he should be hung until dead and so be spared the worst pain of the death decreed for him. And so Henry obliged the old man. But the hanging was too gentle, and it took a terribly long time for him to finally expire." He glanced at Catherine for the effect his words had on her, and emphasized, "Kicking and squirming. Those looking on were so horrified by the sight of the poor man hanging naked from the scaffold, alive and suffering, many turned away. Afterward, of course, his corpse was beheaded and the head stuck on a spike at the bridge. But it wasn't there long. Two weeks later it was replaced by that of Sir Thomas."

Catherine continued to weep.

The ambassador took this moment to press his case for support of an uprising among the conservative nobles. "You understand, Your Majesty, that this has caused deep concern in the north. The conservatives who support you are frightened they will be next and will want to defend themselves." Catherine sobbed, and it seemed she couldn't possibly be listening, but Chapuys continued nevertheless. "But they need a rallying point. A leader. They need you, Your Majesty, to guide them in their struggle for life and for their religion."

Catherine uncovered her face and looked away toward the window that commanded a view of the moat and drawbridge. Tears streaked her lined face, and the years of grief and worry were drawn on it in glistening highlights. Estrella handed her a handkerchief for her to dab her eyes, then watched her pull herself together, more slowly than ever before. The queen was tired. Ill. And this was a crushing blow. The souls of her subjects were at stake, as well as that of her husband, and that harridan Anne Boleyn was winning. But, in a voice that was nearly too low and soft to be heard, she told Chapuys, "I've told you before, I cannot. There will be no blood on my account."

"There has already been blood on your account, Your Majesty. The blood of your friends and supporters. Men who have been your friends and who gave themselves for your sake. You should not allow their sacrifice to go to waste."

"It is not wasted, *mi amigo especial*. Their sacrifice will not go unnoticed."

The ambassador nodded and shrugged and pressed his palms together before him in supplication. "To be sure, Your Majesty. They will both be long remembered, I'm certain. But John and Thomas, not to mention those several monks, suffered horribly for your sake, and what good is it if the Church remains divided? Some are still suffering, such as Thomas Abell imprisoned in the Tower, and more will follow. What will be accomplished if the king is allowed to continue terrorizing the faithful?"

Catherine shook her head in inarticulate denial. More tears rose to her eyes, and when she blinked they rolled down her face to her chin.

He continued, "And what of yourself and Mary?" Catherine pressed her lips between her teeth, and fresh concern lit her eyes in a feverish flame. The ambassador pressed. "Your daughter is at dire risk. Henry is set on his course and will not hesitate to do away with her if he deems it an advantage to himself."

"Henry will not harm his daughter." The terror in her voice belied her words, though Estrella knew the queen wanted desperately to believe them. "But if he does, then she will go to the Lord in grace."

Chapuys was stern as he continued. Forceful. "The king is still listening far too closely to that Boleyn woman, and does her bidding. That is made plain by the recent executions, which she desired. Killing Bishop Fisher and Sir Thomas was a dire political error, and Henry is not so unwise in these matters except where the wishes of his whore are concerned. It is she who pressed him into this, because she hates anyone who supports you. She hates your daughter, and is certainly asking for her death. Mary is a strong, willful young woman and will resist her father's attempts to harm you and the Church. Anne will want her own daughter, or her next child if it is a boy, to succeed Henry. Mary's life is very much at stake."

All the air seemed to leave the queen. She sat in her chair, quite still and staring into space. There seemed no resistance left in her, and Estrella guessed the time had come for her to change her mind and call for rebellion. It seemed the only recourse, for all was lost otherwise. These words made perfect sense.

Chapuys pressed on, "There is a plan afoot to rescue Mary from her captors and spirit her away to the Continent, where she will be safe."

Catherine stared into his face, appalled but curious.

"She is an excellent rider. Men supporting your cause could abduct her while riding and take her to board a galley. And from there to join armed ships from Charles, waiting at the mouth of the Thames. Resistance would be slight, and her pursuers would take no pains to overtake her, for there are few with the heart to see her dead. From there she would be taken to the coast and placed on a ship bound for Spain." Catherine looked doubtful, so he added, "She will then be safe, Your Majesty. But only then."

"It would be treason."

"You would see her dead?"

"No!" Her eyes glistened with pain and grief. "I would not see her harmed in any way. I would not have her threatened, nor spurned by her father, nor chased across England by those who would have her executed. She would not be safe. Nobody would. And to condone such a plan would be treason. *Treason*, and then we would be guilty of the very thing he claims. How can you not see that?"

"It's the only way, Your Majesty. You and your daughter are both far too vulnerable to assassination. It's your life and Mary's I'm trying to protect."

"And what of the men who would die in the ensuing violence? Or even in the attempt? What if Mary would be killed in the chase? Or is caught and executed? No, my dear friend, I cannot agree to this. We must find another way. The pope is the only answer. If he will make his decision, then Henry will be forced to see his error. It's the only way to save everyone."

"I beg you, Your Majesty, to say the word that will prevent tragedy for you all."

Catherine's reply was, "No. I cannot."

Chapuys sighed.

The queen continued, "You must understand, I cannot reject my principles for the sake of convenience. I cannot abandon my belief that God does not wish me to lend my name to war just because it seems the only way to win. I will not ask anyone to die for me. Even more, I cannot ask anyone to kill for me. I will not send men to a conflict they did not make nor wreak havoc on the countryside to protect even my daughter who is the most precious thing to me on this earth. In short, my dear friend, I will not defy the law of God under even the most extreme circumstances. Our Lord Jesus drank from the cup that was given to him, and so shall I drink from mine." Tears rolled down her face, and she gazed steadily at the ambassador.

"Your Majesty, I beg—"

"That is all. I've made my decision. The matter is closed, and you will not speak to me of it further."

Estrella blinked tears from her own eyes and knew all was lost.

Chapuys's grief-filled eyes looked into Catherine's, and he considered her words for several moments, then he said quietly, "Your Majesty, then do me one thing. Do not eat anything that is not prepared in your presence by your own loyal maids." He nodded in Estrella's direction. "Do not allow anyone near you whom you do not trust implicitly. Your life is in danger. I beg you, Your Majesty, take care the king's men do not solve his problem for him."

Catherine nodded. "I understand."

Chapuys fell silent for a moment, plainly wanting to argue further, but then decided against it. He stood, considered speaking again, and once more refrained. Then he bowed deeply and made his exit.

Catherine watched him go, and stared at the empty doorway for a long time after he was gone.

Seventeen

1509

ESTRELLA was not pregnant by Piers Hilsey, and when she realized it she gave a heartfelt prayer of thanks. She withdrew to the rooms over the stables, and though she denied to herself she was hiding, it was true she cringed at the thought of accidentally encountering the earl again. Hilsey disappeared from her life, and in February a rumor reached the apartments over the stable that the most eligible man in the kingdom was now married and expecting a child. Gales of wistful disappointment wafted among the day-dreaming maids of Princess Catherine, but Estrella choked back feelings that were a hard knot in her throat. Several noticed her pallor, and chalked it up to the hard winter weather and poor nourishment. The cold days were long and tedious, as the question of Catherine's betrothal dragged on, and it became the consensus among the Spanish suite that there would be no wedding for her.

Then, shortly after the rumor about Hartford made the rounds, Estrella overheard a conversation that shook Catherine's household to its foundations. On her way to the palace kitchen to see what provisions might be had from a sympathetic cook, Estrella had her head down and her cloak wrapped tightly around her, making her way with utmost discretion. It was shameful. A horror, to be required to beg from the kitchen staff bread and meat. As kindly as was the one old man who sometimes passed to her food that would otherwise have gone to the poor, Estrella despised having to visit him. His eyes held a pity she didn't want, and there was terror that anyone might see her accepting the charity that rightfully belonged to lesser folk. Many of the less wealthy courtiers often sold their sumptuous dinners for cash, and that was all right. They were entitled to the food, and if they chose to sell it that was acceptable so long as the king allowed it. But taking alms meant for the common Londoners outside the palace gates was not only beneath the daughter of a duke, it was stealing. That went against not only the king's law, but it flew in the face of her own dearly held convictions. Perhaps not as dearly held as they had been once, and that tore at her. Once again she felt the stain on her soul, as well as the damage to her pride.

She was sunk deep in these thoughts when she passed the stairwell that led to the apartments above the kitchen and heard a familiar voice talking to an unfamiliar one. It was Ferdinand's ambassador, Fuensalida, discussing Catherine's dowry with a stranger. They spoke Spanish, though the stranger was not a Spaniard. The accent was Italian, and Estrella guessed he might be Grimaldi, the banker who was now married to Francesca. He requested instructions regarding the transfer of funds. Estrella's pace slowed to a halt, her legs obeying an impulse from somewhere other than conscious

thought, and she stood by the entrance to the stairwell to ab-
sorb whatever she might happen to accidentally hear. Not
truly eavesdropping, but unable to proceed to the kitchen because her feet wouldn't move for her.

Fuensalida gave the instructions for the transfer of cash
and went on to discuss the sale of more of Catherine's plate.
Sale, now, rather than pawn, and the proceeds were not to go
to Catherine for the support of her household. Estrella felt the
corridor sway, and the shadows grew even darker as she realized the ambassador was funneling off the money and goods
meant for Catherine's dowry. Large amounts of it, by what
she was hearing. Fuensalida was proving to be the betrayer
Catherine had always suspected him to be.

Stunned as she was, Estrella was slow in realizing the
voices were coming nearer as the ambassador and banker descended the stairs. In a panic she grabbed her skirts and scur-
ried to the nearest corner in the wall, a recessed doorway. But
the door was locked. She murmured a call to Jesus for help and
turned to press her back to the door, as deep in the shadow of
the recess as she could get, grabbing at her skirts lest they puff
outward and betray her. Her heart pounded, and she knew for
a certainty she would be discovered in that shallow space. The
two men would surely know she'd been listening, and God
knew what Fuensalida would do to her if he knew his plot had
been discovered. It would mean his life, and now it would
mean hers to be caught by him. Breaths came hard, and she
forced them to slow.

But God was merciful that day, and the two conspirators
turned the other direction down the corridor, silencing their
talk as they went in the more public area. Estrella listened to
their soft footfalls on the stone fade off down the corridor,
waited until the men were out of hearing, then waited some

more, before emerging from her hiding place with care and hurrying back to the stables. In her distress she quite forgot about visiting the kitchen.

She went directly to Catherine, who was busy embroidering yet more flowers along frayed hems and slashes. "Your Highness, I must speak to you about Fuensalida."

The princess looked up, considered her maid's panicked demeanor, then glanced around the room at the maids. She said to Estrella, "What of him?"

Estrella also glanced around at the others listening, and Catherine took her meaning that the information was of a sensitive nature. Quickly the lesser servants were dismissed, and when the room was cleared of everyone but the chamberlain and her confessor, Catherine looked to her maid again to proceed.

"Embezzlement, Your Highness. He's sending the money for your dowry out of the country with the aid of the banker Grimaldi."

The princess's eyes darkened, and her mouth hardened. She had always been ready to believe the Aragonese ambassador to be a traitor, and it took little from Estrella to arouse her anger at him. "Where did you hear this?"

"From his own lips," Estrella said breathlessly. "I overheard him in a stairwell, talking to Grimaldi. They are selling your plate, and all the money is going to Italy."

Quickly, the princess began to put her sewing aside and said to her chamberlain, "Summon Fuensalida to me. Immediately."

He said, "Are you certain you wish to pursue this, Your Highness? Perhaps there is an explanation."

"Do what I say. I will learn the truth and not be played for the fool by this man." She rested a bland gaze on her chamberlain, as much to suggest he shouldn't side with Fuensalida and be suspected of playing her for the fool as well.

"Yes, Your Highness." The chamberlain hurried to comply.

But the meeting with the ambassador wasn't immediate. It was morning by the time he could be compelled to visit the quarters of the princess, and Catherine's ire grew hot to be kept waiting. When the ambassador did finally show himself, he arrived as if he were on his way to somewhere else and impatient to get there. Neither did this performance sit well with the princess. Estrella eyed him as he made his obeisance in the presence chamber and thought what a poor diplomat he really was. Even the plodding De Puebla had better grace in his calling than this fellow.

The ambassador was bade to rise, and Catherine came straight to the point, her tact blunted by anger. "What are you doing with my dowry?"

Fuensalida paled. No, not a graceful courtier at all, to be so transparent. He faltered a bit, then said, "What do you mean?"

"I mean exactly what I asked. What are you doing with my dowry? Where is it?"

"Well, Your Highness, you know it is no longer whole, for you have been pawning pieces of it these past several years."

"Nevertheless, Fuensalida, most of it should remain. What are you doing with the rest?" Her voice carried the steel edge she'd learned in managing her own affairs since the dismissal of Doña Elvira. She was no longer the malleable girl who had debarked from the Spanish ship in Plymouth.

"Your Highness, you must understand—"

"I understand that you've been sending it out of the country."

"And for good cause, Your Highness." Distress caused him

to fidget, and his eyes darted about. Estrella had never seen a man appear more guilty.

Catherine's eyes went wide. "Then you admit—"

"I *announce*." The ambassador raised his chin, and the princess sat back with a questioning look. "I've been protecting your interests and your father's wealth."

"Protecting? A handy story. And from what could you be protecting the dowry I will need when I marry Henry?"

Fuensalida let his face betray his opinion of the likelihood of her wedding to the prince, and Catherine's face flushed with anger. Possibly embarrassment as well, but Estrella thought not. Catherine was too firm in her conviction for it to cross her mind that Fuensalida could be right. He said, "As a precaution, Your Highness. Only in preparation for the worst, I meant to protect your assets from seizure."

"Why would there ever be such a thing?"

The ambassador hesitated to speak, considered his options, then sighed and addressed an issue he had never bothered to bring up to the princess before. "There are those who believe Henry means to go to war against your father. With support from Emperor Maximilian, and regency over young Charles in Castile—which Maximilian would be happy to give under these circumstances—Henry could assault Aragon while Maximilian invades France. Such an alliance would turn the balance of power in Europe entirely on its ear, and that is a thing very much coveted by King Henry. He would then have all of Spain and France under his heel and the Holy Roman Emperor at his side."

"The king is an old man, and ill. He won't last long."

"He wouldn't need to, and the closer he comes to death the more likely he'll attempt something so drastic. It would be an opportunity to be the victor over the French he hates so well, then to leave that legacy to his son. His final triumph."

"You have gone against my father's—"

"I have power of attorney from your father in this, Your Highness."

That made her go silent, and she gazed at the ambassador. "My father believes there will be no marriage?"

"Ferdinand believes the English king no longer has need of the alliance and will not honor his commitment. He further understands the treacherous King Henry is not likely to give warning of his intention by telling your father to recall you and your household. If that is what he is planning, he will surely be most gratified by the opportunity to seize your dowry and imprison you as a hostage. Indeed, Your Highness, these past several years he's held you as a pawn to assure the good behavior of your father. And so far Ferdinand has been as well-behaved as would be reasonable. The English king is bent on full victory and subjugation of Aragon, whom he hates as much as he hates France. So long as he lives and rules, England will be the enemy of your father."

Catherine gazed long on the ambassador and considered his words.

Fuensalida continued in a grave tone, "I am charged with the safety of your father's assets, Your Highness. I also consider the safety of your royal person. Given the present situation, we must acknowledge the possible necessity of your escape to the Continent."

"No," said the princess, immediately, firmly, and with no room for argument. "Absolutely not. I'll die here before abandoning my commitment."

"Were he to betray you, your commitment would be null. All would be lost in any case."

"Nonsense. I've made my promise to the prince and cannot renege, regardless of what his father might do. I am not the sort to do such a thing, and if I were, I could not expect Prince Henry to honor his own commitment. To be sure, I doubt he would want to have such an irresponsible woman for his wife and eventually his queen. He would be right to abandon me, were I to show myself so faithless."

Exasperation made the ambassador's shoulders sag. "Please consider—"

"No. Prince Henry will marry me. I know it as well as I know there is a God in heaven. Any other outcome is unthinkable."

He fell silent, then nodded. "Very well, Your Highness." He made no further argument, and for that Estrella was grateful. Catherine's conviction that the young prince would rescue her like the knight on a white charger of her romantic heart had long been a thread that held together the suite, and yet it had become a very worn thread. Anymore, Estrella wearied of hearing how Prince Henry was so like the caballeros of old, who held honor above all things and who cherished love nearly as much. Of late, Estrella found the subject of love a painful one.

Fuensalida then assured Catherine he would cease the transfer of cash from the country, and wait until action became necessary. It was plain on his face he feared they would all be taken prisoner soon, but he refrained from repeating himself in the face of Catherine's firm refusal to listen. He then made his withdrawal from the chamber. Once he was gone, Catherine said to Fray Diego, "I do not trust him, and I cannot truly believe his story. I must write to my father."

Her confessor said nothing, and there was nobody in the room who did not take note of that.

Estrella said, "When the old king dies and the prince is free to honor his bargain, will there be enough dowry to satisfy him?"

Catherine's lips pressed together, and she looked over at her maid. "I cannot say. Only my prince can answer that. I must trust that he will accept what is offered."

Estrella had her doubts that any man would accept less than what he thought his due, and knew young Henry was no exception.

Another month passed, during which Catherine encouraged her servants to listen well for indications of the king's health, as well as any preparations for war. She elicited reports from Fuensalida concerning his perception of the situation and conferred with Fray Diego regarding the pros and cons as they both saw them. The king's health was failing, and by all accounts his advisors were hard at work to convince him to ally himself with Maximilian of Austria against Ferdinand and Louis. Catherine and her own advisors tensed in the uncertainty, but she held firm. Estrella waited at her mistress's side, fearful and convinced they would soon be fleeing for their lives.

Then in late March came a message for Catherine regarding Estrella. It seemed a merchant from Cornwall wished for the maid's hand.

When the princess informed Estrella of this with the other maids listening, the room went still, and needles poised in their work. Every eye turned to Estrella for her response, but she had none. She could feel herself go cold and imagined her face was now quite pale, but there was nothing to say.

One of the girls said, "I wish someone would ask for my hand. It's not fair; Estrella's had two proposals now, so where's mine?"

Estrella might have replied that the girl's homeliness might be the problem for her, but she kept that opinion to herself in the interest of harmony with her fellow maids. Besides, a proposal from a merchant was nothing for any of them to be proud of.

Catherine said softly to the girl, "God is saving you for better things, Juana." Then she eyed Estrella to see if the older maid had received her meaning. It was plain the princess did not want her to accept the offer, and Estrella knew why. The entire suite was on the verge of mutiny. Francesca's desertion had shaken them all, and talk of simply giving up and returning to Spain was a low and constant murmur among them. If another maid left, the rest might also leave, and with less suitable places to go. Not that a Cornish merchant was remotely suitable. Plainly Catherine's suite was now seen as a source of beautiful women of noble birth who were desperate enough to be claimed by nearly anyone. That in itself was humiliating. Terrifying for Estrella, who was the one everyone now scrutinized.

The princess addressed Estrella, "The offer is not acceptable, you understand that."

The maid nodded but couldn't help replying, "I have no other prospects." An image of Hilsey came, and heartache curled the edges of her soul. She took a deep breath and let it out slowly.

"You will certainly have better ones soon. I assure you, once I am married to Prince Henry, there will be suitors aplenty for you all."

"Perhaps. Perhaps not."

Maria de Salinas said, "You want to live in Cornwall? Have you ever seen the place?"

"No, and neither have you."

"I hear it's not like here. In London the people are backward enough compared to Spain or Italy. But I hear in Cornwall they are appallingly ignorant of civilized ways and live poorly as a rule. You remember Wales, don't you? The countryside is rough and open, and like Wales the customs are crude beyond comprehension."

The prospect did not thrill Estrella. She had long wished for Catherine's marriage, for the sake of returning to the rich and festive life of the royal court. Marriage to a merchant of any stripe would end all possibility of ever wearing stylish clothes or dining in fine surroundings again. Jewels and fur of any kind would be out of the question, and so would silk. But she said, "It cannot be so bad."

"Indeed it can. I wouldn't do it."

"You are not me, are you?"

"My father is a nobleman, like yours. I cannot believe you would shame your family this way, to throw yourself away on someone like that. And in such a place! Cornwall is the end of the earth; they're barely even English there, let alone anything resembling civilized. You would be the helpmate of a man who is really no better than a laborer. You would be asked to sell in a shop at the very least, if not to carry his merchandise for him. I expect you'd be forced to wear boots, and your dresses would be all woolen and rough."

"Honestly, Maria, it's not as if he were a peddler." Then, in horrified realization, she looked to Catherine to confirm the truth of it.

"No," Catherine said, "He's not a peddler. He deals in wool and flax. Aside from his trading, he also has a shop that weaves some fabric. However successful, it's nevertheless quite small."

"See," said Estrella to Maria. "Not a peddler."

"You'll be asked to labor in his shop."

"I won't."

The princess said, "You would consider this offer, then?"

Estrella couldn't reply. She knew she had to consider it, but was loath to say so to Catherine. The princess would be terribly disappointed, and Estrella wearied of all the disappointments of late. But she said, "I would meet him before deciding whether to consider his suit."

And the princess *was* disappointed in that answer. She sighed, and her lips pressed together. Then she nodded and said, "Very well. An introduction will be arranged."

The others giggled at the idea of being formally introduced to a low merchant. Estrella reddened and bent her head over her work.

The meeting was two days later. Though Catherine discouraged it so soon, the fellow wouldn't be put off and hinted he might lose interest entirely if the meeting were delayed too long. Estrella was horribly grateful the princess didn't let him withdraw his proposal, nor forbid the match outright, nor did she drag heels in arranging the meeting. As much as she frowned on this unsuitable marriage, she was entirely evenhanded about it and allowed her maid to make her own decision.

Wallace Cartwright was his name, and he presented himself at the princess's apartments punctually. Estrella wore her least shabby dress to meet him, deeply embarrassed that even this man might see she was on the edge of desperation. For his part, he at least seemed clean though not nearly presentable as a gentleman. Estrella received him in Catherine's presence chamber, ostensibly in the company of only the chamberlain, but with most of the suite listening from doorways. Her ears perked to hear scuffling and whispering among the other maids vying for a vantage point to hear and possibly even see what would transpire.

Cartwright, of course, was as common as his name, and though his clothes were clean and his person groomed, his efforts at appearing gentlemanly ended there. He was very plain indeed. He was near forty and balding rapidly, his graying hair reduced to a straggly fringe that covered his ears and little else. Perhaps he had been handsome once, a decade or so before, but now Estrella's smile for him was tight and not the least sincere. He had a cane, but she noticed he didn't lean on it heavily. Perhaps he carried it more for show than to hold himself vertical, and she could respect that. He did tend to gesture with it, as if it were a weapon he brandished to intimidate. In the man's eye was a spark of arrogance she found distasteful. Inappropriate. It wasn't going to be easy to say yes to him.

Sitting with her hands folded in her lap, she said, "I'm told you're a merchant, Mr. Cartwright."

He gave a sharp, almost perfunctory, nod of his head. "Aye. Turn a good trade in wool and flax, I do. You won't starve, I promise it."

Estrella blanched, for there had been a time when she'd expected far more from a husband than to merely keep her from starvation. She ventured, "Do you have any children?"

"None at all. Never been married." He said it as if he were proud of it. "Too busy with the trade, building my concerns. I have a mill, you understand. I employ fifty men. Sell the fabric in Flanders, you know. I'm a busy man, and no time for a wife."

"Until now."

He shrugged as if the answer to that must be obvious. "I'll need a son to take the business when I'm gone." It crossed Estrella's mind that he'd left it so late he should hope to live long enough for a son to come of age and not lose the business. "Need a wife for that," he added. It further crossed Estrella's mind that he might simply expect his wife to carry on for his son if he were to die before the child reached majority. She shook off that thought and told herself there must be a brother who would accomplish that if necessary.

Then Cartwright said, "I see no reason the wife in question shouldn't be a comely one, and so here I am." He smiled with a mouthful of blackened teeth, many of them missing, and with a spark of something in his eye even less appealing than the arrogance. Estrella imagined a marriage bed with him, and her mind's eye quickly fled it. Better to not think of such things until she had to. There would be ways to avoid the chore once she'd produced an heir, and worrying about it now would only confuse matters in her own mind. Cartwright's looks were not important, and she would be a fool to think they were.

For a short time she continued to ask questions of him. She learned he was pious, and that was in his favor. He even seemed to be a respected member of his church, for he made contributions well beyond the expected tithe. Not in his favor was that his future wife would have to run the mill while he dealt with the larger business of exporting wool and finished goods. She supposed she could learn how to do such a job but was in despair it seemed she would need to.

The future loomed like a dark thing, incomprehensible and gloomy, an impenetrable forest in which she would be lost if she weren't careful. And lurking there, waiting there for her, was this ugly old man as common as dirt, promising nothing but that he would keep her alive.

Unfortunately, that was better than anyone else was promising.

She came away from the meeting still unsure of what to do, feeling weak and a bit shaken. If she refused Cartwright and continued to wait with Catherine for her own knight on a white charger, she might be left with nobody. Indeed, it was possible she would end up a hostage along with the princess if England were to attack Aragon, for she was one of the several Aragonese in the household. On the other hand, Cartwright was clearly beneath her. Marrying him would be marginally better than if she'd agreed to be Hartford's mistress, and only because it would keep her in the grace of God. Her children would be legitimate, but they would also be commoners. As she would be. The thought of what her father would think made her heart ache.

She moved through the next two days deep in thought. It seemed each moment brought a different feeling on what she should do. Each time she began to think it might not be so terrible a life to be married to a successful merchant, another thought came to remind her it would be a laborer's life. That she would never again attend festive occasions as anyone but an onlooker, that she would be expected to cook and clean, that she would wear the same woolens year after year, new dresses looking exactly the same as the old. No more witty repartee, no more association with well-read friends. In short, she would no longer be around people who thought and behaved as she did. Her life would be among people even more strange to her than the English courtiers she'd known in London. And once these thoughts paraded through her mind and nearly convinced her to refuse the suit, the one hard truth came behind them, and she couldn't deny that this was surely the best prospect she was ever going to get.

After three days of this pondering, Catherine asked her to

come sit by her so they could talk quietly. Estrella came and settled onto a bench near the princess.

Catherine took her hand between both of hers. "Lita, I know you've been thinking hard about what your course should be regarding Wallace Cartwright."

The maid nodded. Her throat tightened as the weight of her worries closed in on her. She wanted to run away from there, to not have to decide and not have to bear the consequences of either unacceptable choice offered her.

"I know you've been hurt by other men."

A surge of alarm coursed to her toes. *Men.* Did the princess know about Hartford? That would be mortifying. Her cheeks warmed, and the redness spread down her neck to her chest.

But without delving into seamy details, Catherine continued, "I know your faith in the future is crumbling, as battered as it's been. I can understand your feelings."

"With all respect, Your Highness, I cannot believe you truly understand my position. Unless someone less suitable than the Prince of Wales has offered to make you his own. A mule skinner, perhaps?"

The princess blinked at that, then she recovered and said, "A point well taken. To be sure, my choices are less ambiguous than yours. You need to decide whether you will regret choosing a life you've never even seen. You don't know what it would be like to be the wife of a merchant. You've never known a merchant, nor a merchant's wife. You've never seen how they live."

"I've heard."

"I have, as well. I understand they work from dawn till dark and sometimes after. They come in contact with all sorts of people who are not gentlefolk. Were you to marry this man, you would be expected to rise before dawn to care for him and your children, then you would spend your day at the work of the mill among men you would never have even spoken to as a gentlewoman. And you should know, Lita, that such men who work in places like that do not respect gentility. We would like to think all the common men adore and respect the nobility, but that would be a mistake. As a merchant's wife you would surely find yourself among many people who will sneer at you for your fall, and will treat you badly for it."

Estrella hadn't thought of that, and her heart sank further. "But Your Highness, I fear there is no choice. I'm already too old to have any prospects, even if I return to Spain. And it's true that I have been hurt by other men." If it became common knowledge she was no longer a virgin, possibly even Cartwright would refuse her.

Catherine lowered her voice until she was barely audible. "If you choose to accept Cartwright, will there be trouble if he asks for a physical examination?"

There it was. Estrella couldn't lie to Catherine. Of all the people Estrella knew, the princess valued truth more than any other. The maid couldn't reply, and only hung her head. She stared at her fingers knotted together on her lap.

Catherine took her answer and said, "Then I assure you there will be none. If you accept him, he will be required to accept you without a fuss of any sort. I promise it."

Estrella looked up, and though she saw disappointment, she also saw that she was not condemned by her mistress. Fresh tears of gratitude rose. "I fear I should be glad for this opportunity to not spend my life an unmarried maid, for I can no longer imagine anyone else wanting to marry me." Then the tears spilled, and the hopelessness of it all crumbled her resolve not to cry. Blubbering like a child and hating herself, she said, "I don't know what to do."

Catherine squeezed her hand. "Lita, look into your heart, and you will know the right course. I think your heart knows this man is wrong for you. I also think God wants better for you than what the merchant offers. If Wallace Cartwright were the man you were destined to marry, you would know it. There would be no doubt." Estrella thought of how sure she'd been she would marry Piers Hilsey, and it sickened her.

But the princess continued, "These years I've spent anticipating marriage to Henry, there has been no doubt in my mind we were meant to be together. Each moment I've spent with him, though they've been few, has convinced me we are two halves of the same soul. Even when I was married to Arthur I knew it was wrong. I knew he was not my true husband, and that is why I never pressed to consummate the marriage." Estrella had never guessed this. She'd always assumed, as everyone else had, that Catherine and Arthur had never shared the marriage bed because of the prince's illness. Her astonishment must have shown on her face, for Catherine nodded. "Indeed. I simply knew in my heart I was not meant to spend my life with Arthur. It was Henry all along."

"Even when he was so young?"

Catherine shrugged, appearing the young girl once again, a tiny smile on her lips as she remembered. "He was a delightful child, and though I didn't know then we would be married, I did know he would grow up to be a fine man. And he is. I know in my heart he will be a wonderful husband and a great king, and God always meant for me to be his queen. There is no doubt of it."

For the first time in years, Estrella thought it might be true.

Catherine's conviction swayed her simply for its strength. She said nothing, but nodded.

"One other thing I hope you'll consider as you ponder your choice," continued Catherine. "In your indecision, if all other things are equal in your mind, I hope you'll consider what God wants for *all* of us. If you stand fast with us, you'll be an example for all the others. They're as afraid as you are, and they have more reason to be, because some have had no offers at all. If you were to show your courage and your faith in a future that does not include the forfeiture of your nobility, you will ease the fears of every maid. Succumb to your own fright, and the suite may panic. They may make decisions they will later regret. You have an opportunity to help your friends."

"And help you keep your household together."

The princess shook her head. "I will survive this in any case. It's not for myself I tell you this. My own course is clear, and I will take it regardless of who joins me. It is for the sake of the maids who are now looking to you to show them their path. It's your responsibility."

Estrella looked at her mistress through the blur of tears and pressed a hand to her mouth. Then she said, "What influence could my actions have? Nobody listens to me."

"Of course they do, Lita. Particularly the younger ones. They look to you because they know how good you are and how beautiful you are in your heart. How filled with grace. They trust that you will decide what's right, and they will follow your example."

"Truly?"

"Yes."

As Estrella considered that, she began to see what Catherine meant. The confusion began to fall away, and a clear path showed itself. For the sake of the others she'd lived with for so long, she couldn't accept the proposal. And as she considered that, she realized how much she did not want to marry Wallace Cartwright. The life he offered would be one of misery for herself and everyone else involved, for she was unsuited to it entirely. God couldn't expect her to become something other than what He'd made her. The pressure to marry dissolved like a sugar confection in the rain, and she was left with one clear choice. She would refuse him and wait with the others. An enormous sigh escaped her, and she nodded.

Eighteen

❧

N OT more than a fortnight after Estrella declined Wallace Cartwright's proposal, the maids were at supper, tense and quiet as always, for there was little to say anymore. A pall had settled over everyone, in which the anticipation of waiting for one shoe to drop had dulled, and the senses become so worn that even the very air seemed rotted. Some days Estrella thought one more whiff of horses from below would send her into screaming madness. Tonight she hadn't much appetite, and hadn't for weeks.

Then into the silence a bell intruded, tolling out across London in a long, low, doleful death knell. Everyone in the room paused, stock still, and listened. For the moment it seemed the entire world was in suspension. Nobody dared breathe, for the news was too fragile. Too dire, and speaking of it might make it not so.

Then Estrella's mind flew. Someone was dead. Someone

important was dead. A member of the royal family. Could it be the king? Though the world was cruel and anyone might die without warning, old Henry had been quite ill for some time; he was the most likely to have expired. Hope rose, and with it the question whether it was a sin to hope the king was dead. Not that she would dare ask, since too much speculation on the death of the king was never taken well by His Majesty. But what if it were the king for whom the bell tolled? Did she dare hope even to herself?

She looked around, and saw by the wide eyes about the table the others were thinking the same thing. Was the king dead? If so, what would happen next? What would the new king do? Their futures hung in the balance.

Catherine gestured to her chamberlain. "Find out," was all she said, then she returned her attention to her meal as if the question burning in everyone's minds was unimportant. But Estrella could see on her flushed face she was excited and pleased by the turn. The princess didn't seem to have much thought for any possibility but that the king was dead and the new monarch would make her his queen. The belief sparkled in her eyes, and she only made a show of eating the rest of her supper. She picked at it and tore the meat apart with her fingers while listening to the maids chatter about the bell, speculating on who it might be other than the king.

The wait for news seemed appallingly long. The messenger sent by the chamberlain returned late that evening, and all he'd been able to learn was that it was indeed old King Henry who had died. A silence fell over the Spanish household, and nobody was eager to express what they felt. It would be unseemly to rejoice too visibly, and though the apartments were far from the center of court life they all chose discretion that evening. Nobody would be able to report against them to the royal family.

On the other hand, none of the Spanish household was able to produce even hollow words of regret for His Majesty's passing. The old *perro sucio* had held them all as hostages for seven years; there was good reason to hate him. And since nobody was willing to speak against him, silence was the only middle ground.

The next morning all the girls found excuses to leave the apartments. Estrella herself went out to the palace proper with Maria de Salinas, to wander as near to the king's presence chamber as they could get. Everyone in the residence was curious to know what might happen, and crowds of nobility milled about, everyone talking but very few with any real information to share. The Spanish girls went ignored, for nobody knew yet what would happen to them and being seen talking to one wasn't a good idea until their status was confirmed.

Standing in the courtyard, doing their best to look like casual passersby, the two women paused to hear a commotion near the royal apartments. The crowd then parted to let through the Prince of Wales and his retinue. No, Estrella mentally corrected herself. He was the new king. Horses were being brought for them, and the tall, strapping young man strode across the courtyard like the king he now was. His visage showed a gravity rare in him, for his father had died only the day before, and there was serious business at hand, but there was no overt grief. His grip on the throne needed to be strong. His stride was brisk, and the ends of his reddish-blond hair lifted as he walked, shining in the spring sunshine. He mounted his horse with an air of command even more powerful than Estrella had seen in him in the mews the September before, and he rode off from the palace at a gallop with his retinue.

Maria spotted Fuensalida emerging from the residence and took Estrella's hand to go to him. "Ambassador, where is he going?"

The ambassador's voice lowered, and he said, "To the Tower. He has much business to conduct today."

"Will he marry Catherine?"

The ambassador glanced at the two young women, drew himself up straight in a stance that, with his lips pressed together and his shoulders tight, suggested he didn't think much of the prospect. He glanced at them again, as if hesitant to bother with the women, but said, "I'm told he was freed by his father to marry whomever he chose, but I'm also told he is unlikely to marry his brother's widow. Given his declaration several years ago that he wouldn't do it, I'm afraid I must agree with my source."

Estrella stared off in the direction the new king had taken and wished she could be a fly to perch on young Henry's hat today.

The Spanish suite waited some more. They waited until evening after supper, when a member of Henry's council arrived at the rooms over the stables to summon the princess. It was the Bishop of Durham, Thomas Ruthall. She was to present herself to the new king at the earliest opportunity in the morning. The young man, apparently, was impatient to confer with his betrothed on the subject of their wedding day and her subsequent coronation.

Some of the girls reacted with a gasp, and Estrella found herself swallowing one herself. For a moment she felt faint with joy, and the room swayed. Then she closed her eyes, took a deep breath, and let it out slowly.

Catherine, however, gave not so much as a blink as she acknowledged the message and asked to have her fondest greetings relayed to Henry, saying that she would hardly sleep that night for anticipation of seeing him in the morning. The council member and his assistants went on their way, and only then did the household dissolve in joyous chatter and talk. The maids gathered on Catherine, each wanting to go with her to the meeting and each wondering when they would move to quarters more suitable to their new stations. Catherine's reply was characteristic: she did not know when or where Henry would send them, but she was certain the quarters would be suitable, and they would be made available as soon as could be reasonably expected. Meanwhile, they would be patient. As always.

The maids then dispersed to ready for the morning. Instead of going to her bedchamber where Maria de Salinas was in charge of working out the princess's wardrobe for the meeting, Catherine sat in a chair by the fire and stared into it. Estrella saw her shoulders slump, and her head tilted to the side in a lost stare. Her eyes glistened, and a moment later a tear fell. Estrella went to her and knelt beside her.

"Your Highness. What is the matter?"

The princess looked into her face and took her hand. "I knew it," she said. "God wanted this for me. I never doubted it." A smile curled the corners of Catherine's mouth. "I always knew Henry would not disappoint me. He is a good man and knows what is right. He would never forsake me, but has rescued me just as I knew he would."

Estrella squeezed the princess's hand. "You were right about him."

"He's my champion." And for a moment Catherine was like a little girl, with hiccupping tears of joy. She dabbed at an eye and smiled. "A true and honorable knight."

The next morning, Catherine chose her closest friends and most trusted advisors to accompany her to the meeting with Henry. They all wore their least shabby clothing, many of them having been up late the night before with their needles, repairing loosened seams and placing fresh embroidery over frayed spots. Every jewel left to the women was on display. Estrella, wearing the ruby given her by John Cranach, accompanied her mistress with her heart pounding for fear of appearing as down at the heels as they actually were. But also her heart pounded with excitement that there would be new dresses soon, and they would be of silk and furs.

The princess and her escort of maids and advisors were admitted to the king's privy chamber. Henry awaited, standing by the hearth when she was announced walking past clusters of intensely interested onlookers. Heads turned constantly, everyone alert to know who was going where and what the status of each seemed to be. Some wore tight smiles of victory and others wide eyes of apprehension. Estrella herself glanced around at the courtiers in the room and saw several familiar faces. Some were men who had been close to the old king, but not very many. Though it seemed the new king was taking care to make a smooth transition and was keeping the best of his father's advisors, most of the men in the room today were younger than the council of Henry VII.

With a frisson of alarm, Estrella spotted the Earl of Hartford amid a cluster off to her left, but he didn't seem to notice her. His gaze was hard on Henry, and he didn't even seem to see Princess Catherine, though she was the center of everyone else's attention. Estrella looked away and focused on Henry as well. She drew a deep breath and let it out slowly to steady herself. Hilsey was no longer important. She was now maid to the woman who would soon be queen.

Catherine was the focus of Henry's attention. The smile on his face as he stepped toward the princess was wide and sunny. Fairly boyish, for he was still only eighteen years old and had led a sheltered life. The roses in his cheeks glowed, and his eyes drank her in with his joy. "My bride!"

"My betrothed," said Catherine, and she curtsied so deeply she seemed to sit on the floor, her skirts pooled around her. Her own cheeks glowed, and the room seemed filled with the happiness of the couple. Estrella had never seen a pair so pleased to be betrothed to each other.

Standing near now, Henry lowered his voice so only those nearest could hear. He said, "I've long awaited this day."

"As have I," replied the princess. Estrella nearly laughed at the gross understatement, but didn't dare even cough.

"You must dine with us this evening. Tell me of your wishes for the wedding. Also, have your chamberlain send a report of your needs to my wardrobe. We will have dresses on loan from my sister and her maids for you until your household can be brought once again to the standard you deserve. Immediately you will be moved to more suitable apartments, which are being made ready even now."

Catherine seemed surprised and said, "Have the details of the agreement been worked out with Fuensalida, then?"

Henry looked over at Bishop Ruthall, who shrugged and said, "We've not heard from the ambassador."

The princess's lips pressed together, and she started to speak, but Henry interrupted her. "No matter. There will be no more obstacles. The terms will be entirely pleasing to him and to your father, and we will be married in good order."

With that, he reached for her hand, knelt, and kissed the back of it. Then, with great tenderness, he turned it over to kiss the palm. He looked up at his future queen with eyes as deep as any Estrella had ever seen, and for a moment she saw the legendary Arthur. A true and honorable knight with stalwart heart and noble mind. Catherine had been right from the start.

Nineteen

1535

HEARING any news at all was a two-edged sword during Catherine's time at Kimbolton. Chapuys continued to contact her through discreet means. Princess Mary continued to live, and that was a relief to her mother, but along with the good news came reports of unrest among the peasantry. Crops failed that year. Land was given over to sheep, and people were turned off their fields and evicted from their homes. Suddenly destitute folk roamed the countryside, and belief grew strong that the bad crops were God's punishment of the kingdom for having put aside its queen.

The dispatches from the ambassador were read in Catherine's bedchamber, in the company of only Estrella, before Catherine would show them abroad to her advisors and discuss their content. Over the years the older maid had learned the queen liked to think before acting, and Estrella was the one she often spoke to first about something she intended to bring up to those who would act on the information. Estrella was a blank wall from which to sound things, and that was all right because it meant the queen felt she was a safe wall as well. That was a trust hard to come by, and it was a good purpose to have in this world.

One morning in late fall, while dressing, Catherine received and read aloud a clandestine message from the ambassador regarding the unrest among the ruling class. She waved off Estrella who held her overdress for her, and sat on the edge of her bed. Estrella stood by with the garment and listened.

"He still wants rebellion," said Catherine. "He's made that clear since he came to England. Once again he's urging a rescue of Mary from that plotting concubine, and to secure my safety as well, but such a rescue could only have an effect if accompanied by an uprising of the disaffected nobility. Were Mary and I to escape to the Continent, Henry would only think well of it, for he would far rather defend himself against Charles than to harm me or our daughter. He knows I could leave this place at will, if leaving it would suit my own purposes. It's the unrest among his subjects that frightens him, and with encouragement from Chapuys he thinks I stay in order to rally the unhappy nobles."

"Why do we not leave, then, and put Henry's mind at ease as well as take Mary to safety?"

There was a sense of weariness in the queen's reply, and she rested the letter held in both hands in her lap. "As I've said before, I cannot disobey my husband even when his commands are contrary to what is best for him. Also, were we to have sanctuary with Charles, my nephew would be forced into war with Henry. Even at the cost of the lives of my daughter and myself, I cannot countenance war and won't allow Chapuys to foment rebellion."

"You may find there is no way to prevent one. The English nobility are a contentious lot, particularly where their own well-being and future prospects are concerned. Not to mention their religion. Many are as disturbed by the changes in the Church as you are."

"And you are not?"

Estrella blushed. "Of course, Your Majesty. But you are so much better an example for discussion than my poor grace. I'm afraid I am not as good a Christian as you are, though I try."

"It's all God asks, Lita."

"Yes, Your Majesty." Estrella quickly brought the conversation back around to the English nobles and away from her own lack of grace. "And the nobles look to you as well. They have strong opinions about who should be queen. And who should be king, as well. Henry is not making himself well loved with his campaign against the religious houses. Neither is that Boleyn woman the sort they want at his side."

"It is well they should want her away." A sharpness came into Catherine's voice at mention of her former maid. "She is not the sort anyone should want in the vicinity, and never mind exerting any influence over the king. She is a tool of the devil, and her evil is destroying Henry's soul. For that alone she must be punished by God. I don't imagine she will ever bear a son. That will be her punishment, I'm certain."

Estrella had no idea how Catherine could be so sure as she sounded, but believed her. The queen had never been wrong about anything where the will of God was concerned.

The queen continued, "My Henry will come to see that one day."

The maid suppressed a sigh of impatience but said, "Why do you think Henry is so innocent of these things?"

"Not innocent. Helpless. The evil influence has his soul imprisoned. The Great Whore has exerted herself on him, seduced him into her circle, and he cannot see how terrible are the things he is doing. And the longer he goes without understanding, the more damage he will suffer. He was not always like this, Lita. Surely you remember."

Estrella thought back, but memory was dim. Henry had always been headstrong and filled with self-interest, and all she saw now was how eager he must have been to be led astray by a woman with no discernible moral standards. "How was he different?"

"Do you not remember him on the death of his father? For so long we'd been at the mercy of the old king. We'd been treated as prisoners, nearly starved, kept apart from the life due people of our station. Old King Henry never wished for me to marry his son and only kept us in England to punish my father."

Estrella's memory sparked, but what she remembered was that those were the things she and Maria and Francesca had been telling Catherine all along when they had expected to be sent back to Spain.

Catherine continued, "But my Henry would not acquiesce to the wishes of his father. He knew what was right in the eyes of God, that he should honor his promise to me. At the time, he was helpless to defy the king, and once he was freed of evil influence, he saw the correct path and took it. He shook off those who would have urged him to marry Eleanor and demonstrated to the world he was the good and true knight I'd always known he was." A soft smile came to her face. "And he was a good king until she seduced him. You know he was a good king."

What Estrella knew was that Henry had never been a particularly good king, but he'd had good advisors before the advent of those currently of his court. And Catherine had been an excellent queen for him. But Estrella thought it best to humor her mistress on this point, for the queen had always been one to credit her husband for every success and his advisors for every failure. She nodded. "He was a very handsome knight. It was almost as if you'd married for love." That much was true. Catherine had always loved Henry.

The glow struggling to Catherine's pale and weary cheeks made clear the queen was even now in love with her knight. "Very much so. We were most fortunate. So happy those first years." Catherine's voice drifted off on a soft cloud of remembrance. "Such a gentleman, and so affectionate. And even after he began to take mistresses he held me in the same regard as ever before."

"Until recently."

"It's that whore. She's seduced him and stolen his will. A siren, and he's steering a course into a rocky shore."

"He should have secured himself to the mast, then, before going near her."

Catherine chuckled. "Indeed. She would be the downfall of England, were I to acquiesce to his demands. So I dare not indulge his folly, and that is why I cannot step aside as he wishes." Her voice turned serious. "But I fear that rocky shore will turn out to be a rebellion. Perhaps to result in overthrow of the Crown, and that would be the most terrible of circumstances."

Estrella cast a nervous glance at the shut and bolted door of the chamber, though she knew none of the king's guard could hear the queen this deep inside her sanctum/prison. Force of habit, for speaking of overthrow was the very thing Henry would love to prove of Catherine, to give him an excuse to execute her.

The queen read further in the missive from Chapuys, and nodded. "See, here, he hints that Henry has begun to weary of his concubine. She has so enraged his advisors, he's begun to see what a disadvantage she is to him."

"Has he a new mistress?"

Catherine seemed crestfallen by the suggestion but examined the letter for an answer. "He doesn't say, but I expect there must be one. Otherwise he would have mounted his charger and ridden straight for this castle to reclaim me."

Estrella tried to picture the fat, aging king riding to rescue his queen once again, and couldn't make the image come. Whatever sort of king—or even man—he was anymore, he was certainly no longer the dashing young knight of Catherine's dreams. "No, I fear there must be yet another woman in the mix."

The queen was silent for a moment, then sighed as if resigned to the fact and looked around the room. There had been other mistresses who had not mattered to Henry. Perhaps she hoped the new woman was one of those. "Well, then, let me finish my toilet and proceed with my day. I can't imagine there is much to be done about this letter, but perhaps my advisors will have some ideas of where to proceed from here." She rose with some difficulty, and Estrella hurried to help her into the rest of her clothing.

An entreaty to the pope was sent, asking for excommunication of Henry, but the measure failed. Nobody was surprised at that, after all the foot-dragging His Holiness had done in the matter all along. All remedies seemed too little and too late, and Catherine's reluctance to let men wage war in her name kept her from the only avenue that might have restored her freedom and safety while keeping her honor. And as the months of 1535 came to an end, so did Catherine's health. By the new year she was seriously ill and bedridden, and her advisors sent for Ambassador Chapuys to see her one last time.

He arrived two days later, bearing a passport from the king. Apparently Henry no longer feared his dying wife. As soon as Chapuys entered the residence, Catherine's entire suite was assembled for a formal meeting in the queen's chamber. She sat up in her bed, propped by every available pillow, wasted and pale, and greeted the ambassador with all the dignity remaining to her. Through the pain of her illness could still be seen her pleasure at seeing her old friend after so much time kept apart. With the suite arranged all around and watching, he knelt by her bed as best he could on aging knees. The chamber was not large by royal standards, and the onlookers stood close. They listened in on the conversation between the queen and the ambassador, who spoke clearly for their audience. Estrella knew it was merely for show. Nothing of consequence would be said here.

Thereafter, throughout Chapuys's stay, the two met out of earshot for long, private talks. The maids heard little of what was said, and most of them would not have understood much of what they heard had they listened. But Estrella, in her close attendance, caught some of the talk and knew enough of the circumstance to understand.

While preparing a drink of mulled wine for the queen, she overheard Catherine asking Chapuys whether she bore guilt for the heresy rampant in England. It was such a surprise to hear, Estrella paused in her task to listen. Catherine had never before expressed the slightest doubt about the choices she'd made in her life.

"In following God's law and obeying my husband," said the queen slowly and with great care in choosing her words, "have I doomed the poor souls of my subjects to perdition?" She smoothed the coverlet at her waist, drawing her fingers along the edge and to the side. "By not going to war against Henry, and so losing my cause, did I choose the wrong course?" Now she looked Chapuys in the eye, with a gaze of deep sadness. "Would it have been less of a sin to fight than it was to ultimately lose the soul of the kingdom?" For the first time ever, Estrella saw doubt in her queen's demeanor. It tore her heart to see Catherine so close to death and so afraid of having chosen the wrong course.

But Chapuys's reply seemed to allay that fear, for he told her that no evil was irredeemable. There would be other ways to retrieve lost souls, and other people charged with the responsibility. She had done what she could and had obeyed the will of God to the best of her ability, and that was all that could be expected of her, for it was not for one woman—even a queen—to save the entire world. Estrella was reminded of Catherine's words to her whenever she felt unsure of her own grace, and it calmed her. His words seemed to calm Catherine as well, and Estrella moved away to let the two special friends continue their talk.

While the ambassador was still at Kimbolton, a woman arrived late one evening to clamor at the gatehouse to be let in. She had arrived muddy and cold, and when the guard declined to admit her to the residence she was adamant and would not be put off. Her driver made loud enough fuss to draw attention from the queen's apartments, and Estrella went with those who gathered at the windows to see the spectacle below in the diminishing evening light. The driver shouted, and a few exclamations were heard from the carriage as well. Estrella smiled; the woman sounded Spanish. The night was dark, the road dangerous, she would not go any farther, and if the guard forced her onward there would be devilish consequences to be paid; she would see to it. The king would hear of it, she promised, and that would be most regrettable for anyone reported to have inconvenienced the countess. Now Estrella was certain she knew who the visitor was in the carriage. The guard allowed her entrance, and the conveyance trundled into the bailey.

Estrella hurried to the stairwell and stood at the top to receive her old friend, Maria de Salinas, the Dowager Countess of Willoughby. It was a bittersweet reunion for Estrella, and she embraced her wilted and muddy friend in the corridor. "You've come in time," said Estrella.

"Ah, Lita, I'm so glad you have stayed with her!" She removed her cloak and brushed it out as well as she could without beating it too much.

"It's good you are here as well, my friend. How long are you here?"

Maria cast a disgusted glance back toward the gatehouse guard. "They expect me to leave in the morning, but they do not know I will never be moved. I'll be here until they take Catherine from this place." Estrella understood her to mean until they removed the queen's body for burial. Maria asked as they proceeded through the presence chamber and toward the bedchamber, "How does she today?"

"She's had a rally and will be able to speak to you. I'm afraid she won't last long, however. Resisting Henry these past seven years has taken so much from her, the strength is quite wrung out. And resisting Chapuys, as well. With all his urgings for rebellion, he's quite worn her down. Even now I believe he might be trying to convince her to call for an uprising after her death."

Maria made a clucking noise of disgust and lowered her voice to a whisper. "You don't suppose he would attempt to use her name after she's gone in defiance of her wishes?"

"No, I don't think so." But Estrella had not thought of that. "I shouldn't think he would go so far. He's more wise than to risk contradiction from those of us who knew her and knew she would never condone it."

"Good." Maria nodded. "Now, let me in to see her. Quickly, for I wouldn't have her leave the earth while I fuss about, making myself presentable."

The two entered the bedchamber, where the queen was resting as if asleep. But the rustling of dresses roused her, and her eyes opened to spark with joy at the sight of her favorite maid. She held out her hand, and Maria took it. Estrella hung back, and tears stung her eyes at the sight of this rare happiness in her mistress. Maria sat on the edge of the bed with Catherine's frail hands inside hers. They talked long and quietly, in a low murmur that Estrella didn't even try to decipher. She only moved about the room, straightening and arranging things that were already in their places. Catherine's voice grew stronger as they spoke, and her spirits rose. Perhaps their mistress would last another few days she might not have had otherwise.

Thereafter Maria and Estrella stayed by the bedside day and night, taking turns to sleep in those final hours. Others came and went, but the two old friends never left for two more days.

Finally, after receiving extreme unction from her confessor

and with much prayer for Mary, Henry, and the people of England, the queen closed her eyes for the last time.

Estrella sat with Maria in the ensuing silence, surrounded by all who were left of Catherine's diminished circle, and felt the great soul leave the room. An emptiness came, a loneliness that made her ache for the days when as a girl Catherine could fill a room with joy and as a queen she could fill it with love.

SEVERAL months later, Estrella stood in the yard of the Tower of London, among a crowd of people who in their restless milling about made the soft ground treacherous with mud holes. She held her skirts to keep them from dragging, but there was really nothing for it. Her hems were a disaster and her slippers hopeless. But it was no matter; this day was an important one, and she would not miss it for the sake of her clothing. Few cared where they stood so long as they could see the block, and Estrella was required to fight to claim a spot that wasn't in a throughway or too far from the center of the yard for a satisfying look.

They'd all come to see the execution. The Great Whore was about to receive her just punishment. Tension was high among the spectators, and people craned their necks to see all they could, to catch a glimpse of the woman the entire kingdom and most of the Continent had been talking about for over a decade. The woman who had nearly brought them all to armed conflict with each other and with the Holy Roman Emperor, who had brought her entire family to a power that was far more readily lost and already on the wane, who had wagered her entire life on the gamble of her child's gender and lost.

Many in the crowd were eager to see what sort of horns grew from her head, for they were convinced she was a tool of the devil and had heard she was deformed for it. Others knew there would be no horns, for executions had been common in recent years, of people who were widely known as martyrs to their religion. There had been plenty of opportunity for the people of England to see that condemnation by the crown meant little in the eyes of God. Most who died did so as ordinarily as anyone else, and even the truly evil did not seem it anymore. When a condemned man or woman approached the block or the scaffold, the only difference between one and another was whether the fear of death and pain was overcome. They either balked or they went gracefully, and that was the standard by which the crowd judged an execution.

Estrella did not have a good vantage from which to watch, for her status with the Crown had been severely impaired during her recent service with Catherine. But she could see the headsman and the block, and so was satisfied with her position. The executioner stood waiting, wearing a black hood over his head and a suit of black clothing. He was a muscular fellow, and strangely relaxed for a man about to kill. He stood with his sword ready, its tip resting easily on the boards at his feet. Everyone knew who he was; he'd been brought from the Continent, a swordsman skilled at this work. He was as calm and still as the curious crowd was not.

Though the thrust of Boleyn's conviction was treason, the woman was to escape a traitor's death, and Estrella reckoned that also was justice. A hard knot of confusion clutched her chest in spite of her clear anger and knowledge that the condemned deserved death. It had been years since she'd seen the woman to be killed on that block, and she had never liked her, but there was a strong apprehension at this event. She was about to watch a woman die, and at the hands of her own husband. A queen executed by a king. Regardless of how much the evil Boleyn might deserve this, and how hated she was by the onlookers, particularly Estrella herself, there was nevertheless a tension over what they were all about to witness. She wondered how she would feel about it after Anne was dead. Would it be a sin to rejoice? To gloat that this execution was made possible by the far more natural death of Catherine? Knowing that Anne would have survived as long as Henry's first queen was alive to return to her place by his side would have made it easy to feel vengeful today. But Estrella resisted the thought, for she deemed it unseemly. Revenge wasn't for her; it was God's place to judge Anne Boleyn. So Estrella pushed her thoughts away from the temptation to gloat and waited patiently for the appearance of the condemned.

Instead she thought about Henry and his reaction to Catherine's passing. He'd certainly gloated. Stories circulated all through the peerage about the crowing he'd indulged in at the news. Hearing about it made Estrella heartsick. He'd behaved as if Catherine had been the one to deliberately give him trouble. As if she'd tricked him into the marriage and had gone out of her way to cause unrest over his attempts at dissolution, when she'd never done anything but obey him and follow the law. And had in fact done everything she could to quell the unrest caused by his selfish ways. Estrella considered how Henry had changed since the day he rescued Catherine from her impoverished life, and knew he was not the hero he'd once been. Nor had he been for a very long time.

But there had been other heroes, she realized. The men who had come to Catherine's aid in recent years were many. John Fisher and Thomas More had stood by their queen— given their lives for her and for their principles. Stalwart

Thomas Abell had risked everything and now occupied a nearby cell in this very Tower for his championship of the queen. By all accounts, Abell was not expected to ever see freedom again. There was the interpreter Montoya, who had contributed to the cause in his own inimitable way and as bravely as anyone. Chapuys himself, who had struggled tirelessly in his efforts to restore the dignity and position of the queen who had outlived her usefulness to both her husband and her nephew. The faithful Francisco Felipez, who had outrun assassins and who had risked his life more than once to deliver messages for his queen. Each of these men had championed Catherine as surely as if she had given each a kerchief or ribbon to tie to his armor before charging into battle. Not one knight, but many. Few women could claim so much adoration from chivalric men. Few real princesses could claim that. Queen Catherine of England had so lived by her principles that she had become inseparable from them. To defend the Church was to defend her. To attack her was to attack the Church.

Henry surely realized her importance to his subjects. The funeral he'd provided for his first wife had been lavish, in keeping with all due a Dowager Princess of Wales, though he had balked at allowing honors due a queen, even though he'd won the struggle against her by outlasting her. Estrella herself had participated in the ceremony, as part of the long train of black-clad ladies following the casket to Petersborough. Chapuys was not in attendance and made it clear to all who would listen he stayed away because Catherine would not be buried as befitting a queen. Cisco had been nowhere to be found, either, possibly for the same reason. Estrella herself had qualms but agreed to be part of the ceremony because it was one last thing she could do for her queen and her friend with whom

she'd shared so much joy and heartbreak over so many decades. Estrella had never known anyone else so firm in grace
as Catherine. Wistfully she considered her own less uplifted
state and knew her only hope was that God was as merciful as
they said.

She thought about the men in her own life and of how little adoration she'd herself won. Other than the lukewarm attention of Piers Hilsey, there had been nobody she could call
"champion." That thought was disheartening enough to tinge
her soul with darkness. A sigh escaped her, and she glanced
around to know if anyone had heard her melancholy.

"Lita! Estrella, there you are!" The voice was familiar, and
in Spanish. She looked up to find Cisco Felipez nearby in the
crowd, making his way toward her. "Lita!"

She held out her hand as if ready to pull him from the sea
of people milling about them. He did grasp it as he drew near,
then gave a small bow within the constraints of space and
touched his lips to her gloved knuckles. "Cisco, so good to see
you. I was just thinking about you."

A wide grin crossed his craggy face. "Cursing my name, no
doubt."

Estrella smiled. "You know better. I must say I didn't expect
to see you here today."

"I would not miss this for my life," he said, a bitter edge to
his voice. The years had not mellowed him much, but rather
had made him hard toward the world and those who ruled it.
He turned to Estrella with a tight smile and said, "I knew you
would be here as well. Isabel is with her husband, off near the
gate." He indicated with a thrust of his chin. "We all deserve
our revenge."

Estrella opened her mouth to protest the unchristian sentiment but realized he was right. She couldn't deny the part of

her that relished the justice to be done here today. So she said nothing.

He said, "Do you suppose she'll bawl?"

Estrella gave that a bit of thought, then said, "I think she'll go with nary a whimper. She's a tough bit of hide, that one." At once an insult and a compliment for Anne, and fitting for that, given Estrella's suddenly mixed feelings about the whole affair.

"Tough enough with the king burrowing beneath her skirts. But now, I think she will disgrace herself. The woman is an irredeemable coward. I wish she would show herself; I would like to see the spectacle." Now the hatred was thick in Cisco's voice.

"We're about to learn the truth, I think." She nodded toward a disturbance in the gathered crowd. Those standing in the yard near the exit from the quarters were moving aside to make way for the condemned and her escort. Estrella was too short to see anything other than a shifting of bodies, which she didn't exactly see but rather sensed in the movement of people around her. "What do you see?" she asked. "What is happening?"

Cisco grunted, then said, "She's carrying herself rather well in fact and appears to need no help. Pale, but otherwise in command of herself." He watched her for a moment, then added sotto voce, "She should trip and fall in the mud."

"Oh, come, Cisco. You cannot hate her so much."

"I can, and I do. And I shall for all my life. The evil she has wrought brought destruction to many good men. And to a good queen. She drew astray a king who otherwise might have done well for his people, and she nearly brought this country to insurrection. 'Tis not my country, to be sure, but for the English this woman has done nothing but evil. And her most unforgivable evil was to the Church. God is punishing her for it, and she will burn for eternity. She goes to her judgment, and I know it must be a harsh one."

"Well, whether it will be or not is not for us to say. Nor even know, I think, for the damned never seem to come back to tell us of their punishment. In any case," she nodded toward the progression of the condemned woman, which she could only follow by the movement of heads in the crowd, "she does seem to be keeping her dignity." Estrella didn't know whether she should be pleased or disappointed at that. Something in her rather wished the woman would collapse in a disgraceful display, kicking and shouting like a lunatic. Perhaps she still would, but it was unlikely. Estrella should have known Anne Boleyn would not crumble.

Finally she saw the condemned as she mounted to the block. As Boleyn reached the platform, she turned to look out over one of the towers as if she'd heard something. Or was searching for someone. But whatever it was she sought she didn't seem to find it, and after a moment of alertness, she turned back toward the headsman without a change of expression.

The hair rose on Estrella's arms, for in a stunning moment of clarity she fully understood the utter finality of what was about to happen to this woman. She grasped the edges of her cloak and hugged herself in it as the chill ran through her. She tried to imagine how it might feel to have one's head severed from one's body, and couldn't. It certainly could never happen to her. It would be impossible to believe anything else. She would never have done the things that had brought Boleyn to this, no matter what the stakes. She had to believe that.

Boleyn faced the crowd with far more grace than she'd ever displayed in Henry's court, pale but with a calm demeanor. After a short speech absolving all but herself for this turn of events, the condemned removed her cloak, handed it off to one of her escort, and knelt before the block.

The execution was almost too quick. Without dramatics or any other display, and with an economy of movement that bespoke the smooth expertise for which he was known, the executioner raised his sword and brought it down in an instant. The body collapsed to the platform, the head rolled away, and that was that, except for the blood which seemed to go everywhere. There was a collective sigh from the onlookers, and low talking began.

Estrella looked to Cisco, who was silent. His lips were pressed together, and his jaws stood out in knots of muscle. He opened his mouth to speak, but instead of the curse she expected she heard him mutter in a husky voice, "May God have mercy." Then he took a deep breath and turned to offer a helping hand to Estrella as the crowd began to make its way from the yard. She took it, and followed him away from the destroyed queen. Patiently she stepped along in the muddy yard as the well-dressed onlookers moved away from the scene. A box was lifted to receive the headless body, and Anne's head was placed with it. The thing was an incongruous object, no longer seeming to be a part of her, but only something that looked a little like her. It was spattered and smeared with blood, as were the shoulders of the body. Blood in payment for the suffering of Catherine, and for the deaths of those who had inconvenienced the king in his pursuit of this woman.

For several days Estrella remained in London, preparing to return to the current Duke of Whitby and the rest of her husband's family. There, in the house she'd presided over for fifteen years, she would live out her days as dowager in comfort and relative security. The young maids she'd taken on after

Catherine's funeral were now hard at work to pack the trunks, and Estrella presided over them with a distracted manner, not really paying attention but rather sifting through wonderings about what lay ahead.

So much had changed these past months. For the past few years her life had been so caught up in the matter of Catherine's struggle with Henry, she'd given almost no thought of anything else. Suddenly there was no struggle. No longer any involvement with the royal court. No need to even be in London, no purpose to be about. The unaccustomed calm was nearly unsettling. She was so used to trouble arising at frequent intervals, she now found herself tensing, waiting for something bad to happen. There was no telling what that might be, but life had taught her there was no rest until death forced it.

As if to prove her right, there came a knock at her chamber door. Estrella really didn't wish to see anyone today, but this would be her last day in London—possibly for her entire life—and it would be unfair to turn the visitor away. She nodded to her maid to greet whoever it was. The girl hurried into the next room, and Estrella waited.

The voice from the entrance gave her gooseflesh. It was the Earl of Hartford. Accompanied by a friend, she could tell by the voices. Her maid came to announce them, but Estrella wanted none of it. Her mouth opened to tell her to send the men away. But she hesitated. The words wouldn't come. They stayed glued to her tongue and paralyzed it. *Hilsey.* What could he possibly want? She told her maid she would be in momentarily.

It felt good to make him wait. Even more satisfying than watching Anne die. She stepped to the window of her bed-chamber and looked out over the London streets abustle with folks going about their business, none of them concerned with her. Her palms were damp, and she dried them on a handkerchief. Deep breaths. He would wait. He *should* wait. Finally she was composed enough to make her entrance.

Hilsey stood with his friend, of calm demeanor, as if he had all the time in the world to wait on her. He was chatting in a low voice with the man but broke off in midsentence when Estrella showed herself. His gaze went to her hard, and she could almost feel it on her. It alarmed her, and she hesitated before approaching him.

But he said nothing alarming. He introduced his friend, but the name flitted past her, and she forgot it immediately. The thing foremost on her mind, she couldn't help but blurt: "What brings you here, my lord, of all places?"

A smile lit his face. Still so disarming. "I've come to see you, of course."

A small sound of frustration escaped her, and she said, "Of course. However, I can't imagine why you would want it."

"I can't imagine not wanting it."

The friend, who may have been a relative—a cousin of some sort perhaps, for there was a resemblance—straightened and intervened. "Lady Whitby, I hope you will pardon this abrupt approach, but we fear time is short and the earl would be hard put to persuade you once you'd left London."

"Persuade me of what?" Now she was truly puzzled.

"My brother wishes me to present his suit for your hand in marriage."

Astonishment took all words quite away from her brain, and she was left with no response whatsoever.

The brother waited, and when she said nothing he continued as if picking up the pieces of a failed conversation. "We realize this is rather sudden."

"And highly irregular."

Piers said, "Are we not a little old to be dancing 'round the maypole? Lita—"

"My *lord*," Estrella said with a harshness she regretted, but then continued in a softer voice, "surely you cannot mean to approach me in this manner, considering recent events."

"The only recent event that has bearing on this happened last fall, and that was the death of my wife. You know she's passed away."

Estrella knew it, but had pushed it out of her mind along with everything else about Piers she'd heard over the past decades. And now she had no response for this.

"Estrella—"

"Countess."

"*Estrella.*" His voice held an intensity that alarmed her further. "You know I never stopped loving you."

She glanced toward the brother, whose gaze was on the floor.

"He knows," said Piers.

Her heart leapt into her throat. "And who else—"

"Nobody. And he only knows because I asked him to come today and lend some propriety to this."

"Propriety? Indeed? And what is this in truth?"

"A sincere and forthright proposal of marriage."

In frustration Estrella turned to the brother and said, "I apologize, my lord, but will you please excuse us for a time? I'm afraid the possibility of propriety is quite beyond us anymore, and I would prefer to express myself freely on this subject." She glanced sideways at Piers. "Though I'm certain he'll tell you everything once he's rejoined you."

They both looked to Piers, who was frowning at Estrella. But then Piers gave a slight nod to his brother and said, "I'll meet you downstairs shortly."

The brother bowed to Estrella. "Very well, my lady. I'll be happy to take some fresh air while the two of you air some very musty discussion."

Piers threw him a cross look, but received only a grin as his brother took his leave. Once the door was closed behind him, and Estrella's maids were sent away, surely to listen from the other room, Piers reiterated, "You know I never stopped loving you."

"You've said as much, more than once. Not that it matters a whit. Nor should it, as you so succinctly put it nearly thirty years ago." She went on, as tartly as possible, "How very fortunate for you that your wife has passed, what with her being a Howard and all, related to the late, unlamented whore and therefore not in terribly good odor with the king."

Piers shrugged. "Nonsense. Norfolk has been distancing himself from his niece for some time, and the Howards are in no particular danger just now. I have come through this unscathed so far. Whereas you have not."

Estrella's ears warmed with embarrassment, and her anger grew sharper. "I am as comfortable as I've ever been, and will continue to be so. I am no longer the poor little Spanish maid."

"I know that. I'm hoping you might still have feelings for me."

"You mean, you hope I've pined for you all these years?"

He blinked at that, thought a moment, then said, "Why, yes. Just as I've pined for you. I hope you've thought of me every night of your married life."

She certainly had not, though he'd risen to her dreams often enough. She admitted nothing, however. Her reply, though she knew it would be a mistake, was, "Why?"

"Because—"

"I mean, why should it matter? What could possibly become of such a thing? What's done is done. Our lives have been spent."

A smile broke free from his intense expression. "We're not dead yet, Estrella. What time is left to us might be better spent than aching after each other." His tone had a "don't be silly" quality that made her redden.

"Speak for yourself, Piers."

"And what would you do with your remaining days? Lurk about the household of your husband's nephew? Exist as the wife of a ghost?"

"'Tis a better existence than you ever offered me."

"Not a better one than I'm offering you now."

"How so? I have money, and as much influence as I care for. I have friends, most of whom are true friends and trustworthy. I expect to live out my days in a security heretofore unknown to me. Over the course of my life I've come to appreciate security. Marrying you would only take my life back to court and its vagaries and intrigues."

"No, it would not. I wish to retire to the country and leave Henry's court."

Once again Estrella was made speechless. To hide her astonishment she sat on a nearby chair and stared into the fire flickering in the hearth. When she didn't reply he continued, "Though I'm not dead yet, I am an old man, and I would husband the years left to me with care. While Norfolk has distanced the Howards from the Boleyns, I reckon putting distance between myself and Henry will increase my time on this earth."

"A truth for most people, I daresay."

"Then you understand my intent. For the first time in our lives we're free to live the way we please. My sons are grown, my heir waiting for me to die, and now I wish for some happiness. A spot of peace before my life would be over. Perhaps even joy."

For a long moment she thought hard on his words. He made it all sound so gentle. So filled with the sort of peace she'd only hoped for in heaven. The sort she knew never existed in earthly life. Slowly she said, "I would marry—if I marry—for the sake of respect as well as affection. My first husband respected me, and I him. At my age I've come to appreciate it, and I cannot settle for less."

Hilsey's smile widened, and he nodded as if she'd just said exactly what he'd been thinking at the moment. "Yes. I would come to know you as he did, something I've long regretted losing in my marriage to Beth, for she was a shrew, and a bane upon my soul our entire marriage." His head bent to look into her eyes, and he searched them. She knew he was telling the truth. "I envy Whitby his years with you, as I'm certain some other poor fool envies me my life with Beth. And from afar I've come to admire your courage in your service to Catherine. I would have such a woman on my side. *At* my side." His voice went soft. "To love as I never could before."

Now she looked at him, and her heart clenched hard enough to tighten her throat. At nearly sixty years of age, his eyes still held the spark of hope for the future. It was a strength—a sense of invincibility—that heartened her. She opened her mouth to speak, but it took a long moment to find the courage to say what she was thinking. The words came ever so slowly. "I never stopped loving you."

He knelt beside her. "I know. I can see it in your eyes. They haven't truly changed for me since the day I first saw you in the stands on Arthur's wedding day." Her eyes closed, and he chuckled. "I could see into your heart, even from my saddle. It shone among the crowd and captivated me entirely in an instant." She looked up at him again, stunned at this revelation. She'd had no idea, and had thought his interest in her had begun the day he'd brought her the horses and carriage for Catherine.

He took a deep breath, grasped her hand in both of his, and pressed on with his suit, for they both knew this conversation was the only chance he would have to convince her. He would do it now, or never see her again. "Estrella, *mi pájara d'España*, listen to me. You could spin out your days in a nunnery, or living among your husband's relatives as dowager, or you could marry me and become the Countess of Hartford. You could spend the rest of your days treasured as you were meant to be. Marry for a love that has already proven true over time." He folded her hand in his and kissed it.

The image of him in his burnished armor, riding to the lists and proving his mettle, made her think of how Catherine had also seen Henry that way, how it had caused her great grief, robbing her of her righteous anger. And it made her think of how wrong that had been. All men were carpet knights, in armor corroded with self-interest. Piers' was no different. There was no such thing as the Arthurian ideal, and probably never had been. She'd been a silly girl to ever have thought there could be. They had all been silly girls those many years ago, bound across the sea on a journey to a kingdom that only existed in a poem.

Now, however, she was no longer a silly girl. She could see Hilsey's offer with far clearer eyes than she'd had in her youth. Though he was no champion riding to her rescue—for she no longer needed rescue and he had never been the one for it in any case—he nevertheless was offering something she desired: himself. For what that was worth anymore, he had offered himself to her in a proposal that was not the worst she'd ever had. In some ways, she considered, it was better than some she'd accepted. This thought also fitted into her understanding of the reality of the world.

He was right. Though she cast about for a reason to tell him no, that she did not wish to marry anyone, there was none. She still loved him, there was no impediment of any kind, and indeed they would both benefit from quiet retirement and each other's much-desired company. She believed him when he said he would treasure her, and it was an attractive prospect. A curiosity rose in her to learn what that might be like.

Her throat was nearly closed, and she had to clear it to say, "Very well, then. I will marry you, Piers."

A smile broke out on his handsome face. His eyes closed, and he kissed her hand again. Then her lips, with a passion Estrella hadn't felt in what seemed an eternity. There was a flittering moment when she felt young again, and the future was a gift waiting to be opened. She smiled in return and fell into his embrace.